COOL WATER SPLASHED AROUND THISTLE ...

A heavy dose of chlorine burned her eyes.

"What the f . . . !" Thistle tried to open her eyes. It hurt too much to move her neck. Sun dazzle through her closed eyelids intensified the daggers lancing into her mind.

Where had she landed?

Oh, yeah. That was Alder getting even.

Except Pixies weren't supposed to play tricks on other Pixies. That's what humans were for.

Shivers racked her entire body. Wet. She was wet, wet, wet. Cold and wet weather sent Pixies into hibernation. She needed to find a warm spot to dry her wings. Then she'd fly back to Alder and give him a taste of his own warped sense of justice.

Without thinking, she started her wings fluttering. All the extra moisture and the chills racking her body would slow her lift.

She'd really let Alder have it.

Nothing happened. Unique and lovely green wings in the shape of double thistle leaves failed to flutter through the air.

What had happened to her wings? Gone!

Her eyes flew open. The remnants of sparkling Pixie dust settled in the pool of water around her legs, taunting reminders that Alder was king of her tribe and more powerful than any three Pixies combined.

She wasn't in The Ten Acre Wood anymore. . . .

THISTLE
DOWN

Irene Radford

DAW BOOKS, INC.

<u>Donald A. Wollheim, Founder</u>
375 Hudson Street, New York, NY 10014

Elizabeth R. Wollheim
Sheila E. Gilbert
Publishers
www.dawbooks.com

*To cancer survivors everywhere who
don't let the disease define them.*

ACKNOWLEDGMENTS:

I may write in isolation, but even before *The Glass Dragon*, I relied upon a cadre of critique partners and beta readers. The list grows longer every year and with every book. Sara, Lizzy, Maggie, Jessica, and Bob top the current list. I couldn't do this without you.

Prologue

DUSTY WATCHED A GLIMMER of light creep under the wooden mini blinds of her bedroom. The pink ballerinas on her curtains began to take form. A tiny bit of breeze crawling through the open window on this hot August morning made them flutter as if they truly danced. Like the way Dusty imagined herself dancing in the recital last spring. Only, all she and the other preschool girls got to do was bourrée and turn a bit. In her mind, she had flown around the stage like a fairy.

Dusty was five now. Next spring she'd get to really dance in the recital. And she'd let her sandy blonde hair grow long enough to pull back into a proper ballerina bun.

The floorboard in the hallway groaned, right outside her doorway. She held her breath and scrunched her eyes shut, pretending to sleep. Her brother Dick wanted to wake her on this most important day.

"Dusty?" he whispered as he scratched on the white-painted door.

She put her hand over her mouth so he wouldn't hear her giggle.

The door inched open and almost eleven-year-old (he took pains to remind everyone he was not ten or ten and a half, but almost eleven) Dick peeked around the edge. "You awake, Dusty?"

She held still, playing the game all the way to the end, like he'd told her she had to.

The door creaked a bit on its hinges. Dusty watched

Dick cringe at the noise. He froze in place, peeking over his shoulder to see if Mom and Dad woke up.

No shouted warning from Dad. No whining scold from Mom. Dick came farther into the room and shook Dusty's shoulder. She stirred and opened her eyes. A smile already spread across her face and made her tummy glow. "Is it time?"

"Shush." Dick held a finger to his lips. Early as it was, he'd combed his dark hair and put on clean shorts and a plain T-shirt the same color as his blue eyes. He looked very handsome.

"I'm ready," Dusty whispered and climbed out of bed already wearing her pink shorts and a T-shirt with Tinker Bell on the front. She stuffed her feet into her sandals, not caring that the heel strap got twisted.

"You can't wear that!" Dick said, too loudly.

"Why not?" Dusty dropped her voice to a barely breathing whisper.

"Because Tink's a Faery. We're going to visit Pixies. It's an insult."

"Oh." Dusty looked down at her favorite shirt and wondered if she'd ever wear it again. Dashing tears from her eyes at her mistake, a big, bad mistake, she ripped a purple shirt from her drawer. This one had a bouquet of lavender roses with clear glitter on the petals.

"I guess that one's okay. But hurry. We may be too late as it is. Girls. They're stupid."

"I am not stupid. I already know how to read almost as good as you. And I know my pluses up to ten and my minuses."

"Okay, okay. You're smart. About some things. Now hurry. We have to go now."

Dusty pulled off the horrible pink faery T and dragged the purple one on as she and Dick tiptoed down the back stairs to the kitchen. Once outside, Dusty adjusted her sandals before the rubbing raised a blister. She had to run to catch up with Dick who was already through the gate. Then he took her hand and ran with her down the block, around the corner, across another block, past the big old log cabin that had grown up and down and sideways and was now a museum. A little light shone from the basement window. Someone was working very early. Or very late.

Then they were at the edge of The Ten Acre Wood. All she could see were tall trees, sword ferns, and the beginning of a path. The barkdust on the path had been beaten down and pushed aside so it looked like dirt; like a real game trail entering the wilderness.

Her heart did a bit of a flip in fear and excitement at the adventure that lay before her. The sun was just peeking over the ridge to her right, coming at the trees from the side and sending the long shadows along the museum lawn. The trees looked like a very tall fence with no gate, just that narrow path that suddenly looked like a pirate's gangplank, or the trail to a dragon lair, or . . .

Dick grabbed her hand and forced her to face him. "You're going into kindergarten next week, Dusty. It's time you found out about The Ten Acre Wood. All the other kids will have been here and they'll expect you to know all about it." He looked old and wise.

Dusty nodded her head to make sure he knew she understood how important this outing was.

"Now keep hold of my hand and walk only where I walk. There are traps in the woods. Pixies love to play tricks on humans. If you wander off, you could get lost forever and drown in the pond because the nasty old Faery who refused to go underground and who rules everything can make it look like solid ground."

Dusty gulped and bit her lip, but nodded again.

Together they stepped onto the path. Dick looked right and left and up ahead and behind, making sure they never strayed away from the trail. His hand got sweaty. Dusty tried pulling her fingers free of his to wipe them on her shorts. But he just held her tighter. She could no longer see the lawn behind them, or where the twisted path led them.

Frightened, she clung to him and watched her feet to make sure she stepped only where he stepped. After a bit, that felt like all morning, she could see more than just her feet and the bracken ferns that waved over the path. The fronds bounced as if someone very tiny jumped up and down on the spines.

She giggled, less afraid.

Then there was more light. The trees took on distinct shapes, less fuzzy from shadow. Suddenly the trees spread farther apart, stood straighter, became less frightening.

Dusty looked up and saw the pond. Ugly brownish-greenish water in the center with a broad muddy bank that showed how big the pond was in winter when it rained all the time. But now in summer, when they hadn't had any rain in weeks, the mud sprouted grass and weeds and tall wildflowers.

Off to one side, just above the mud line stood the biggest oak tree she'd ever seen, or imagined. Its gnarled bark looked like it hid a face—just like the Grandmother tree in that cartoon movie about an Indian girl. Only this face frowned and disapproved of human intruders.

Flitting from flower to flower were flying things. Bigger than any bugs she'd seen, and more colorful; blues and purples, pinks and greens, tipped in gold and silver like the jewelry in the store window downtown.

"Hold out your hand," Dick said quietly. He dropped his clutch on her and showed her how to offer her palm.

A flock of the flying jewels separated from the flowers and circled them. Dusty thought she heard them singing.

She smiled in delight, and hummed back at them. *Dum dee dee do dum dum*.

As if a mist blew away from her eyes, she saw that the flying bugs looked like tiny people with wings. They had pointed ears and slightly slanted eyes like Tinker Bell, and they wore flower petals and cobwebs instead of clothes, but their skin and hair were colored to match their clothes. And their wings! Oh, those pretty wings looked like the jeweler had carved leaves out of precious gems and set them in the sun to catch the light and wink it back at her.

She gasped in wonder, spinning on her toes, like a proper ballerina, so that she could see them all at once.

"Dusty, meet the Pixies," Dick said with pride. "Pixies, meet my baby sister Dusty."

A purple Pixie separated from the flock and settled on Dusty's outstretched palm. She cocked her head and looked first from Dusty to Dick and back again. Her song, *dum dee dee do dum dum*, grew louder in Dusty's ears. "Dusty is not your real name," she chirped. Her hair and clothes were darker purple than her skin, but matched her eyes.

Dusty was so caught up in the happy expression in those eyes, she barely noticed that her green wings were jagged and prickly like a thistle. Then she realized the Pixie's wild mane of purple curls that stood out from her head like a small pom pom resembled a flower.

"I bet your name is Thistle," Dusty said. Her esses whistled because she forgot that one of her front teeth had fallen out and she didn't push the sound around the gap like Mom insisted she do.

"You guessed right!" Thistle clapped her hands and hopped up and down, her wings angled so she didn't catch the air and lift too far away. "I'm Thistle Down. So, what's your real name?"

"Desdemona Carrick," Dusty said on a frown. She hated the name Mom insisted belonged to her and only her.

"You don't like the name any better than Dick likes to be called Benedict," Thistle giggled. "Don't blame you. Dusty suits you. Dusty you are." A bright cloud of sparkling dust dropped over Dusty.

She felt lighter, bigger, important.

Something big crashed through the underbrush

across the pond. Dusty jumped back, but she didn't close her hand into a fist. She had to let Thistle fly to safety on her own.

Dick laughed long and loud as Chase Norton, his best friend, stomped on ferns and kicked aside blackberry vines. Chase wasn't quite as tall as Dick—he was four months younger after all and wouldn't turn eleven until March, where Dick's birthday was in November—but he was broader all over and had thick blond hair that always flopped into his greenish-brown eyes—lighter and prettier than the pond water.

"I can't believe you still believe in Pixies," Chase snorted. "I thought you'd outgrown that, Dick."

Dick shrugged. "Had to show my sister The Ten Acre Wood. She's five now."

"He doesn't want to believe in Pixies anymore," Thistle whispered in an aside to Dusty. "Adults are like that, expect for a special few. He can still see me and hear me, he just won't admit it." She rolled her beautiful purple eyes, but they sparkled with mischief at the same time.

Chase humphed something rude as he clomped around the edge of the pond to join them.

Dusty wanted to clamp her hands over her ears to shut out Chase's language. But Thistle still stood on her palm, hands on hips, a scowl on her lovely face. Dusty didn't dare move, or she might frighten her new friend away.

"We're special friends now, Dusty. I won't desert you just because Mr. Muscles doesn't believe anymore," Thistle said proudly.

"Special friend?" Dick asked. He looked like he might cry.

That scared Dusty more than the noise Chase made tromping through the woods.

"Does that mean you and I can't be friends anymore, Thistle?"

"You don't need her as a friend. You got me." Chase pounded his chest importantly. "We're guys now, going into fifth grade. We don't need no girls hanging around."

That was scary, too. Just since Dick was almost eleven now, did that mean he didn't need Dusty, his sister, anymore? Would he still help her with her arithmetic and reading? Show her baby birds in their nest hidden under the eaves of the garage, or point out what was a weed, and what was one of Mom's favorite plants? Or hold her hand during a rare thunderstorm to keep her from being too scared?

"Dick," Thistle said gently. "Dick, as long as there is trust and love, friendship knows no boundaries. I can be your friend, and Dusty's friend. You can be my friend and Chase's. Though I don't know why you'd want such a logical and clumsy oak as a friend." Quick as a blink, she flew over to Chase and kicked his bangs down to flop into his eyes and returned to Dusty's hand, almost before any of them realized what she'd done.

Dusty giggled.

"I am not clumsy!" Chase proclaimed, brushing his hair back again. "And the word is oaf, not oak."

Thistle and Dusty giggled.

"You guys go on and play pirates. I'm going to dance with my new friend," Dusty said and waved her brother and Chase off, deeper into the woods.

The huge old oak continued to frown. But Dusty didn't notice.

One

A LONG JOLT OF PAIN arced from Thistle's pert little backside to her shoulders, then up into her neck and over the top of her skull into her eyes.

Cool water splashed around her. A heavy dose of chlorine burned her eyes. But the water cooled the itching flush on her skin.

"What the f . . . !" She tried to open her eyes. It hurt too much to move her neck. Sun dazzle through her closed eyelids intensified the daggers lancing into her mind.

Where had she landed?

Oh, yeah. That was Alder getting even.

Except Pixies weren't supposed to play tricks on other Pixies. That's what humans were for.

Shivers racked her entire body. Wet. She was wet, wet, wet. Cold and wet weather sent Pixies into hibernation. She needed to find a warm spot to dry her wings. Then she'd fly back to Alder and give him a taste of his own warped sense of justice.

She shivered in the unnatural weather. Wasn't this August?

Without thinking, she started her wings fluttering. All the extra moisture and the chills racking her body would slow her lift. Pixies weren't meant to sit for long on hard stone with their legs splayed in front of them.

Everything hurt.

She'd really let Alder have it.

Nothing happened. Water lapped her waist and continued to pour down over her head. Her legs remained stretched straight. Smoothly curved stone cradled her bottom while jagged and warped rock pressed into her back. A huge itch clawed her entire spine from butt to neck.

Unique and lovely green wings in the shape of double thistle leaves failed to flutter through the air.

What had happened to her wings? Gone!

Her eyes flew open. The remnants of sparkling Pixie dust settled in the pool of water around her legs, taunting reminders that Alder was king of her tribe and more powerful than any three Pixies combined. The old Faery in the oak had given him that power just before he left for . . . wherever old Faeries went when they no longer wished to live in this realm.

She wasn't in The Ten Acre Wood anymore.

Then she noticed black hair—very wet black hair—tangled over her shoulders and chest. Chest? She had boobs! Big ones. When had that happened? Bad enough Alder had stolen her wings. What had he done to her lovely lavender skin and deep purple tresses!

And he'd given her human tits the size of watermelons—well maybe only the size of pomegranates. But still, compared to Pixie evenness, those globes would throw her off-balance. She'd be too heavy to fly.

If she had wings.

Fat, salty tears mingled with the water dripping down her face.

Blaring horns, angry shouts, the pelting of water hitting a rippling pool slammed against her ears as she grew more aware of things beyond her own pain and confusion.

"This isn't Pixie," she gasped.

"I don't know what you're on, lady, but dancing naked in Memorial Fountain during morning rush hour isn't going to help," a rough male voice said from somewhere near her left shoulder.

Thistle peeked in that direction, trying not to move her aching head.

A big, callused hand extended toward her. It was covered with sun-bleached blond hair on the back and knuckles.

She followed the line of the hand up a muscular arm to the hem of a dark blue, short-sleeved shirt with three gold stripes in an inverted chevron embroidered on it.

Gulp.

"You gonna get out on your own, or do I have to carry you?" the man asked.

Thistle placed her hand in his. He closed his fingers around it, hard, and yanked her forward.

She stumbled to her feet, unsure how to balance with all that extra weight up front.

She tried to compensate with a little lift.

Her missing wings failed her.

She almost sat back down again. The man pulled on her arm harder, keeping her upright.

"Okay, everybody back to business!" the man shouted. "Get those cars untangled and moving. Nothing to look at here. Haven't you ever seen a naked woman before? Eight o'clock and it's already hotter'n Hades. I'd like to dance naked in the fountain to cool off, too! Pioneer Days nonsense. It's going to be a bad Festival this year."

Thistle risked looking around.

Behind her, Florentine swoops and curls carved into a stone urn. Water spouted up and out from the top. All around the fountain, dozens of human automobiles sat at odd angles in the six-way intersection. They should be flowing in a smooth circle around the fountain.

Oftentimes, in her delightful Pixie size, she'd flitted from car hood to rooftop to trunk, diverting a driver's attention and causing him to swerve oddly for several moments.

But she'd never done anything to cause this much chaos before. This looked like a masterwork of Pixie tricks.

Would she get the credit for it, or would Alder?

She smiled at the tall blond man in a police uniform. Not a man alive had resisted that smile, especially if she threw in a few Pixie sparkles. He towered over her, glowering.

Not a good sign, nor a bit of Pixie dust in the air.

"Will someone get the phone!" Dusty Carrick called up the basement stairs.

The shrill ring continued.

"Lazy, self-centered, know-nothings, can't remember the date of the Oregon Provisional Government in 1843," she muttered as she dashed up the steep and dusty risers to the kitchen of the historic-house-turned-museum. She had to hike her long calico skirts and apron above her knees to keep from tripping. A very modern, cream-colored wall phone blended into the sprigged wallpaper of the pantry at the top. Dusty had painted tiny sprigs of pink flowers on the Bakelite to make sure it didn't stick out like a sore thumb.

She reached around the corner and grabbed the receiver on the seventh ring, just before it clicked over to the answering machine. Where was everybody? A half hour after opening on a summer Friday morning, there should be a full crew of tour guides and administrative staff around.

Hadn't Joe Newberry said something about an appointment first thing this morning and that she was in charge until he got back? That notation should be on the wall calendar in the employee lounge that she hadn't bothered checking when she came to work at six. If there had been something about the archaeological dig or reference documents, she'd have noticed.

She inhaled sharply, bracing herself to talk to someone she didn't know about something other than history. Still, carrying on a stilted business conversation had to be better than listening to the slightly accusatory tone of a message on the machine. Or confronting the person face-to-face.

Her inhalation caught on a dust mote and pushed it deep inside her. She sneezed horrendously before she could say anything. Her wire-rimmed glasses slid to the end of her nose, teetered a moment, then settled without hitting the floor.

"That you, Dusty?" Police Sergeant Chase Norton asked from the other end of the line. She'd know that voice anywhere.

"Excuse me, Skene County Historical Society," she said stuffily and sneezed again. This time she managed to stick a finger under her nose and keep the glasses from falling off.

"Your brother named you right," Chase chuckled. "You been mucking about in the basement of that old mausoleum again? More dust than artifacts down there."

"Benedict has a foul sense of humor," Dusty said. Actually, he'd done her a favor in nearly eliminating her full name from people's memories. She'd done the same for him. Most of the world, except their mother, knew him as only Dick Carrick, from his business cards to his phone listing.

Their mother, Juliet, was too enamored of Shakespearean character names. Thank God she hadn't named her two children Shylock and Hero. Benedict and Desdemona were bad enough.

Dusty also thanked whatever deity might listen that her parents had gone to Stratford-upon-Avon, England for the first summer of their retirement to absorb even more Shakespeare.

They could have stayed home and spent their time finding blind dates for Dusty.

"Look, Dusty, as much as I'd love to chat, I've got a problem only you can solve."

Her heart sped up. Did Chase want a date for the Historical Society Fund-raising Ball next week?

"What do you need, Chase?" She didn't dare say she'd do anything for him. If only he'd made this call twelve years ago when he was a senior in high school and she a lowly, and lonely, homeschooler. Maybe if he'd asked her out then ...

No sense in living in what ifs and maybes.

The past was past.

"I've got a young woman in custody who asked me to call you as her one phone call."

"Who?" Dusty couldn't think of anyone she knew well enough, other than her brother, who would call her for help.

"She says her name is Thistle Down."

Dusty's mind spun in puzzlement. "I don't know anyone named ..." No, it couldn't be. Five years without a word or a glimpse ...

Dusty hadn't ventured into The Ten Acre Wood since ... since she started working full time at the museum as assistant curator.

"Don't tell me she's four inches tall, has lavender skin and purple hair with green wings in the shape of thistle leaves," Dusty said, half hoping. She held her breath.

"Nah, don't be ridiculous. She's got black hair and white skin and not a stitch on her when she landed in Memorial Fountain."

"That will give local gossips something new to memorialize."

"But her eyes are the most amazing shade of purple ..." Chase drifted off almost dreamily.

Dusty's heart caught, then beat again loudly in her ears.

Chase was falling in love again.

"If she puts on sunglasses, will you remember the color of her eyes?"

Then a new thought caught her in a sucker punch.

"Purple eyes?" Dusty asked.

The clatter of a big tour group gathering in the front lobby jangled along Dusty's nerves.

"Look, Chase, I can't get away from the museum right now. Isn't there someone else you can call?"

"Nope. This is her one and only call. Don't know why she chose you."

Dusty had her suspicions.

"Well, I guess you could drop her by here . . . just to see if I know her."

"If I turn her over to your custody, she stays with you. Otherwise it looks like I'll have to charge her with drunk and disorderly . . ."

"I am not drunk!" a female voice chimed delicately in the background. "I haven't had a drop of honey."

The world came to a screeching halt around Dusty.

"Bring her by in an hour, after I deal with the current tour group." She hung up. Where were those girls who were supposed to do the tours?

Dusty gritted her teeth and went to greet the noisy crowd of tourists with their equally loud bevy of children.

For the next forty-five minutes, Dusty led the group of five adults and six children through the pioneer home. She explained as clearly and succinctly as possible the exhibits highlighting the history of Skene County, Oregon, and the city of Skene Falls on the Skene River. If she made the tour comprehensive, she wouldn't have to answer questions.

Of course a child had to ask: "How come there aren't any bathrooms?"

"When the house was first built in 1845, no one had indoor plumbing. Washing clothes or taking a bath was a big deal that required a lot of work and planning." She crouched to be at eye level with the eight-year-old boy. Much more comfortable communicating on this level than dealing with sneering adults who kept staring at the dust stains on her apron. She imagined she felt the waves of judgmental disdain emanating from them.

"They didn't have electricity to heat the water, or pump it from a reservoir back then. When the Historical Society moved the house from river level up here to the plateau to become a museum in 1937, we stripped out some of the more modern conveniences."

"Like bathrooms," the boy said. He began a telltale sway from foot to foot.

Time to get this group out of here.

"Life was really different back then; no electric lights or TV or telephones, no hot and cold running water. No X-rays or antibiotics to help you get over sickness." Or chemo and bone marrow transplants.

"My grandma died of cancer," the six-year-old girl said solemnly.

"I'm sorry to hear that. Some things we don't know how to fix yet. I bet your grandma lived a lot longer than she would have back in 1845. Because of vitamins, and good food trucked in from all over the country, and medicines, she lived long enough for you to get to know her. That's something to be grateful for." She'd fought cancer herself when she was about this girl's age. She had won the battle with a lot of help. She knew the ache in the middle the little girl showed by clutching her stomach as she spoke.

Dusty pasted a bright smile on her face as she stood to face the parents. "This concludes the organized tour. Feel free to browse the gift shop next door where you bought your tour tickets. There are picnic tables on the grounds, along with some hands-on exhibits like the covered wagon, and public restrooms at the corner of the park on the Center Street side."

"The little log cabin?" the father asked.

Dusty nodded. "The Ten Acre Wood is part of the park and open for exploration. We ask that you stay on the gravel paths and not damage the native ground cover. There are leaflets in a drop box behind the carriage barn that will guide you through a treasure hunt. The pink papers have trivia questions based on local history, the green ones are about movies, and the blue ones are general trivia."

"Is that where all the tall trees are?" one boy asked. He strained his neck peering out the nearest window toward the towering Douglas firs.

"Yes. And I hear there's pirate treasure buried there. Or was that a dragon hoard? I'm not sure. Maybe you should find out."

The children dashed out the door, followed more sedately by their parents.

Dusty exited as hastily as she could without seeming to run. On her way back to the sanctuary of the basement, she found the two teenage tour guides relaxing on the back porch that had been enclosed for an office and employee lounge—and private restroom. Both girls wore modern sundresses, had their feet up on the long worktable, and had cans of cola in their hands.

The sight of thick condensation dripping off the cans reminded Dusty she hadn't had anything to drink in a couple of hours. She threw a roll of paper towels to the girls and pointed to where their cans dribbled on the sheaves of papers on the table. Then she poured herself a glass of iced tea sweetened with agave nectar from the pitcher she'd made when she first arrived.

"There are two more groups approaching the front walk, girls," Dusty said at the dark portal to her underground hiding place. "Your turn to guide the tours. You might spend some time talking about the spinning wheel and whale oil lamps."

"Ah, Ms. Carrick, it's hot out there," Meggie complained, rubbing the cold soda can over her brow. "Can't you take them?"

"Your job," Dusty reminded them. "Remember the internship credit, and recommendations you'd *like* to get for your college applications?"

Meggie, the willowy blonde who looked too much like Phelma Jo Nelson for Dusty's comfort, dropped her feet to the floor and stood as if the action took every bit of energy she possessed. "I guess." She heaved a sigh, letting Dusty know how much of a burden work was. "I haven't given a tour to a cute boy in like ages."

Unlike Phelma Jo, Meggie was unmotivated, and not a bully.

"Pioneer Days officially starts with the parade at ten AM tomorrow. Traffic all over town will pick up any minute now. And you'll have to wear costumes all week. The volunteers delivered a whole stack of them yesterday, cleaned and pressed. Now, I have an appointment in," Dusty looked at the watch pinned to her bodice with an antique enameled bow brooch, "fifteen minutes. I'll need this office since Mr. Newberry locked his and hasn't returned from his appointment. You girls need to be elsewhere before then. Now get to work."

Dusty escaped to the cool depths of the basement and the broken crockery from a tribal archaeological dig performed by the community college. The artifacts needed cleaning and piecing together. The crockery dated the dig to post-European contact. The remnants of shell beads and leatherwork suggested an earlier time. An interesting puzzle.

Artifacts didn't judge a person unfairly on first impressions.

TWO

"LIFE'S A BITCH AND THEN YOU DIE," Phelma Jo Nelson spat at the stooped man. She leaned back in his comfortable office chair and propped her feet on his massive desk. Once tall and robust, her opponent now sagged and wavered.

Vulnerable. She could make some money off his new fragility. A more attractive prospect was that, in replacing him, she would be in a position of power to close down Dusty Carrick's precious museum. The collapsing pile of lumber without plumbing or electricity had no place in this modern town. Phelma Jo had managed to acquire the lot where her mother's shack had stood. It hadn't had plumbing or electricity either, only empty booze bottles. The lot now held her modern offices and condos.

She needed to be in a position to control growth in this town, control crime by ridding it of hiding places for criminals—like The Ten Acre Wood—and control her own life.

"So you have to retire," she reminded the man. "You've had a good run, honey. Now it's time to step aside for a younger and more aggressive generation."

"I have no intention of allowing my failing body to dictate . . ."

"You don't. But I do. Now sign this press release, and I'll make sure it gets to the proper reporter. Not that Digger fellow. Someone who will show respect for you and your position in this town and know that I am the only person you trust to continue your good works." She slid the single sheet of paper across his desk.

He made no move toward acquiescence.

She selected an antique fountain pen from the leather cup holding several fine writing instruments and rolled it onto the paper.

"Sign it."

"PJ . . ."

"Don't call me that."

"Phelma Jo, surely we can work something out. I'll appoint you to any position you want, name you my heir. But I am not retiring."

"Yes, you are." She retrieved a fat file from her soft leather document satchel and waved it at him.

He blanched. "You wouldn't release that information. You're in as deep in the land deal as I am."

"Yes, but then I'm a real estate developer. Everyone expects me to push a slightly shady deal. You've cooked the town's books and skimmed taxes, *my taxes*, into your own pocket. I've never done anything overtly illegal."

"Yet."

Dick Carrick bounced up the steps of the Skene County Historical Museum. He stepped into the deep shade of the long porch across the front of the pioneer house, then paused and blinked a few moments to let his eyes adjust to the shadows.

Only eleven o'clock and already the summer sunshine beat hot and heavy upon his back. He whipped a silver-colored silk handkerchief from his breast pocket and dabbed his face clear of perspiration. His custom-made gray silk suit, a shade darker than the handkerchief and his tie, rode easily on his shoulders. Nothing on the front porch or inside the museum seemed to match. It was all a mash-up of odds and ends collected over decades.

The scientist in him screamed for order in the semi-chaos. The chaos and disorder of childhood games and magical imaginings beckoned to him from The Ten Acre Wood at the far end of the museum grounds.

Strange, he never noticed the heat back when his days were full of imagination.

He shook his head to clear it. Time to relinquish the treasure of the wood to a new generation of children. Big brothers had been introducing their younger siblings to the wood, and its inhabitants for generations.

But a guy could grow up too much. His job as a representative of a major pharmaceutical company suited him much more than his original career in medicine. He could be flamboyant and glib and not have to worry about studying.

"Dusty!" he called, as he breezed into the museum lobby—just a narrow space between two velvet robes that led past the parlor toward the offices at the rear. He was surprised at the emptiness.

The blonde teenager who worked summers poked her head out of the back room. "Oh, it's you. Ms. Carrick is in the basement. As usual." Then she disappeared again.

Dick heard the dulcet tones of the other girl, the African-American one with her beautiful, thick hair, done up in beaded cornrows, upstairs giving a tour.

Down, boy, he reminded himself. *They're both jailbait.*

The roar of the air conditioner in the office beckoned him with the promise of coolness. The only concessions to modern conveniences in the museum proper were a few carefully disguised safety lights. In winter, Dusty turned on gas log fires in every hearth and free-standing iron stove.

He didn't expect to find Dusty anywhere except the basement at any time of year. When tourists abounded, Dusty hid.

"Hey, Dusty, you down there?" he asked at the top of the staircase. A shiver of disgust ran the length of his spine at the thought of actually having to touch the filthy railing beside the steep descent. He didn't dare use his handkerchief to protect his hands. The accumulated grime would ruin the silk.

Instead, he turned slightly sideways so that his feet fit nicely along the length of each narrow step.

"What's up, Dick?" Dusty's voice drifted upward, as if it came from a long, long way away.

"You aren't. Can't you come up to the light of day for a change? I'm beginning to think you're a vampire or a werewolf or something equally hideous that can't stand daylight hours." He backed up two steps to the landing and the security of the doorway.

"Oh, all right," Dusty grumbled.

Dick retreated another two steps and waited for her.

"Do you need Dad's pickup on Saturday? I promised to help the guys at the firehouse haul flowers for the parade," he said to fill the time she needed to climb. "I can march with the volunteers, but I'll have to duck the reception afterward and work."

"Let me look at the calendar. I might have to help haul tables and chairs from the library for registration and refreshments."

"I can do that while I'm bringing tubs of flowers from the nursery." He spotted his sister on the landing, in her dull green calico pioneer dress and filthy apron.

The front door banged. It sounded as if someone had shoved it with a good deal of anger behind the thrust. Muted grumbles followed the reverberations.

"Um, Dusty, sounds as if trouble is brewing up front."

"What time is it?" she asked, wiping her hands on her work apron. It had been white once but never would be again; no amount of chlorine bleach would get out the ingrained dirt. She negotiated the steps confidently, without using the railing. But her petite feet fit perfectly on the steps.

"It's, uh, eleven o seven." Dick checked his cell phone. He wore a watch, an expensive one, but never thought to look at it now that he had access to everything on the phone.

"That will be Chase Norton, then," Dusty said. She

paused, one foot hovering above the next step like she didn't want to proceed any further, but had to.

"Is something wrong?" Dick asked. "Can I field the interrogation for you?"

"Thanks, anyway. But this is something I've got to do myself." She shoved her glasses back up her nose and settled her shoulders, bracing to face conflict as if approaching the guillotine.

When she reached the doorway, though, her shoulders slumped and she didn't seem capable of lifting her gaze above the baseboard. The thick lenses of her glasses distorted any possibility of reading her expression.

Dick threaded her arm through his and flashed her a big smile. The top of her head only reached his shoulder, emphasizing to him just how fragile she was. Chemo at age nine had stunted her growth and left her vulnerable to fatigue at odd moments. She was an inch shorter than their mother. Chemo had also destroyed her appetite. She never ate enough to put some meat on her bones. She looked as frail as a Faery from underhill. Or underground, considering her time in the basement.

"Okay, Sis, I'm right here to help."

She looked up at him with the same look of grateful admiration she'd used when she was eight and a half and he'd rescued her from Phelma Jo kicking dirt in her face after knocking Dusty over in a rough game of tag in the schoolyard.

The scrapes on her knees and arms had gotten infected and not healed. That was the first sign of the leukemia that had almost killed her.

He held that look in his mind and let it swell his chest with pride. He took care of his baby sister, protected her when no one else would. His bone marrow, no one else's, had saved her life.

Together, they walked through the antique kitchen to the parlor and lobby. Chase Norton stood before the reception desk, bulky in his uniform with a light Kevlar vest beneath his shirt, loaded utility belt and a thigh holster for his Taser. Dick knew the bulk was artificial. Beneath the equipment, Chase Norton was as lean and strong as he'd been when playing college quarterback. A chick magnet. A great companion for picking up girls in bars. Sweat darkened his light Nordic-blond hair to sand.

The heat . . . or extreme anger?

Dick was betting on anger.

Behind Chase stood the most beautiful woman Dick had ever seen, wearing one of Chase's black T-shirts. Long legs stretched below the hem, giving hints of more lovely curves beneath the thin fabric. From the shape of her ample breasts, and the puckering of her nipples, she wasn't wearing any underwear. Blue-black hair gleamed against her milky white skin.

He licked his lips, anxious to get to know this lady.

Then she turned and lifted her deep purple eyes to his face. Laughter sparkled just beneath the surface.

He forgot to breathe. Thistle looked a little different from the last time he'd seen her. But he'd never forgotten those eyes. The eyes of the first girl he'd kissed. The eyes of the woman who haunted, or was that taunted, his dreams every night.

Thistle studied Dick and Dusty with an eye for the possibilities of a round of mischief. They'd both given her new insight into her purpose in life—spreading confusion and chaos with wild pranks—as they all grew up together. Now her friends looked like they needed a heavy dose of Pixie fun.

How had they gotten so old? And so solemn? She should have checked back on them more often during their teen years, but there was always a new generation of little ones to introduce to the joys of Pixie.

Something had to be done about Dick and Dusty. Soon. Chase had probably been a lost cause since he was ten.

Thistle was just the Pixie to help them out of their funk. Maybe even the angry and pragmatic Chase.

Those happy thoughts sank to her middle at the sight of Dusty's frightened form cowering half behind her brother.

Before Thistle could frame a question or murmur a phrase of comfort, the policeman grabbed her arm and thrust her forward. "Take her. Just get her out of my sight for a long, long time," he said. "If I never see her again, it will be too soon."

So much for tricking him into a better humor.

"What's the matter, Chase? Didn't you enjoy having your siren go on and off fifteen times on the half-mile ride here?" Thistle batted her eyelashes, feigning innocence.

"I don't know who you are, or what kind of drugs you're on, but stay away from me." He backed up, hands held in front of him. "Bad enough the blasted siren's on the fritz, the seat belts wouldn't stay fastened, and the radio only broadcasts static. The minute she got out of the car, everything cleared up fine. I nearly had to cut the seat belt to get out of it, though." He shook his head in disbelief.

"Strange magnetic fields," Dusty whispered. "Some people are like that."

They all heard her.

Thistle looked back and forth between the men. She expected Dick to have half his senses tuned to his sister. He'd always been overprotective, even before she got sick. But Police Sergeant Chase acted as if every word Dusty uttered fell like pearls of wisdom from a queen to her grateful subjects.

Stars above, when had that happened? Not good. Not good at all.

Dusty, of course, spoiled the regal image with a smudge of dust that clashed with the spray of freckles across her nose. That childlike smudge was good.

"I've got to do something about Chase," Thistle said to herself. "Can't have *my* best friend trapped with a humorless bully of a man." She rubbed the bruise on her wrist from where he'd grabbed her to drag her out of the fountain.

With that thought, she flounced over to Dusty and put her arm around her shoulders. Yee gads! Thistle now stood half a head taller than Dusty. Last time they'd been together, Thistle fit into Dusty's hand or atop her computer mouse. But she only rode the mouse when Dusty got tired and Thistle got bored. The computer made interesting noises, and the screen flashed in odd colors when Thistle got too close.

And as for Dick . . . well, well, well, didn't he clean up pretty with his sun-streaked brown hair, light tan, and brilliant blue eyes, so much like Dusty's but more . . . more intense and defined.

Dusty just looked crumpled and, well, dusty. Sort of like this whole house.

Oh, I've got a lot *of work to do,* Thistle thought. Since it looked like Alder intended her to stay here for a while, best she get started. And she couldn't do that with Policeman Chase Norton hanging around.

"I'll launder your shirt in Faery tears, Sergeant, and have Dick return it," Thistle said. "Unless, of course, you want it back now." She reached for the hem and began tugging the garment over her head, exposing her butt to them all.

"That's okay." Chase blushed all the way from his neck to the tips of his ears. "Call me later, Dick. There's a preseason Seahawks game on the big screen at Old Mill. Friday night, free Buffalo wings with a pitcher. And Festival in full swing." He practically ran out the door and down the steps.

Thistle threw back her head and laughed; the only way she could keep from crying. But the tightness in her chest continued to squeeze her heart and she couldn't swallow past the lump in her hot throat that burned like Faery fire. She'd lost Pixie. Maybe forever. Now she had to make do with *humans*!

The irony of Alder's punishment wasn't lost on her.

Nor the cruelty.

Three

CHASE MOPPED THE SWEAT from his brow on his shirtsleeve. He wished he could start work on the cold pitcher of beer right now. He had a lot of explaining to do to the captain.

He should have kept the naked woman in lockup and processed all the paperwork on about fifteen counts, from drunk and disorderly to public nudity to . . . laughing at him. But lockup, with air-conditioning, had become a shelter from the heat for the elderly, poor, and homeless. Since he had a place to dump Thistle Down, or whatever her real name was, he'd grabbed it.

The captain could chew his hide. But part of Chase's promotion to sergeant included the authority to step slightly outside the box when necessary. Today was necessary.

Besides, dumping Thistle Down on Dusty had given him a chance to talk to her, to elicit more than just a few mumbled words from her. She hadn't graced him with a complete conversation since . . . since he broke her music box, the pink one with the twirling ballerina inside, fifteen years ago.

He shook his head. He thought he'd given up trying to attract her attention. Dating his best friend's sister would complicate his life too much.

But that Thistle woman. Wow! Gorgeous. If she weren't so much trouble, he'd love to escort her to the fund-raiser Masque Ball next week.

One more short-term flirtation in a long list of them.

Dusty probably wouldn't even notice that he'd come, alone or with someone.

One of these days he'd forget Dusty's pert little turned-up nose and the endearing smudge of dirt on her cheek.

His gaze drifted toward The Ten Acre Wood, imagining it lit with Faery lights on the night of the Ball. He sighed. Not this year. He planned on skipping the Ball, unless he had to run security. No sense in spending the evening longing to hold Dusty in his arms while they danced when he knew that would never happen.

"Hey!" he yelled at a couple of kids running around the picnic tables in the museum grounds. "Stop throwing rocks!" The clatter of broken glass from the vicinity of the restrooms followed by a yelp of surprise punctuated his command.

He took off after the kids as they dispersed into the bushes and down the steps to Main Street. He had 'em cornered. The only way off the stairs was over the cliff and a roll through poison oak.

Thankfully, they hadn't disappeared into The Ten Acre Wood. He'd never find them in that tangled overgrowth.

➤➤

"What happened, Thistle?" Dusty asked over her shoulder as she fished for a cola in the employee fridge. She wiped the can top with a sanitized wipe and handed the cold drink to her charge. Then she washed her private glass and poured another iced tea for herself.

Dick had hastened away to his sales calls. He'd left today in a bigger hurry than usual, as if something, or someone, in the museum bothered him.

Dusty laid blame for that squarely on Thistle's shoulders—one of which was showing too much skin as the neckline of her oversized T-shirt slipped, and then slipped some more.

Thistle stared at the pull ring on her cola as if it was a bit of alien technology. All the years Thistle had kept

Dusty company during her recovery from leukemia with the chemo and bone marrow transplant, and then homeschooling, Dusty had never had a soft drink to show her how to use the pull ring. Mom hadn't allowed any junk food in the house, not even organic soft drinks. None of the other kids, including Dick, appreciated snacks of whole wheat crackers and organic goat cheese with home-pressed fruit juice or soy milk to wash it down. Thistle had been her only company.

Dusty pulled the ring on the can, showing Thistle how to do it.

Mom would love to dress Thistle up in sixteenth century clothing and teach her the part of Arial in *The Tempest*. With her light bones and long limbs, she looked the part.

"Why are you here?" Dusty prodded.

"Because I couldn't think of anywhere else to go but to you." She opened those fabulous purple eyes wide in innocence. Feigned?

"Back up. Why do you need a place to go? You could just go home." Dusty took a long drink, never taking her eyes off of Thistle. She watched carefully for any tic, or telltale flicker of expression that might give her clues.

"I can't go home." Thistle looked longingly over her shoulder. Where her wings should be. "At least not for a while. Alder will come to his senses in a few days. Then I'll be away from here as fast as I can fly."

"Who's Alder?"

"The new king of my tribe."

"And what did you do to him to deserve trimming your wings and exiling you?" Dusty turned toward the whiteboard with its lists of reservations and Chamber of Commerce notes of things to promote during tours. And the schedule for setting up and tearing down the parade tomorrow. She had too much to do to babysit a Pixie in exile.

But Thistle had been her only friend for too many years for Dusty to desert her now.

"I didn't do much. Just a prank. Alder has a short temper and more magic now that he's king. What are we going to do this afternoon?" She took a sip of her cola and spat it out. Sticky drops sprayed far and wide, clinging to the fridge, the walls, the chairs, the papers on the table. "What kind of poison have you given me?"

"It's not poison. It's a diet cola. People practically live on them."

"There is nothing natural or clean or even interesting in it." She held the can up, reading the ingredients. Dusty had taught her to read during those long hours of lonely homeschooling.

A clatter of bright voices interrupted Dusty's thoughts. "Suzie!" she cried in delight. "Sharon!"

Dusty dashed to the entry hall and knelt to give big hugs to her two favorite children in the world.

"Auntie Dusty, we got lollipops." Three-year-old Suzie held up a sticky red blob on top of a paper stick. It listed sideways at an alarming angle.

Dusty grabbed a tissue from her apron pocket and held it under the candy just as it decided to plop off the stick.

"I didn't get to finish it," Suzie wailed. A fat tear appeared at the corner of her eye.

"It's too hot for lollies, my girl. How about a nice cold drink instead," Dusty offered, using a second tissue to mop up tears before they grew too plentiful. "I've got lemonade in the fridge. Homemade, just for you."

"Daddy promised us ice cream after dinner," six-year-old Sharon confided. Her lollipop disappeared into her mouth before it collapsed. "Will you cook dinner for us, Auntie Dusty. You cook better than Daddy."

"And where is your daddy?" Dusty asked, searching the walkway through the open door.

"Parking the car," Sharon replied, obviously bored with adult chores.

"Well, come on back to the lounge. I've got someone I want you to meet." That ought to fix the problem of babysitting Thistle. Suzie and Sharon could entertain her while Dusty talked to their father, Joe Newberry: her boss, her mentor, and a good friend.

"Go wash your hands, girls, and I'll be with you in a minute," Joe said as he entered the museum. He nodded to Dusty, looking weary and worried. He headed straight for his office, a tiny cubicle off the pantry that served as curator's office and document storage. He barely had room for an antique writing desk and straight chair. Fortunately, the room borrowed air-conditioning from the adjacent lounge.

Last year they'd considered giving him an office in the attic rooms of the gift shop—another historic house, but newer and smaller than the museum. Joe had lasted less than a week before he moved back. He didn't like being away from the core of the exhibits. And the gift shop didn't have air-conditioning. Only a couple of fans in the front parlor.

"You look tired, Joe," Dusty said, following him in and closing the door behind her. Deep lines radiated from his eyes. His naturally pale skin had an almost gray tinge beneath the high color on his cheeks from the heat.

"That's only half of it," he muttered, flopping into his chair and letting his legs sprawl. He ran his hands through his thinning brown hair. Then he loosened his tie with a frustrated yank. He wore a suit today, his good navy one, instead of his usual khakis and polo shirt.

"What's wrong? Trouble with our grant from the state?"

"I wish it were that trivial." He choked out a laugh.

Dusty held her breath. Keeping the museum in good repair had occupied most of Joe's life since . . . since Dusty couldn't remember how long ago. He'd befriended her during her junior year in high school when she started hanging around asking too many questions about history and how the house was built and who built it. Soon after that, he'd given her a job cataloging the books and documents the Historical Society kept in storage without knowing what was there. By the time she'd finished her BA, she was running the place behind the scenes and he was her best friend.

"Don't look so scared, Dusty. The grant's in good shape, though the state's going to ask for a bigger chunk of matching funds. We just have to pass the inspection tomorrow morning, before the parade starts. The committee could have chosen a better time."

He straightened a little and began fussing with the piles of reference books, papers, fat folders, bits of cloth, and other detritus of museum work that overflowed every flat surface available. "The parade participants are supposed to show up around nine and start marching at ten. So if we meet the committee at seven, we should be in good shape. I just wish they'd postpone the inspection until after Festival," he continued, filling the silence with banal words rather than coming to the heart of the matter.

"The Ball? Are the plans falling apart without Mom overseeing them?" The annual Masque Ball held in the park at the end of Festival provided a large portion of operating funds for the museum. Townsfolk, and a growing number of patrons from nearby Portland, paid good money for tickets, then dressed in outlandish or elegant costumes and danced the night away to live music in the gazebo. Dusty loved stringing tiny Faery lights through the trees to add a magical flavor to the evening.

"Actually, the plans are going better than usual without your mother's interference." He looked down sheepishly.

This time Dusty laughed. "Yeah, Mom does get carried away sometimes."

"Like the year she tried requiring costumes of Shakespearean characters that all had to pass her scrutiny for authenticity?"

They both laughed at that fiasco.

"You're doing a good job, Dusty. You've managed to keep all the committees on track and out of each other's hair."

"The magic of email," she explained. "Mom prefers face-to-face confrontations . . . er meetings. I don't think I've even met any of the committee chairs."

"Your mom is a force of nature, not necessarily a good leader and organizer."

Joe stopped laughing abruptly and pinched the bridge of his nose.

"So spill it. What happened that you're in your best suit and have the girls with you?"

"I don't suppose you'd consider marrying me?"

"Joe, the only time you propose to me is when your ex starts playing nasty games about custody and you think marrying again will look good to the courts. What's she done this time?"

"Monica has left her lover, the Italian count turned chef, finished her fancy cooking school in Florence, and gotten herself a very good job in Seattle at a four-star hotel restaurant. She has followed her bliss. Now she wants the girls back."

Dusty didn't need to see his deadpan expression to know how much hurt he hid behind the mask. She'd held his hand more than once while he worked through the grief of Monica's desertion after reading some damn self-help book. The break she "deserved" grew from a three-week vacation to two years of finding herself.

One of these days Dusty might accept one of Joe's offhanded proposals just to have his children full-time. She babysat them three nights a week while Joe taught a high school equivalency class at the community college. But she knew Joe didn't love her. Part of him still pined for Monica.

"I guess she found herself, 'cause now she's suing for full custody, claiming I can't support her precious children on my salary and that I'm neglecting them."

"If her children are so precious to her, why'd she walk out without so much as a good-bye, leaving you with two toddlers and a mountain of her debts?" Dusty couldn't understand how anyone could leave those girls.

"She said I was undervaluing myself and my education by settling for the museum job instead of teaching at a university. I know she never understood the total lack of glamour in faculty politics."

Monica didn't deserve him or Sharon and Suzie.

Dusty wished she had a place to sit. The office didn't have a second chair.

"Will you accept the full-time teaching job at the community college? It pays better than the museum." Dusty knew to the penny how much it paid. She'd turned down the position when the college offered it to her based upon her academic work and the application her parents had filled out in her name—without telling her because they knew she'd never do it herself.

Her stomached roiled at the thought of facing classrooms full of students every day.

But Joe would thrive there.

"I may have to. That would leave you in charge here. I wouldn't trust anyone else to love this museum as much as I do." He grinned at her. "Think how much fun you'll have working with the county commissioners, the tourists, all the grant committees, designing field trips for school children, teaching special classes for teacher in-service days. . . ."

Dusty ran out of the tiny room, bile burning in the back of her throat. Her hands grew clammy. The moment she cleared the doorway to the basement, her breathing eased. Two steps down into the cool dimness, her stomach settled. She hastened back to her dirty potsherds.

She barely noticed Thistle playing jacks with the girls in the lounge. They hummed an almost familiar tune that followed Dusty all the way to the bottom of the stairs.

Dum dee dee do dum dum.

It reminded her of her favorite music box, broken for fifteen years now. But not quite.

Four

"WHAT HAPPENED TO DUSTY?" Thistle asked no one in particular.

The young girls kept bouncing their little ball and collecting the oddly shaped metal stars.

"Oh, some bully beat the crap out of her in the schoolyard about a billion years ago," the blonde teenager replied, just returning from her tour. She shooed the children into their father's office.

"Everyone in town knows that story," snorted the darker girl. "One of the advantages of living in a small town. We all know each other's dirty laundry."

Gossip! Thistle wiggled with excited anticipation. Good gossip provided food for Pixies when pollen was rare. But were these girls *reliable* gossips?

She eyed them closely: exact opposites, tall and fair, short and dark, heavily made up and bare-faced, careful embellishments of lace and jewelry to the blonde's pioneer costume, the other's stark and prim. Yet they seemed joined at the hip, true friends. Like Thistle and Dusty used to be.

"Pretend I'm not from around here," Thistle prodded the girls. "Pretend I was born and raised by wild Pixies in The Ten Acre Wood."

Both girls giggled. "If it was The Ten Acre Wood, then you were raised by pirates. More barbaric and unlettered than Pixies. Pixies have better manners," M'Velle said.

"What about Dusty?" Thistle prodded before the girls went into a gigglefest about childhood games. "I know she was really sick for a while, but I thought she got over it."

"She beat the cancer with chemo and a bone marrow transplant, but her mom insisted on homeschooling her-even after she got better. They always eat organic, take their shoes off at the door, and wash their hands like a hundred times a day. Dusty tutored us last summer, but she did most of it by email. I'm Meggie, by the way." The blonde tossed the words over her shoulder as she reached inside the icebox for a cold drink. She didn't clean off the can top as Dusty had.

"And I'm M'Velle," the brunette with milk-chocolate skin added. "Ms. Carrick takes books from the library around to old folks in town who don't get out much. And she helps her mom organize Garden Club meetings and stuff, again by email. The old folks, and those of us who work at the museum, may be the only people she sees face-to-face."

"Her mom went ballistic over the cancer thing," Meggie took up the story. "Blamed the school system for letting Dusty 'catch' it when her scrapes and bruises from a playground dustup didn't heal. As if you can 'catch' cancer." She rolled her eyes in disgust.

"Sounds like guilt to me," M'Velle snorted. "Mrs. Carrick blames herself for not being able to protect her child from cancer, and then she couldn't heal her because she wasn't a perfect bone marrow match. Anyone who has passed high school biology knows that a full sibling has the best chance of being a match." M'Velle rolled her eyes. "Ms. Carrick plays in the dust down in the basement rather than face reality. And her mom encourages it because she's still afraid she'll catch something from another person that will kill her precious baby girl."

"You know, if Ms. Carrick got out more, she'd learn a few social skills and feel less awkward in public. She'd learn to talk about something—anything—but history and this museum," Meggie said quietly. "She tells us all the time that practice makes perfect. She should take her own advice. Maybe she'd make a few friends if she took the trouble to go find them."

Thistle hummed a bit of displeasure into the tune that clung to the back of her throat. *Dum dee dee do dum dum*.

"What she needs is a date with a bunch of people. Have a few laughs with a guy before she goes on a solo date," Meggie said.

Thistle wandered around and around the room, her gaze flitting from this to that. Starshine! She missed her wings.

"She needs more than a few laughs. She needs to find someone she can take a mating flight with," Thistle mused. The music inside her soared in memory.

"A what?" both girls asked in chorus.

"In Pixie, when you fall in love, the truly, deeply, forever kind of love, you both fly up to the tallest branches of the Patriarch Oak in the center of The Ten Acre Wood, the one with mistletoe. Then the female flattens her wings, the male grasps her from behind, and they plummet downward. His wings will slow the flight, but aren't strong enough to actually fly them both. The girl has to trust him to get her to the ground safely." Thistle settled on the floor in a corner with her legs crossed. Her middle ached so badly she couldn't stand up anymore. Her internal music died on a sour note.

"Before you can love that deeply, you have to be friends. There's responsibility in friendship."

"Wow! That sounds like the best kind of love ever." Meggie's eyes glazed over, lost in a dream.

"Wouldn't it be easier to face each other, so both of the Pixies can support the flight?" M'Velle asked. She sounded a bit bewildered.

"Oh, that's fun, too," Thistle brightened a bit. "But the other, the mating flight depends on that deep and abiding trust. You have to trust the man with your life as well as your heart and soul. He completes you, and fulfills you. There's nothing else like it."

"What a beautiful metaphor. Pixie love. I'll have to use that expression, start a new fad," Meggie said dreamily, still lost in her imagination. "Maybe I'll write a story about it."

"Sounds like you've had one of those kinds of relationships." M'Velle's eyes narrowed in scrutiny. "What happened? I mean why did the police drop you off here with nothing but a borrowed T-shirt to wear? Seems to me, if you had a guy you trusted so much, you should have called him rather than Dusty Carrick."

"He betrayed me," Thistle replied softly. *And I'll have my revenge on Alder yet.*

"If my boyfriend ever did that to me, I'd kill him," M'Velle insisted.

"Killing is too good for him," Thistle said, an unmusical chuckle formed in the back of her throat. "I gave him a comeuppance. A really good one." She laughed long and hard in memory of her best trick ever.

Then she sobered as she remembered how Alder had lashed out in anger. He'd blasted her so hard she'd landed in Memorial Fountain, stark naked in the middle of rush hour without wings to fly her back home.

No Pixie ever plays tricks on another Pixie. Ever. Go live with humans a while and learn to appreciate being the victim of Pixie tricks, Alder had said.

"Dusty needs to learn to trust people again. I know just the man she belongs with," Thistle said instead, looking toward Joe Newberry's office as the sound of childish giggles erupted in the background. "And you girls are going to help me teach her." Maybe then Thistle Down could find a way home.

"What? No way."

Thistle loosened her clenched fists, hoping she had a little Pixie dust left. With a sharp flash of her arms she flicked her fingers at the girls. A satisfying shaft of lavender, pink, blue, and gold sparkles shot forth from each fingertip.

Meggie and M'Velle gasped in wonder. "What was that?" they asked in unison.

"A diversion to get your attention. Now listen to me," Thistle insisted.

"Well why didn't you just say you had, you know, like something important to say," Meggie grumbled.

"This is important. Dusty is your friend."

Both girls rolled their eyes in response.

"Believe me, she is. How else did you get your jobs this summer? She spoke up for you. She helped you both get better grades in school, so you'd qualify for the jobs." She silently thanked the network of Pixie gossip for that bit of information.

"Yeah, she did," M'Velle admitted. "And I appreciate it. She showed me the best way to get away from prejudice is to get an education."

"So now it's time for you to be a friend to her. Go talk to Dusty. Nothing special, just be friendly, recount your day, laugh at the antics of the children in your tour groups. Let her know that you trust her with your secrets. Be as good a friend to her as she has been to you," Thistle instructed. "I just wish I could go downstairs and help, but underground is death to a Pixie," she mumbled to herself.

"No, I'm afraid you can't assemble your float on the museum grounds tomorrow. The rules say you have to bring it here complete for judging." Dusty said anxiously into the phone in Joe's office. The room was too quiet. She needed background music to keep her from listening to the old house creak as it settled. Or strain to hear how Thistle was getting on with Meggie and M'Velle.

Her boss had taken his daughters to day care and then gone home to change to casual business clothes. She had the place to herself for a couple of minutes until Thistle or Meggie or someone else came looking for her with a problem only she could solve.

"But we just can't get everyone assembled at the garage and then transport them all to the museum by nine!" wailed the chairman of the Chamber of Commerce.

"I'm sorry, sir. Those are the rules you agreed to when you sent in your application for a place in the parade. You signed the agreement. Besides, there will be another activity on the grounds that won't be clear until nine. You cannot show up early just to assemble your hay bales and park benches on the back of a flatbed truck."

The man complained and grumbled with a threat to take the restrictions to the City Council. Dusty held firm, happy that she could conduct this conversation over the phone and not have to face the man. One scowl, and she knew she'd cave in to his demands and ruin the inspection for the grant.

Eventually, he hung up on her.

No sooner had she replaced the phone in its cradle when it rang again.

"Ms. Carrick, I really must insist you open your parents' home for the Historical Tour Wednesday night," Janelle Meacham, chair of the Historical Preservation Committee, demanded without preamble. "It's bad enough that Mabel Gardiner won't open her home. We can't bypass yours as well."

"I'm sorry, Mrs. Meacham. I can't do that. My parents are on sabbatical until September. No one will be home to decorate and show the public rooms." Dusty bit her lip. She began to shake at the idea of playing hostess to hundreds of strangers wandering through the big Queen Anne style home and gardens.

"Nonsense, what else have you and Dick to do with your time? I'll email you the recipe for those shortbread cookies . . ."

"No. I can't eat white flour or processed sugar. I will not bake for your tour, nor will I cancel several meetings and appointments to be there. You will just have to do without stopping at the house. You can admire the gardens from the street."

"But your mother always . . ."

"I am not my mother." This time Dusty hung up first.

Hands shaking as much as her middle, she made a note to make sure Dick mowed the lawn.

Her lunch wanted to come up. She wished now she hadn't eaten the second half of the chicken salad on homemade whole wheat bread. She'd eaten no red meat and only organic fruits and vegetables, free-range chicken, or wild-caught fish for so long she didn't think she could digest anything else. But today, even her wholesome diet felt like a lump of processed glue.

She needed a long walk in the fresh air. But the emails for the coming week of festivities kept piling up.

The phone rang again.

"Damn." Dusty stared at the malevolent tool of society. She blushed at her own bad language. Thought a moment. "Double damn. Skene County Historical Society," she answered sweetly.

"Desdemona, why didn't you answer your cell phone? I've left several messages today." Her mother's voice sounded fuzzy over the long-distance connection.

"Sorry, Mom. I turned it off while I was doing a tour. We're very busy to today with the start of Festival and all." Dusty pulled her phone out of her pocket and flicked on the power. Sure enough there was one, and only one, message from an unknown overseas prefix.

"Oh, well, I won't keep you. I just wanted to make sure you made time to go to the Health Food Market. You can't trust the local grocer to have truly organic food. And the farmers' market isn't much better. They say they use natural fertilizers, but you never know. And did you find the bottle of hand sanitizer in the back of the pantry? It's not as good as soap and water, but in an emergency . . ."

"Yes, Mom. Dick went to the store on Monday." She crossed her fingers at the little lie. She'd bought organic foods from the local farmers' market last Saturday and found they tasted no different and felt no different from the more expensive specialty market. "I know where the hand sanitizer is. Now I really have to go. We're very busy . . ."

"Of course. Just checking. See you in a couple of weeks. Oh, and my college roommate's son will call you. He wants to escort you to the Ball ..." The rest of her words dissolved in static. She dropped the receiver into its cradle.

Dusty breathed heavily and resisted the urge to run to the basement. She really did need to tackle some of those emails. But the privacy she craved wasn't about to happen in Joe's office. Was Norton's Family Diner any less private than this! Everyone in town ended up there at some point in the day, even if only for coffee on the run.

"Can I talk to you a minute, Dusty?" Meggie opened the door a crack and spoke meekly.

"Um, I have twenty-seven, no make that thirty-one emails to answer." Dusty bit her lower lip.

"This will only take a minute." Meggie squeezed into the office, keeping the door closed as much as possible. She kept looking over her shoulder as if needing to keep this visit secret.

Curiosity replaced Dusty's annoyance at the invasion of her space.

"What's up, Meggie?" Dusty leaned forward, forearms braced on the desk. "This hesitancy isn't like you."

"I know. It's just that ... just that I need some advice and you're a friend."

"Huh?"

"Look, I know I don't usually bother you with this kind of thing, but ... but you see, there's this guy. This guy from school. He's really cute and everything. We could have true Pixie love, I think ..." She trailed off, looking as puzzled as Dusty felt.

"And you're asking *me* for advice, why?" She decided to ignore the reference to Pixies.

"You're a friend—and an adult. It just seems like you know a lot about people, even though you don't get out much and all."

Like never, Dusty thought.

"I know a lot about the people who founded this town," Dusty hedged.

"But people are people, whether they live now or a

hundred fifty years ago. And I need to know how to make this guy notice me."

"Invite him to the Ball," Dusty said flatly. "Girls are allowed to do that now. Especially since it's work related and you work here." That was stretching it a bit. Meggie rarely worked even though she showed up every day.

"That's a good idea. But how do I know he'll come?"

"You don't. Not unless you ask." Dusty had answered similar questions from the girls, but usually through email and their tutoring sessions. She smiled a bit inwardly. These girls were her friends. Sort of. And, just like friends, they . . .

Oh, God, this was starting to sound like a setup. Who was going to be the one to comment that Dusty should follow her own advice and ask Chase to accompany her to the Masque Ball?

"Thanks, that's a really good idea." Meggie retreated with her usual determination and eagerness to return to the lounge and her can of cola. She left the door open a crack.

Dusty shifted to look at the computer screen. Her eye caught the blinking red light on line two. She hadn't heard it ring during her conversations, and the girls had strict orders not to tie up the lines with personal calls.

She pushed the chair away from the desk to go investigate—she dismissed the urge to lift the receiver and listen in—when M'Velle slipped into the office with the same furtive over-the-shoulder-glances as Meggie.

"May I speak with you?" M'Velle asked. Dusty noticed how her diction and grammar were more precise than Meggie's more casual style.

"Yes." Dusty dragged out the word, suddenly suspicious that someone wanted her distracted and off the phone.

"It's about my college application essay," M'Velle said, approaching the desk more decisively than her initial entrance.

At least this was something Dusty felt qualified to

discuss. "What about the essay? I thought you'd finished it and were just waiting for a work recommendation from Mr. Newberry."

"Well, yes. But now there's this scholarship I found out about and I want to change my essay to fit."

"What scholarship?"

"DAR."

"Daughters of the American Revolution. They don't usually give those to anyone who can't prove they had an ancestor who fought in the Revolutionary War."

"I know. And finding documentation for blacks prior to 1864 is almost impossible. There are only a few book-keeping entries of the purchase and sale of slaves, often without names. But I'm not all black. My grandfather on my mom's side is white, and very proud of being able to trace his ancestry back to the Civil War. I think I can prove his family owned land in South Carolina back to the mid-1700s."

"So what about your essay?"

"I want to write about the difficulty in tracing my black ancestry because slaves weren't citizens and re-cords of births and deaths, and parentage is so spotty, especially if a baby was sired by a white. It's worse than trying to trace the kings and queens of Pixie. And then I want to compare it to how easy it was to find out about my grandfather's family." M'Velle's eyes lit up with excitement.

"Sounds like a great topic." Dusty leaned forward, equally excited. She wanted to bounce ideas off the wall with this girl and help her come up with a solid research plan and outline.

"But will the DAR approve of it?"

"That's another question entirely. My mom might know. She's a member."

"Oh. I thought you knew about every scholarship available." M'Velle's expression fell, and her eyes grew dark with resentment and disappointment.

"Let me send out a couple of emails to people who

might have some answers for you," Dusty offered. "Mom's in England for the summer, and she's never been good about checking her email or answering it." Though she called every week. Sometimes twice. Or three times.

"You'd do that?"

"Of course. You do good work; study hard now that you're over your sophomore slump. I want you to succeed."

"Thanks, Ms. Carrick." M'Velle looked as if she might reach across the desk and hug Dusty. Then she thought better of it and straightened her posture again. "Can I run my research notes past you? Make sure I'm not jumping to conclusions without facts to back it up?"

"Certainly. Bring them to work tomorrow."

The girl waved blithely and retreated. She, too, showed much more determination in her step upon leaving than arriving.

"Uh, M'Velle, is this sudden interest in consulting me a setup?"

M'Velle paused at the door. She looked over her shoulder, directly into Dusty's eyes. "No. We just want to let you know that we value your friendship." Then she vanished and closed the door with a firm snick of the latch.

Dusty checked the phone. The red light on line two had blinked off as she stared at it.

"Mission accomplished, whatever you two are up to." Now to call Dick and figure out a way to send him to buy Thistle some clothes and then figure out what to do with her. She almost wished Dick was still dating Phelma Jo occasionally—though their relationship had been more off than on since high school. PJ Nelson had an innate sense of fashion. Not something learned because she didn't have anyone at home to learn it from. But when it came to sizes, colors, and cut, PJ was the one Dusty wished she could consult.

Five

PHELMA JO NELSON PEERED over the top of the résumé she held in front of her face. The applicant, who stood so straight and yet so casual in front of her desk, certainly delighted the eye more than the neatly typed words on the paper. Haywood Wheatland. What kind of name was that?

"I don't need an assistant," she said finally. As enticing as this man was, her organization was as complete as she wanted it to be. Adding another body, or a too inquisitive mind, would upset the balance she'd built. Her plans were too close to fruition.

"Yes, you do," Haywood Wheatland said in a light baritone that seemed to sing the words. Then he smiled.

Phelma Jo found her gaze glued to his marvelous teeth and full sensual lips. She couldn't look anywhere else if she wanted to. Daydreams of stripping off his clothes—the epitome of style without shouting expensive, a look she had perfected—and throwing him onto her desk seemed so simple and right.

"Why do I need an assistant?" she finally choked out, breaking the thrall of his physical beauty.

"Not just any assistant. You need me." He paused, the animation in his face and posture froze for half a heartbeat, barely long enough to notice.

But Phelma Jo noticed. She'd trained herself to take note of, and advantage of, every change in body language.

"Not just any assistant. You need me," he repeated with a widening of that ingratiating smile.

Phelma Jo forced herself to read the résumé again. An associate degree from a community college she'd never heard of. Standard word processing skills, including minor bookkeeping. Nothing exceptional. Just another wannabe business major looking for a job to fund the next degree.

"You can't do anything for me that I can't hire out of any high school class at half the wages you request." She threw down the résumé, letting it slide across her pristine desktop as a signal the interview was over.

But, oh, he was delicious to look at. He'd add something decorative to her very functional staff of real estate agents, accountants, and paralegals, all hired for their skills and because none of them outshone Phelma Jo herself.

"You need me because I know how to put a crimp . . ." Again that annoying frozen pause. "You need me because I know how to put a crimp in Desdemona Carrick's Masque Ball forever, and at the same time fund your campaign in the next mayoral election."

Haywood Wheatland planted himself in the guest chair in front of the desk without invitation, as if he belonged there, had always belonged there.

"How . . . how did you know I plan to run for mayor?"

"Gossip." He smiled, flashing those gleaming teeth that seemed to reflect every color in the office. "Gossip. Besides, it's the next logical step for you."

"Tell me more about this gossip." Phelma Jo leaned forward eagerly. "And your plans for Dusty Carrick."

"Am I hired?"

Phelma Jo fished an employment contract out of her desk drawer, made a few adjustments to it, and handed it to him for his signature.

"You've heard, I presume," Haywood said, leaning forward conspiratorially, "that Ms. Carrick has taken under her wing, a beautiful and mysterious woman . . ."

"Don't be ridiculous. Dusty is incapable of talking to a stranger, let alone aiding one. Unless she can do it online."

"Ah, but she volunteers at the senior center ... volunteers at the senior center talking about history and gathering stories from them about olden times. And she gives tours to the public. She may not like it, but she does it. She does it if she can talk history and nothing else. And now this Thistle Down woman is her newest best friend."

"I can't see why everyone in town thinks the world of Ms. Timid who talks to shadows and jumps into them at first sight of a stranger. She's pathetic and so self-involved she doesn't know the meaning of true friendship," Phelma Jo snorted. She should know.

"This is pretty?" Thistle held up a brassiere by one end with two fingers, skeptically examining the sturdy elastic, sheer fabric, and filmy lace. "I could make a great game of launching Pixies to the far side of The Ten Acre Wood with this."

Dusty suppressed a deep laugh. "It ... um ... is designed to support your ... um ..."

Thistle twisted the undergarment so that it hung correctly. "My boobs," she said flatly.

"Yeah."

Thistle looked from the bra to her chest and back again. "How do you balance with all that weight up front and no wings to lift you from the back?"

She looked totally bewildered. She kept rocking back on her heels and widening her stance as if afraid of falling forward. Good thing Dick had bought only flat-heeled sandals for Thistle instead of the high-heeled torture devices he usually admired on women.

"Well, they grow slowly." Dusty glanced down at her meager display. Thistle was much better endowed, but not out of proportion to her height and slender frame. "We get used to it gradually, I guess," Dusty replied. "Look, most of the dresses Dick bought for you have halter tops or spaghetti straps. You can't wear a normal bra with them. The straps will show and that looks ugly."

"Yeah. I have noticed a lot of teenage girls with that look. I wondered what the extra straps were for."

They giggled together as Thistle mimicked the girls who constantly fussed with their straps, trying to hide them, when the action only attracted more attention to their dishabille.

"But the fabric?" Thistle shook her head. "It feels hot. I don't think I'm going to wear this contraption." She flung the bra into the corner of the room.

"Try this dress." Dusty pulled a creamy sundress printed with big splotchy purple flowers out of a plastic bag from a large discount store. "It's cotton, so the fabric will breathe, unlike the polyester in the bra. The colors are right for you, and the top is relatively modest. You won't flash a lot of cleavage."

Thistle obediently lifted the hem of her borrowed black T-shirt, exposing her entire body without a flash of embarrassment or modesty.

Dusty lowered her eyes as she fished in the other five bags for panties. Her face grew hot, and sweat trickled down her back. Body modesty was something Thistle would *have* to learn living in this household, with Dick's bedroom just across the hall.

What would they do if Thistle was still here when Mom and Dad came home from England next month?

Her fingers flipped aside several dresses, packages of hose, another bra. Two more pairs of sandals, one beige, one dark purpley blue. No panties. None! How could Dick forget such an essential item?

This enterprise was getting to be too much. Way too much.

"Let me get you something from my room." She dashed out of the spare bedroom of the big old house that had been in her family for at least four generations. The room she'd slept in for as long as she could remember was positioned on the other side of the bathroom, across from the master bedroom, and close to the back stairs that led to the kitchen. For the first time in a very long time she noticed, actually noticed, the matching pink curtains and bedspread covered in twirling ballerinas. The bed ruffle and bolster pillow ruffles were white eyelet. Chipped white paint graced her headboard, dressing table, and bookshelves. She hadn't changed a thing since she and Mom had so carefully selected the furnishings for her fifth birthday.

Had her life stagnated as badly as her décor?

From her own underwear drawer she found an unopened package of three pairs of white cotton panties. As she pulled them from beneath neatly piled, still serviceable garments she began to laugh.

At herself. At Dick for forgetting to buy panties. He probably never noticed if women wore them or not, even the women he so casually bedded.

Something to taunt him about. In private. Still laughing, she returned to Thistle's room and presented her with the underwear as if bestowing the crown jewels.

With more laughter, and no embarrassment, she explained their usage. And while she was at it, she found a box of tampons and demonstrated the toilet and sink.

Their laughter felt natural; embarrassment fled.

Suitably clad, Thistle began rummaging through the plastic bags. She jerked her hand away before she'd touched a single garment.

"What?" Dusty asked. She grabbed Thistle's hand and watched a burning flush spread from her fingers to the back and across the palm. "Let's get some cold water on this."

"The bags, and the second dress, they're fake." Thistle sighed with relief as cold water from the bathroom tap flowed over her hand and arm.

"Synthetics. Of course! I bet you'll have trouble with preservatives and processed food, too. Good thing you came to me. Most every other home in town would poison you in about three minutes."

"Why do people poison themselves?" Thistle asked, cocking her head.

Dusty shrugged. "Convenience, shelf-life, laziness.

I'm not sure. But since I was sick, Mom and Dad have done their best to keep me from getting sick again. We eat only natural foods and use only natural fabrics. It's hard eating out and harder buying inexpensive clothes or towels, or even upholstery that aren't synthetic. Mom took out all the wall-to-wall carpeting because it holds dust and mold and is largely artificial fibers."

"I bet that's why so many people are so fat. They can't walk!" Thistle mimicked a man who had come to the museum that afternoon and had to sit every five steps, wheezing and out of breath.

Dusty'd had to restrain Thistle's natural tendency to roll the little rubber ball from her game of jacks underneath him, just to watch him hop about in fright.

"He needed the exercise," Thistle reminded her.

"What else do Pixies do besides play tricks?" Dusty asked upon returning to Thistle's room.

"Oh, Pixies are the best matchmakers of all. And I know just the man for you!"

"Really." Dusty's bright mood faded. "Who?" If Thistle played her matchmaking games as poorly as her mother, Dusty needed to stop it right here and now.

"Joe Newberry, of course. He really needs a wife, and you really need to be a mother to his daughters."

Dusty nearly doubled over in laughter. "Joe's my best friend. Not my lover. Besides, I don't think he ever played in The Ten Acre Wood. We have no shared memories."

"We'll see about that. Think about the new memories you will build together around the Patriarch Oak."

Thistle lay down upon the bed, amazed at how the mattress and coverlet cradled her body. Much nicer, if lonelier, than curling up with seven other Pixies in a tangle of moss. Life was so different among the humans; so strange. And yet she had observed them for decades. She should know how they lived, how they thought, the appliances they took for granted.

The red numerals on the black box on the small table beside the bed must mean something.

"Five, two dots, four, five," she mused. "That sounds like a time. Humans are obsessed with time. But I'm not sure what it means."

The color scheme depressed her. It hadn't worked ten years ago. One might graciously call it eggplant and evergreen with heavy dark wood accents. Thistle had never seen those kinds of trees, and to her the colors looked more like bloody mud and algae green atop alien and dangerous forests.

She closed her eyes and absorbed the scent of the room. Much nicer than looking at it. Roses, lavender, and cherry in the pomander on the dressing table. A bit too heavy and sweet, like the paint scheme. Maybe take out the cherry and add cedar?

Her hands caressed the soft coverlet and her dress. Sort of like the silky texture of the cobwebs, embellished with feathers and flower petals, which she usually wore. And much more substantial. But then, humans were also obsessed with keeping their bodies covered, or at least portions of them.

How was she supposed to get used to all this?

How was she supposed to sleep alone? Pixies slept in a tangle of legs and arms and wings, finding security in the gentle breeze of a dozen breaths all working in rhythm, a dozen hearts beating in time. Nothing sexual about it. Sex was sex and sleep was sleep. Unlike humans, Pixies didn't mix the two.

The loneliness of living in a human body among humans who closed themselves off from each other was perhaps the cruelest punishment of all.

Moisture crept out of Thistle's eyes and down her cheek. She missed the light breeze supporting her wings, drifting around her with the information about the weather, about her surroundings, and who trespassed within The Ten Acre Wood.

Memory grabbed hold of her, taking her soaring, playing

tag with oak leaves, tweaking the tail of a squirrel, dancing just out of reach of the frog's tongue. She hungered and took a sip of pollen. Dewdrops clinging to the bottom of a fern or in the cup of lupine leaves quenched her thirst.

A shimmer of movement above her, bright green and tan, the color of alder leaves and branches. She giggled. A deeper, enticing laugh was the only reply. More a challenge than any words.

Thistle rose to the occasion and chased the source of the laughter around a tree trunk, skimmed the top of fern fronds, dashed beneath a rhododendron, and skipped across the gentle wind-driven currents of the pond. He laughed and escaped. She chortled and dove beneath him, then looped around and came at him from the side. With one last burst of speed and a new round of bright laughter, she caught the tip of Alder's left wing with her left hand. As he slowed in their game of tag, she flipped him around to face her.

Hovering within the shadows of the Patriarch Oak, with only a whisper of air between them, they came to rest in the joint where a stout branch met the trunk.

He cupped her face in both hands and kissed her deeply. "The ancient Faery living in the heart of the Patriarch Oak has died," he whispered.

"What does that mean?" Thistle couldn't remember a time when her tribe had anyone other than the nameless old one as their king. He'd stayed when the rest of the Faeries went underhill, taking their abundant magic with them.

"We need a king, someone to make rules and protect us from predators. No one else knows how to do the job, so I volunteered. The old one has been teaching me. I am going to be king," he whispered. "Tomorrow I will be king. And I will need a queen. Today, right now, you and I will fly to the top of this tree, the center of the universe, and take our mating flight."

Thistle returned his kiss and spoke aloud. "In full daylight where all can see and know that we belong together. Forever."

Six

DICK CHECKED THE CALLER ID before answering his phone on the second ring while he sipped cold lemonade in the kitchen. A foreign code preceded the long line of numbers.

"Hi, Mom," he said brightly.

"How did you know it was me, sweetie?" Mom's breathy voice came clearly over the thousands of miles of cell phone signals.

"Caller ID, Mom. What's up?" As if he didn't know.

"Oh, just checking up on you kids. What's Dusty doing? Did she get a call from my college roommate's son?"

"Actually, Mom, we're going on a double date tonight." Dick bit his lip, hoping his all-too-perceptive mother wouldn't catch the lie.

"Why, that's wonderful, Dick. I hope she likes Ted Summerfield."

Nothing about Dick; all she ever asked about was his reclusive sister as if she were still a teenager, just venturing back into reality after chemo-induced isolation. Heavy sadness settled on his shoulders. He wondered briefly if maybe Dusty truly was only an adolescent emotionally. She'd never grown beyond the restricted life appropriate to a twelve year old.

"Dusty and I are meeting Chase and a new girl at the Old Mill tonight. Just pizza and beer and maybe some dancing. We'll be home early. I haven't heard anything about a Ted Summerfield."

"Oh, well. I guess he hasn't had a chance to call her

yet. I trust Chase. You keep an eye on your sister, though. Make sure she orders the vegetarian pizza with whole wheat crust and organic soy cheese . . ."

"Yes, Mom." *The Dusty special, the cooks called it.* He scratched his fingernails over the receiver. "Um, Mom, I'm losing you. Cell phones, you know. They aren't really reliable over this kind of distance." Though he could hear her perfectly well, and he ran his business entirely from his phone.

"Of course, dear. Just needed to check on you and Dusty. We are having a wonderful time. Saw two plays yesterday. I'll send a postcard." She spoke over-loud, spitting her consonants as if she recited lines from a stage without microphones. "See you in three weeks. Bye, sweetie." She made kissy noises and rang off.

Dick closed the phone and rested his forehead against the long farm kitchen table. Nothing ever changed. Dusty was still Mom's sick baby, and he was her wayward son charged with his sister's care.

What did he have to do to make a life of his own? Mentally, he added up his savings account and investments. Next month, he'd have enough money for a down payment on his own house. Moving back home for the summer had helped a lot. He'd wasted a lot of money these last five years on rent and expensive but insignificant dates.

He'd buy a house and move into it just as soon as his parents returned from England. There were a lot of good buys out there now with foreclosures and short sales. He couldn't leave Dusty alone before then.

That new house would be awfully empty without someone to share it with. He closed his eyes trying to picture his ideal house and roommate. Thistle was the only one he could think of.

"Too bad Joe couldn't make it tonight," Thistle said blithely to Dick and Dusty as they entered the Old Mill

Bar and Grill. She scuffed her new leather sandals through the sawdust and peanut shells littering the floor.

Dick preened a bit at how well he'd chosen clothing for her. He'd taken his time, compared prices and quality, looking for just the right color combinations and simple styles he thought a Pixie might wear. All the while he stayed pretty close to the budget Dusty had given him. He'd hardly made a dent in his checking account.

"No Pixie would ever let her den get so dirty. Doesn't anyone ever sweep this place?" Thistle wrinkled her elegantly narrow nose at the smells of spilled beer, salty peanuts, and too many people packed together.

"That's called ambiance," Dick replied for his sister. "Joe's a nice guy, but he'd be a fifth wheel tonight." He held the swinging door open for his sister and her friend. His friend, too, he hoped. Damn, she smelled good. Nothing like lavender soap and shampoo to set his senses ringing.

"Actually the sawdust hearkens back to the days when the saloons had dirt floors," Dusty said. She looked more confident talking about history than approaching a crowd of strangers. "The earth was dampened and packed as solid as baked clay. The sawdust helped absorb spills—especially blood from bar fights."

Thistle's eyes sparkled with mischief.

"Do you want to go home, Dusty?" Dick asked softly.

"No, she does not!" Thistle insisted. "I spent almost an hour getting her ready and persuading you to bring us." She grabbed Dusty's arm and nearly dragged her into the dim bar.

Dick opened his mouth to protest. Thistle shot him a glance that froze the words in his throat. They felt like a solid and jagged lump pressing against his voice box. He couldn't breathe around it.

He coughed and coughed again, trying to dislodge it.

Thistle slapped his back in a time-honored attempt to free him of the spasm.

"Are you okay?" She sounded genuinely concerned.

He forgot any kind of protest in the warmth of her concern. And the obstruction dissolved.

"Chase is already here," Dusty said. She pressed backward against the wall beside the bar, observing the crowd.

"Good. He'll have ordered beer," Dick said, his voice still a little wobbly.

"And so is Phelma Jo." Dusty turned to leave.

Thistle blocked her exit. "If you leave, she wins."

"She always wins."

"She doesn't have to." Thistle put one hand against Dusty's back and the other in the crook of Dick's elbow and marched them both over to where Chase had claimed a large table at the edge of the dance floor. His pale blond hair reflected the light from an overhead chandelier made of deer antlers and bulbs shaped like candle flames.

As they moved toward him, the noise from the jukebox playing country tunes, the clack of pool balls hitting each other, and dozens of people trying to talk over each other slammed into Dick like a wall. Off to the left, Judge John Pepperidge presided at a large round table with a birthday cake in the center. Judge Johnny's oldest nephew blew out the twenty-one candles. Then the chant was begun by the bartender, and was picked up and echoed by every patron: "No ties, no ties. No ties."

The nephew looked up, a little perplexed. Judge Johnny took the opportunity to produce a pair of large shears from the shadows beneath the table. With one deft movement he cut the young man's tie off just above the knot and brandished it above his head like a trophy. The crowd burst into a round of applause. The bartender came out from behind his barrier, bowed to the birthday boy, took the severed tie from the judge's hands and promptly nailed it to the wall behind them, one of hundreds.

Tommy Ledbetter, otherwise known as "Digger" snapped photos of the whole proceedings.

Thistle cast him a puzzled look. "A rite of passage," Dick explained.

"Oh. Oh!" Her eyes lit with understanding and mischief.

"We have something similar in Pixie, the younglings have to prove their ability to fly the full length of the waterfall from bottom to top before they are considered adults and ready to mate."

He burned with jealousy at the idea of her mating with anyone else, human or Pixie.

At that moment he realized that he had never doubted her story. Thistle was a Pixie stripped of her wings. She was the girl he'd fallen in love with when he was fourteen, the girl he'd held as a standard that no other woman could measure up to.

And she had to return to Pixie.

Chase noticed Phelma Jo showing off her new boyfriend as they made the circuit of the room. Where had she found him? Not locally. Chase made of point of recognizing faces around town. Part of his job. With the downturn in the economy, fewer people moved here from Portland, thirty miles north. Newcomers were rare. And he should recognize his contemporaries who'd moved back to town to live with their parents.

So where had this guy come from? Maybe Phelma Jo bought him for the night. Something about the too ready smile and too white teeth of the stranger made the fine hairs on Chase's nape stand straight up.

Phelma Jo and her escort stopped to exchange greetings with Big Mike, the mechanic who owned the car care center at the south end of Main St, and Jim Butler, his landlord, before they wandered into the back room. Mike and Jim shook hands, sealing some kind of deal. Digger snapped a photo of that, too. Neither one would be able to renege on whatever they agreed upon tonight. That's how business got done in this town.

Not parading a trophy boy around the bar.

Chase couldn't see PJ and her newest acquisition from his vantage point. He'd chosen this table because he could see the entire room from here. But not the back room. Not much ever happened back there. Three pool tables filled most of the available space. Players barely had room between them to maneuver their cues without putting out the eye of an opponent or clonking a neighbor in the back of the head.

Thinking only of gaining a line of sight into the room, Chase grabbed Dusty's hand before she could completely settle in the chair next to him. "Let's dance," he ordered and set her on her feet with his hands on her waist.

"But ... but ..."

The jukebox thundered out a quick two-step. He raised his right knee and began clomping around. He whipped his head about, making sure he circled the dance floor. Just as he got the back room in full view, Phelma Jo and her trophy emerged and took seats on the opposite side of the dance floor from the table Chase had claimed. The stranger seemed to steer Phelma Jo on a broad circuit so that they never came close to the table where Dick and Thistle sat.

With a quick shift of direction that left him half dizzy, and Dusty stumbling in his arms, Chase side-stepped back the way they'd come.

Right in front of Phelma Jo, he twirled Dusty under his arm and reclaimed her just as the music tweetered to a halt.

Not knowing what else to do, he looked down at Dusty.

"That was—exhilarating," she said somewhat breathlessly.

"Yeah." A smile crept up on his face. "Want to go again?"

The next tune turned into a lovelorn ballad set to a waltz. Waltzes were good. Easy to dance to. A good excuse to draw his partner close within the circle of his arms.

Out of the corner of his eye, he caught a glimpse of Dick and that Thistle woman flitting about the floor. Dick guided her masterfully through the dance. She glided gracefully but didn't seem to actually follow his steps.

"I didn't know Dick could dance," he muttered.

"Mom taught us both the basics when we were in grade school," Dusty said. Her gaze caught the graceful couple and stayed there. "No proper and polite education is complete without ballroom dancing."

Chase made a mental note to run a full background check on Thistle Down. He had her fingerprints. The rest should be easy.

"I'd like to·dance," Phelma Jo said quietly to her escort.

"Sorry. I don't dance," he replied.

"You're my assistant now. I like to dance. I suggest you learn. Quick."

"Trouble in paradise already," Chase muttered. He had a clue to the man's identity. He could mine the gossip mill tomorrow. Then he whisked Dusty across the floor.

He took a moment to look at her, feel the warmth of her back where he held her, appreciate the slight flush on her upturned face. Her eyes shone with an excitement he hadn't seen there for a long time. Not since she got sick.

He wanted to see that glow of happiness more often. He wanted to be the one to help her grow into her self-confidence so she could look beyond her fears.

Seven

"PIZZA'S HERE," THISTLE SAID. She wiggled out of Dick's dance pose. A ridiculous and awkward stance. To truly dance, one needed only space and wings to catch the wind in pure joy.

She recognized the hold as part of human, unnaturally strained, courting rituals. Pixies rarely bothered with more than a few flirtatious flits around their territory. If a couple liked each other, they went off to a private glade and explored the possibilities of a potential mating flight.

Oh, well, she wouldn't be here long enough to follow up on the interesting way Dick's hand clenched against her back, or the way his fingers entwined with hers as they made their way back to their chairs and the fragrant and steaming dishes a waiter had plopped down in the center of the round table. Dick's hand kept her from stumbling on every imperfection in the floor.

Chase and Dusty joined them a moment later. They looked flushed and happy.

Thistle narrowed her eyes in speculation. She could definitely see their energies reaching toward each other. At least that part of her magic hadn't faded along with her other Pixie traits.

This wouldn't do at all. Chase was not the man for Dusty. He'd kill her imagination and overshadow her intellect with his energy and lust for life. Dusty needed to match up with Joe. But Joe didn't have a sitter for his daughters tonight. So he stayed home while Dusty danced with another man.

Hmm. What could she do about that?

Dusty's aura retracted deep within herself as she sipped at the foaming brew in her glass. Good. Chase wasn't the right man for her. Thistle needed to direct Dusty's attention back toward Joe. There was a man who truly needed her. And so did his daughters. Two little girls at just the right age to be befriended by a Pixie.

Hmmm. Ideas spun in her head.

Besides. Chase had a mean streak. Thistle had been his victim when he was eight or nine. He couldn't be trusted. Nope. No way.

"Anyone ever see Phelma Jo's companion before?" Chase asked.

The two men's attention fixed on a long-legged beauty across the dance floor. She wore a dark gray straight skirt and plain pink blouse as if they were royal robes, created to enhance her personality. Something was just a little off about her ...

"Do you mean the woman with the fake blonde hair?" Thistle asked, directing her gaze across the room.

"She dyes her hair?" Dusty asked incredulously.

"Of course she does. Her roots are almost as dark as my hair," Thistle replied.

"She was blonde when we were kids." Dusty brightened considerably as she reached for a piece of the bread and cheese and tomato sauce confection piled high with semi-cooked vegetables.

"Never seen him before. He certainly seems attentive to Phelma Jo, though." Dick shrugged and snagged his own piece of pizza.

"Something about him bothers me," Chase said quietly. "Can't put my finger on it."

"Maybe you're just jealous," Dick laughed.

That made Thistle turn her attention across the dance floor. If Chase were truly jealous, then he needed to stay away from Dusty and not hurt her anymore than he already had.

"He reminds me of someone," Thistle mused. "Can't wrap a wingtip around the memory, though." She tapped her teeth, trying to place the square face with hair the color of wheat ripening in August sunshine.

"That's an interesting metaphor." Dusty looked puzzled. "Not a phrase most people would use."

"Who said I'm most people? Now what's this on top of the pizza?" Thistle pointed to a brown blob that looked crumpled and nasty.

"That's Italian sausage. Try it, very tasty," Dick informed her. He picked a similar nugget off his piece of pizza and ate it separately, smacking his lips and smiling at the delicacy.

"Um . . . no thanks." Thistle put her hands in her lap, though her tummy growled with demands for food. Not a bit of pollen or a mosquito in sight.

"Stick to the mushrooms and olives, you can pick off the meat. Or try my veggie special," Dusty whispered. "Do you eat cheese?"

"Cheese? Of course I like cheese," Thistle replied with enthusiasm. And mushrooms. She knew about mushrooms and the delicious things they could do to dizzying flight with or without a mate. Alder knew where the best rings of them grew and how to snatch them out from under the noses of the Faeries. But olives?

"Olives are those little black circles. They're a kind of berry, but they're savory and salty—not sweet, " Dusty explained.

"If I eat human food, will I be forced to remain human?" Thistle whispered to Dusty.

"I don't know. That's the Greek myth of Persephone, and some tales of European elves who trick humans into staying with them. The theory could extend to Pixies. But if you don't eat, you will get sick and die. So eat and enjoy." Dusty took a big bite of cheese and bread.

Die of sadness because she couldn't return to Pixie, or die of hunger while she held out hope? Thistle felt heavy with no wings to lighten her. Her throat grew hot and nearly closed. Moisture gathered in her eyes. Tears. She'd seen children cry often enough, and helped them get over their hurts. But Pixies didn't cry.

The savory food no longer enticed her. She lifted the glass of beer someone had set in front of her. One long swallow. She almost spat out the bitterness. But the liquid felt good on her convulsing throat.

She took another more cautious sip. If she ignored the first impression of bitterness, and sought the undertaste of grains and fruit and sweetness, it tasted like something Trillium would add to a festive dinner back home.

Before she realized how much she'd drunk, the glass was empty and Chase was refilling it from a pitcher. Much of Thistle's heaviness lifted away.

Then Phelma Jo and her blond companion paraded toward them. The companion hung back as Phelma Jo approached their table.

"I didn't receive an official invitation to the Masque Ball, Miss Carrick," she said arrogantly. Her overbite nearly covered her lower lip and she scrunched her nose in distaste, making her look like a rabbit with wounded dignity.

"You didn't?" Dusty asked, opening her eyes wide with innocence. "I'll look into that in the morning."

Thistle heard Dusty's reply from across the room. She looked up and found herself facing the far wall filled with hats made of fake raccoon fur. She shook herself and tried to remember how she got here. Her mind wandered away from that bit of information as quickly as her feet wandered toward the door as she tried to go back to the table.

She had to watch her friends from a distance, it seemed. Thistle knew Dusty's expression of furtive eyes and a quiver in her jaw as she fought to hide a smile. She had deliberately removed Phelma Jo's name from the guest list.

"My assistant will come to your office first thing and pick up my invitation," Phelma Jo spat.

"All the invitations went out by email this year," Dusty replied. "Perhaps I no longer have a valid address for you."

The tall man standing slightly behind Phelma Jo's shoulder leaned forward to whisper something in her ear. His eyes sought and held Dusty's gaze. He smiled at her and then backed away.

Thistle tried to return to the table so she could hear more. Three steps later she was at the front door, and Dick had to guide her back toward their table.

What was going on?

"I expect a written invitation. Have it ready for Haywood at 9:15 tomorrow morning." Phelma Jo marched away, tossing her thick mane of bleached blonde hair. Her companion had already retreated.

"The museum doesn't open until eleven, after the end of the parade," Dusty called after them.

Phelma Jo didn't acknowledge the correction, but Haywood Wheatland flashed that glorious smile directly at Dusty.

"Like I'm at her beck and call!" Dusty protested. "She's never come to the Ball before. Why now?"

"I remember her," Thistle mused. "Nasty child who trapped me in a jar with a wolf spider. Almost as nasty as the boy who glued my wings together with dog drool." She speared Chase with a glance.

He choked and tried to bury his blushing face in his glass. He remembered.

Thistle turned her attention back to Phelma Jo. A pattern of energy grew around her, linking in a long chain back to . . .

Thistle dropped her sandal in front of the couple dancing a vigorous two-step right in front of her. They stumbled, bumping into a passing waitress, who reared back against the jukebox, knocking a listing music lover against the bar. The bartender reached to grab a line of bottles. But they cannonaded into each other, dropping in a line the full length of the bar. At the end, another patron lunged to grab the last bottle to keep it from spilling. He lost his balance and stuck out his foot behind him, catching a waiter in the crotch. He doubled over, spilling a full pitcher of beer on top of Phelma Jo's head just as she returned to her chair.

The beer bounced off of Haywood Wheatland. What the . . . ?

Dusty's jaw dropped in amazement. Then she had to bite her cheeks to keep from laughing out loud. Her eyes sparked with amusement.

"See, PJ doesn't always win," Thistle whispered.

Phelma Jo spat and spluttered and dripped. She loosed a stream of curses worthy of a Faery drunk on honey.

"Ah, I feel much better," Thistle said and grabbed the last piece of pizza on the tray. She ate it in five big bites, not bothering to pick off the meat.

Eight

❧

SOMETHING ABOUT THE HOT NIGHT AIR, high humidity, and the smell of spilled beer on her now ruined silk blouse played tricks on Phelma Jo's vision as she drove home to her condo overlooking the river and the railroad tracks. The buildings blurred, overlapping the shacks she'd torn down for the expensive development.

"I am in control of my life. I am rich and successful. I don't owe anything to anybody—except a few mortgages. No one tells me what to do. I don't have to remember my god-awful childhood. It's in the past. It's over. I'm not that scared child anymore." She repeated her personal litany over and over as the blocks grew longer and her mind kept drifting to the past when the smell of beer on a hot night ruled her life.

Her mind drifted back to where she'd started twenty years ago, back when life was one long pain in the ass . . .

"I'm theven now, you are thuppothed to take care of me!" Phelma Jo yelled at her mother through her oversized and gaping front teeth. "You're thuppothed to make sure there'th food in the houthe and cook it. Not me!" At least that was what the latest foster mother told her before Mom had sobered up and taken her away from the family that had fed and clothed her for six months.

Mom actually took care of her for almost six weeks before she brought a new boyfriend home, and he bought a bottle of the clear liquid that smelled so awful. That was five bottles and three days ago.

Now the boyfriend was trying to play Daddy and help Phelma Jo take her bath. It didn't feel right having him touch her where she knew no one was supposed to touch her.

Before Mom could take another swig out of the latest bottle and the boyfriend could drag her back to the bathtub, Phelma Jo stomped out of the tumbledown one-bedroom house beside the railroad. The moment her feet hit the pavement, she started running, her too-small sandals scuffing against the street. Hot tears ran down her face. Her breath came in short gasps around the huge lump inside her.

Five blocks away, straight up the cliff, The Ten Acre Wood loomed tall and dark and mysterious. A hiding place. She didn't even look back to see if the boyfriend followed her. Or care.

The quiet coolness welcomed her on the hot summer evening. Birds chirped happily. A frog croaked from the muddy spot that in winter was a small pond. The scent of hot fir sap and sweet thistles filled her nose. Her sweat dried along with her tears as she picked her way along a faint trail to a hollow stump. Deep inside, she found the cracked and stained mason jar she'd stolen from one of the old ladies who lived across the street from the park. She unscrewed the cap and crept toward the little clearing where dragonflies rested, soaking up the last of the sunshine for the day.

Something moved in the shadows to her right. She froze in place and looked only with her eyes, suddenly afraid. The kids in school said these woods were haunted. They said that weird things happened to kids who came here alone.

Most of the time, Phelma Jo didn't believe them. But now . . . the shadows grew long and the evening winds came up to chill her arms and her knees.

The shadow moved again. She dropped her gaze to a small tree that lay across her path. The biggest spider she'd ever seen crawled along the rotting wood. Brown and hairy. "I bet you're mean ath well ath ugly," she whispered. "As mean as the boyfriend. Well, I'm meaner. I have to be meaner."

Cautiously, she stooped and rested the jar on the log with the open mouth toward the spider. Inch by inch, she nudged it closer to the bug. The glass bumped up against one of the hairy brown legs.

The spider raised that leg and waved it about, kinda like it was sniffing. Then it crawled inside, pausing with each step.

Phelma Jo remained as still as still could be until her prize had climbed all the way inside. Then in one swift motion she scooped the lid over the opening and screwed it tight.

"Just what I need to make life interething. Should I turn you loothe up my mom'th thkirt while she thleeps? Maybe you'll bite the boyfriend when hith handth get too clothe to her."

A faint buzzing drew her attention. She batted at whatever bug dive-bombed her ear. Jewel-bright wings caught the sunlight in the clearing just ahead.

Phelma Jo watched the purple dragonfly swoop down to the mudhole, tagging the top of a frog's head. She followed cautiously, still holding her prized spider inside the jar. Her hand unscrewed the top but left it in place as she took a wary step crossing over her previous wary step.

The birds stopped singing. The breeze faded away. All was still.

She watched as the dragonfly spread its wings and settled on a broad fern frond overhanging the dried mud at the edge of the pool. Not much water left this time of year.

Watching where she placed her feet, making sure she didn't rustle a leaf or crack a twig, Phelma Jo moved up beside the colorful bug. She slid the jar beneath the fern, right below where the dragonfly perched.

As quickly as she'd trapped the spider, she caught the

bug with the lid and forced it into the jar, along with the fern tip. The plant made a ripping noise as it lost the bit of its leaf.

The dragonfly beat frantically against the glass with wings and tiny feet. It flitted about, desperate to stay away from the spider.

"Let'th play that you're my mom and the thpider ith her boyfriend. When he eats you, my fothter mom and dad can come get me. They'll make sure I get thupper. They'll make sure no one touches me where they shouldn't."

"Help, help. Let me out!"

Phelma Jo thought she heard a cry. Only her imagination. Imagination would get her into trouble, just like the kids who scared themselves with ghost stories about The Ten Acre Wood, then tripped and got hurt trying to run away too fast to look where they were going.

She held the jar up to the slanting sunlight, admiring the bright colors and wondering how long the bug could evade the spider. Wouldn't it be funny if she let them both out under her mom's skirt as she lay on the sofa too drunk to move?

"That's not really a dragonfly, you know," Dick Carrick said from right behind her. He reached an arm over her shoulder and grabbed the jar away from her.

"Hey, that'th mine!" Phelma Jo shouted. She jumped, trying to snatch the jar back.

"It's not nice to hurt spiders and Pixies and things," Dick admonished her.

"Juth cuth you're older and bigger than me, doethn't mean you can tell me what to do. No one can tell me what to do." Phelma Jo jumped again.

Dick held her still with one hand on top of her head. At the same time, he tucked the jar under his arm and unscrewed the lid with his free hand. The dragonfly slipped through the first opening before the spider had a chance to follow.

"Hey, I worked hard to catch my peth," Phelma Jo protested.

Dick just watched the dragonfly circle his head and flit away into the woods. "You're welcome," he said quietly, almost in awe of the bug.

"You're ath crathy ath your thithter, talking to bugth." Phelma Jo stomped away in disgust.

She waited in the shadows of the old railway shed for the boyfriend to turn out all the lights and fall asleep before creeping back into the house. She washed her hands and face from the cold water in the tub. But not her whole body. She wouldn't take off her clothes and give him the chance to spy on her. Or touch her.

"What are we going to do about Thistle, Dick?" Chase whispered to his friend as they stood on the wraparound porch of the Carrick home. The Queen Anne style pile of gingerbread and turrets had been in Dick's family since it was built over a hundred years ago.

Chase thought it an eyesore with Mrs. Carrick's most recent paint job of pink with white trim and yellow highlights. Not just any pink either. A screaming harem-pink worthy of a whorehouse.

He hated that Dusty had to live with that image. But then she lived so quietly she'd never found the need to move out on her own. Did she even know how ugly the house was?

Dick thrived away from his mother's stifling influence. But he'd finally decided he needed to save enough money for a down payment on a house. So he moved in with Dusty for the summer while their parents were away.

Or maybe he moved back home to protect Dusty from being alone. That would be just like him.

"What do you mean, 'what are we going to do about Thistle?'" Dick asked. He kept looking over his shoulder.

"Dick, look at me. The girls don't need you to put a very drunk Thistle to bed." Though Dick looked like he really wanted to do just that. "She knows too much about things she has no business knowing. Things about us. How'd she find out?"

"Huh?"

"How'd she know I glued a dragonfly's wings together with dog drool from my red mastiff when I was eight? Remember the posters I used to glue to the wall with Julia's dog drool. Better than superglue."

Dick smiled. "Yeah. Who'd of thought it would work."

"Yeah. And how'd Thistle know Phelma Jo tried to capture a very similar dragonfly in a glass jar in the same stretch of The Ten Acre Wood?"

"You believed in Faeries and Pixies when you were little," Dick said. His eyes finally focused on Chase. "I remember."

"I gave up that notion by second grade. The same time I stopped believing in Santa Claus, the tooth fairy, and the Easter Bunny. I thought you did, too."

Dick looked as if he wanted to say something, but he clamped his mouth shut instead and let his gaze drift up to the waxing moon. "We'll have a full moon for the Masque Ball. Magic happens under the full moon. Especially in The Ten Acre Wood."

"Only for dreamers and lunatics. You're no help at all."

"Should I be? Think about all the wonderful things we did as kids, all the pirate games and exploring the wonders of finding a bird's nest or watching frogs hop from tuft to tuft in search of the perfect bit of mud."

"All natural. Except the pirate games. And that's just kids playing. You're a trained scientist. You, of all people, should know that Faeries and Pixies exist only in children's stories."

"Ever think we might be living inside one giant story?"

Chase snorted. "Just keep Dusty safe. That Thistle woman is a con artist if I ever saw one. Too bad I can't arrest her without evidence." He started down the broad stairs. Then he had another thought and returned to

Dick's side. "What made you invite Dusty and her new best friend to the bar tonight? I thought it was supposed to be just us men watching the game."

"It seemed like a good idea at the time. We had fun, didn't we?"

"Yeah, we had fun." Chase's mouth quirked upward despite his best efforts to remain stern. "Especially when the waiter stumbled and spilled an entire pitcher of beer on Phelma Jo. I've wanted to do that to her more than once."

Dick burst out laughing. "Like the time she ran your boxer shorts with red hearts up the flagpole at City Hall the morning after she broke up with you?"

Heat flashed from Chase's toes to his ears and spread across his cheeks. He was just glad the dim light over the door was behind him. "We were never going together, so we didn't have anything to break up from. She always got rid of her boyfriends before they got tired of her and left. Always in control of the relationship. That's PJ. I was a senior in high school and she was a football groupie, sleeping her way through the entire team like we were trophies. She only stayed with the guys she could control."

Or she was a notch in his own belt of experimentation.

"Wouldn't have been so bad if she hadn't scrawled my name along the fly with magic marker."

"That is one vengeful woman, Chase. Best not get on her bad side."

"She doesn't have a good side," Chase grumbled. Actually she did, but that was one secret he was sworn to keep. The health and well-being of a lot of troubled teens depended on Phelma Jo staying anonymous in helping them.

She made certain teenage runaways didn't follow the same self-destructive path her mother had.

"Amen to that. I've had my own run-ins with her. But damn, she is hot, even with the squirrely overbite and mean temper."

"Well, I'm going to keep careful watch on her and her new assistant. What kind of name is Haywood Wheatland anyway?" Chase shook his head in puzzlement.

"I'll ask around. Discreetly. See if anything comes up on Google."

Chase had his own databases on his work computer. He added Haywood's name to Thistle's for deep background checks.

"Anyway, can you find out if he's a patient of any of your doctor clients? I've never seen him around before."

"Patient confidentiality will rule. But there's usually a talkative nurse or two leaving a computer screen untended." Dick flashed a wide grin.

"Let me know if you find out anything. I don't like strangers in my town associating with a woman of questionable morals and business ethics." And that went for Thistle Down, too.

He bounced back to his pickup whistling a catchy tune. What was the name of the music? He couldn't remember it. Great. Now it was stuck in his head until he figured it out. Something to do with May flowers and honey wine.

Nine

DUSTY DRIFTED ON THE LIGHT BREEZE wafting along the river. She looked about with lazy curiosity, not at all concerned with the distance between herself and the water that would cradle her. For now she was content to allow air to lift her wings and take her wherever she needed to go.

A slow smile spread from her mouth to her eyes to her fingertips as the huge white swallowtail wings carried her along. *Freedom.* No duties or responsibilities or fears chained her to the earth.

No one judged her. No one threatened her. She didn't fear saying the wrong thing or laughing at the wrong moment. She was who she was and the wind did not care.

She laughed. What were the worries of the world when she could talk to the wind and listen to the river from stupendous heights while her wings took her to new places and marvelous sights?

Slowly, lazily, and carefree, Dusty awoke. She stretched in the small white-painted bed of her childhood and relished the lightness left behind by her dream. And confidence. If she could fly with the wind . . .

Next time she felt the need to hide in the basement, she should remember that dream and face whatever troubled her.

A shaft of sunlight showed her dust motes that could easily be Pixies dancing.

She rolled over just as the alarm clock clicked over to

six o'clock and an obnoxious beep reminded her that freedom and self-confidence were only a dream. She had a museum to run and the grant committee to impress. And then a parade to manage and a Ball to organize.

She just had to remember the dream. Remember it and float forward.

Yeah. Right.

Dick backed up his dad's half-ton truck into the loading bay of the nursery while dawn was just a promise on the horizon. He yawned hugely as he set the brake. Just two minutes. All he needed was two minutes with his head on the steering wheel and his eyes closed.

"Hey, Carrick, get the lead out!" Tom Ledbetter, otherwise known as Digger, yelled from right beside him.

Dick jerked awake, swearing.

"We've got a pumper wagon to decorate and horses to hitch before we can march in the parade."

A flash nearly blinded Dick. He pressed his fingers against his eyelids to calm the dazzle. "Did you have to take a picture of me asleep?"

"Candid shots are the best for the social pages." Digger shrugged and let the camera rest on its vividly striped neck strap.

"Yeah, yeah. Let's get those flats of flowers loaded while they're still fresh. Did anyone bring coffee?" Dick yawned again. A bug fluttered against his lips.

A big bug.

He spat it out.

"Hey, watch it, buddy." A blue splotch twisted away from the inside windshield. "Phew, you musta had garlic for breakfast."

The blue splotch took on definition. Dick saw large green wings and a blue body. And ... and ...

He froze in place, moving only his eyes. Digger had retreated to the rear of the truck to release the tailgate.

"Who ... who are you?" Dick whispered. Maybe he

was only dreaming. He'd had a short night's sleep on top of too many beers and too much salty pizza. With garlic.

"It's about time you noticed I hitched a ride with you," the blue Pixie stood on the dashboard while he waved his arms about like a semaphore. He stretched and flapped his leafy wings slowly, as if he needed to work the kinks out of them.

"Do I know you?" It was one thing to tell himself that Thistle was a Pixie grown to human form, quite another to confront a real-life Pixie.

"Nah, I don't hang out in The Ten Acre Wood much. But I know you, and you really—*really*—need to brush your teeth."

"Um, thanks, buddy. What's your name?" Though Dick could guess, with the multiple thin blue-purple petals that made up his jaunty hat. "You must be Chicory."

"You guessed it. Now, quick, tell me what's up with Thistle, so I can report back to my boss."

Dum dum do do dee dee dum. A bright tune surrounded Dick with a sense of well-being and cooperation.

"Who's your boss?"

"Can't tell. I'm sworn to secrecy."

"Nope. We trade information."

"It's just gossip, Dick. Gossip is my job. I've got obligations," the Pixie whined.

"So do I. I need to load those flats of flowers."

"Better water them first. The pansies are looking a little limp. Kinda late in the year for them."

"That's why the nursery donated them." Dick unfastened his seat belt.

"Hey, you can't leave me in the lurch!"

"Wanna make a bet?"

"What are you betting on this time?" Digger asked as he shifted a cardboard flat filled with four-inch flowerpots topped with a rainbow of blossoms.

"I bet a buck the parade finishes eighteen minutes late."

"Sucker bet. The parade always takes longer than planned." Digger dropped the flat and pushed it into the far corner of the truck bed.

"Dick, grab those snapdragons. They'll make a nice contrast in height and color to the pansies," Chicory whispered from the region of Dick's left ear.

Why not? He selected a flat from the array on the loading dock.

"Not that one. They're full of bugs. Get the one to your right," Chicory advised.

"Have you noticed how many bugs are around this morning?" Digger waved his hand in front of his face, chasing off some yellow flying things that might be Pixies, or dandelion blossoms floating through the air. "Loud buggers." Digger's gesticulations increased as the swarm of yellow grew to ten and then fifteen.

"Dandelions," Chicory whispered. "Always a dozen or more in the tribe. We call them by number; they're too dumb to have names. Too many of them to bother naming."

"Just like weeds," Dick mumbled. Then he spotted a flat filled with waving blue flowers. "I thought chicory was a ditch weed."

"That's a low blow," Chicory replied. "See if I help you again." He lifted off Dick's shoulder, grabbing a fistful of Dick's hair. The swarm of yellow followed him.

"It's going to be a long day," Dick sighed, slapping the stinging place on his scalp.

"You got that right," Digger replied. "Let's grab some coffee at Norton's on the way to the station."

❧

"Dick, where's Thistle?" Dusty asked as she wolfed down peanut butter toast and a cup of strong tea.

"How should I know?" he replied on a yawn, running his hands through his rumpled hair. He'd shaved and pulled on his buff knickers with bright red suspenders, but not his blue fireman's shirt for the parade. "Coffee.

Don't suppose you made coffee?" He looked at her hopefully. "I didn't take the time to meet the other volunteers at Norton's before they start decorating the wagon. Too noisy and bright for my hangover."

"In the pot." She pointed to the coffeemaker full of his favorite exotic blend—organic and free trade, of course. She couldn't stand the taste of the stuff even diluted with cream and sugar.

Dick poured a big mug full and swilled half of it down, hot and so strong it almost had a life of its own. He kept looking at his left shoulder as if missing something.

"You should have noticed if Thistle left before my alarm went off. The guest room is right across the hall from yours," she reprimanded him. "The bathroom is between her room and mine, so I wouldn't hear her even if she made a racket."

Besides, Dusty had been drifting in that lovely dream before the alarm brought her back to the real world.

"Sorry. I was down at the nursery hauling plants long before your alarm went off. I'm back only long enough for a shower. It's already hot, but not as humid as yesterday." He shrugged and shuffled back up the kitchen stairs to the second floor.

"I don't have time to look for Thistle. The grant committee is coming to the museum early," Dusty called after him.

"Parade duty and then work," he mumbled.

Dusty took one last swallow of English Breakfast tea with just a tiny bit of honey and freshly-squeezed lemon, grabbed her purse, and dashed out the door to her little hybrid car.

"I shouldn't spend any more time with exiled Pixies. Nor will I believe I can fly. That's as ridiculous as . . . as me having a date with a real man and not some lame fix up." But, oh, it was a nice dream of flying. She sighed wistfully as she guided the car toward the museum on the ridge overlooking downtown. "I don't think I'm going to accept the date Mom arranged with whatever his name is. It will be just like all the others: dull, embarrassing, and a disappointment for all concerned."

Most days, when the weather was fine, she walked the few blocks to work. Today she wanted to look professional for the grant committee. Two-and-a-half-inch heels, hose, and a tight navy blue skirt did not take well to walking any distance. At least not for her.

A quick survey of the museum grounds told her that the herb garden planted in a knot design had been carefully weeded and watered. The signs on the outdoor exhibits looked straight, clearly visible, and legible. The City Parks Department had mowed the grass and raked it two days ago.

The sprinklers turned on their automatic timers as she bent down to reset the strap of her navy sling-back heels.

Fat droplets swished across her back and head. The spray of water passed on in its wide circle. The droplets hit in a distinctive rhythm. A tune, that might be the same one her old music box played but was catchier and brighter, caught the back of her mind in time with the sprinkles.

"Who reset the timer?" she shouted to anyone who might hear. Hastily, she rolled up the car windows and scuttled toward the sidewalk where the watering system didn't dare threaten potential customers.

The tune seemed to dance along with her heels clacking against the cement.

Dum dee dee do dum dum.

The line of water followed her like a malicious and living monster. It broke every rule of high summer water conservation and plastered the sidewalk as she ran away from the museum grounds toward the place where the road dead-ended by The Ten Acre Wood and the curving cliff.

Chiming laughter followed her every step until it suddenly choked on a sob.

Dusty looked up, realizing the water had turned itself off, leaving her slightly damp around the edges but not seriously soggy.

There, where the parkland grass met the first line of trees and sword fern underbrush stood a lone figure in a wilted purple-and-cream sundress. Her long dark hair flared out from a very pale face.

"Thistle, what are you doing here?" Dusty wanted to yell at the woman. Something in her slumped posture and bedraggled appearance made Dusty soften her tone.

"I can't go home," Thistle whispered. "I ache all over, my tummy is upset, and the light hurts my eyes. I need to go home to our den and let Trillium take care of me. I need to grow my wings and be purple again."

"You've got a hangover. No wonder, with the amount of beer you drank last night. Come on into the offices and I'll get you some orange juice and aspirin. Dick swears that's the only way to get over a hangover."

"You don't understand. I'm stuck in this ugly, lumpy body forever. I can't ever go home." Fat tears trickled down her pale face, blurring her fabulous purple eyes.

"Thistle, you are the only person alive who thinks that's an ugly body. And most people admire the lumps. Stop whining. Come on. You can stay in the museum lounge today. I've got meetings and the parade and a bunch of scheduled tours today. But tomorrow you need to look for your own place to live and a job. I can't afford to support you."

Though life would be duller and less bright without Thistle around. Years ago, all the color had drained from Dusty's life when she got sick. Thistle had been the only bright spot in her life for many years after. Gradually, as Dusty grew older, Thistle stopped coming. She checked in once in a while, but it had been years since the tiny Pixie had graced Dusty with her presence.

She deliberately called up her dream and the feeling of carefree flight. When she opened her eyes, the world seemed a bit brighter and less threatening.

"Pixies don't need to work," Thistle sobbed. "A Pixie's purpose is to befriend children who need us. We live on pollen and morning dew, gossip and an occasional mosquito. What will I do, Dusty? I need you and Dick. Without you, I am nothing. Without you two, it's as if I don't exist."

"I'm not a child anymore, Thistle. I've grown up. Now you need to do the same."

"But I can't. Pixies can't grow up. We just wither away and die when children stop believing in us."

"I still believe in Pixies, Thistle. I'd go insane if I didn't hold our friendship deep in my heart."

Ten

❧

"**H**AYWOOD, WHY ARE YOU SITTING at your desk?" Phelma Jo tapped her foot in annoyance, hands on hips and chin thrust forward. Her first husband had told her he was afraid of her when she took that pose.

Haywood maintained that strange frozen pause when she finished speaking. Then he answered her as if no time at all had passed. "I'm at my desk checking on some local ordinances . . . I'm checking on some local ordinances before you file documents on your latest project," Haywood replied calmly, flashing his heart-stopping smile. "It's Saturday. No one will be in City Hall to notice me snooping through their databases and City Council minutes. I don't think we'll be bothered with state laws unless someone knows where to complain and bothers with acres of paperwork."

"I need you to go to the museum and get me my invitation to the Ball," she reminded him.

"I will be on Desdemona Carrick's doorstep thirty seconds after she opens the doors to the public." He returned his attention to his computer screen and frowned.

"What?" Phelma Jo demanded.

"Just a law we'll have to get the City Council to override. I'd rather manipulate the mayor into signing off on the project before taking it to the City Council. But his authority may not extend to this."

"The self-serving bastard is retiring. Our less-than-illustrious mayor is always vulnerable to bribes. I'll take care of the override."

"If anyone finds out what you did, you could be vulnerable to fines and possible jail time. That would make you ineligible to run for mayor."

"Not to worry. I've got the mayor under my thumb. My name will never come up in an investigation. If there is one. I'm running for office because I can't be bribed or blackmailed. All my misdeeds are common gossip. Only half the gossip is true."

"In the meantime, the City Council is restless and in a mood to override the mayor. Let's see if we can divide and conquer a committee of five. I'll just work on the wording of our filing until the museum opens."

"Haywood," Phelma Jo said softly.

"Yes?" He turned half his attention back to her, still typing, still keeping one eye on his screen. "Yes?"

"Look at me when I talk to you!"

"So you can intimidate me into adoring you?" This time he turned his smile on her full force. His gaze locked onto hers.

Phelma Jo read his admiration in his expression and knew it was all fake. He loved only himself and his agenda. She was his tool.

Life in Phelma Jo's world wasn't supposed to work that way. Her employees needed to obey *her* agenda.

So why couldn't she bring herself to fire him on the spot?

"Don't worry, Phelma Jo. We'll bring Desdemona Carrick and her brother down in a wave of humiliation so deep they'll never show their faces in your town again."

"You promised to break her heart."

"Winning Dusty's heart is extra fragrance in the flowers, or a twist to the mushroom high. Or a twist to the mushroom high."

Odd phrase, that. And why did he keep repeating himself?

She smiled to herself. A flaw. She didn't know what it meant or why he did that, but it was a flaw she could exploit to deepen her control over him.

"There is a weed in the knot garden, Mr. Newberry," Samuel Johnson-Butler, PhD said, looking over his half glasses toward Joe.

Dusty's face flamed. The herb garden was her responsibility. She should have seen the weed before the grant committee could find fault with the management of the museum grounds. Especially since the committee was chaired by Dr. Johnson-Butler, the head of the Business Department at the local community college.

"The city landscape department is responsible for mowing the lawns and policing the grounds for out-of-place plants and litter," Joe replied with firm calmness. "I shall call it to their attention."

He flicked his head toward Dusty. She took the hint and withdrew from the pack of three committee members to inspect the garden. Joe led them from the neatly labeled plants to the long barn housing antique carriages and wagons. The potting shed, moved here from one of the first farms in the region, stood between her and the committee. The original county jail, a single-room shed sunk three feet down with only one tiny window in its uninsulated plank walls was next on the agenda. That favorite children's attraction (topping even the replica covered wagon they could climb on) had a clear view of the knot garden. She needed to work fast.

At a first cursory glance, nothing looked out of place along the neat serpentine paths around bunches of medicinal and flavorful herbs. Then she spotted the obnoxious intruder. A single blade of grass poked one half inch above the freshly turned dirt around the lemon basil.

Dusty stooped to yank it out by the roots, careful not to trip in her heels. "That's it? A single blade of grass?" She wasn't aware she'd spoken until she heard her own words.

"From a single blade of grass comes a forest of uncontrolled weeds," Dr. Johnson-Butler admonished her from halfway across the grounds and behind the wagon barn.

Couldn't the committee content themselves with a tour of the inside of the museum and gift shop? A full two acres of grounds and he found one blade of grass out of place.

A clatter of iron-shod horseshoes and wooden wheels on the blacktop announced the arrival of the first of the parade floats. She checked her watch, half an hour early and the grant committee was still here. She didn't dare divert to show the Historical Society where they should place their covered wagon.

Cursing under her breath, Dusty rushed to catch up with Joe.

Thistle emerged from nowhere, right in front of her. "Want me to teach him a lesson?" she giggled. Chiming music seemed to enhance her words. She looked neater and fresher than when Dusty had first found her. But dark smudges hollowed her eyes. They seemed nearly cadaverous and empty.

"No," Dusty whispered. "We need him happy and appreciative."

"He doesn't appreciate anything he doesn't initiate himself," Thistle said, watching the man carefully.

"The jail is a favorite exhibit with the children," Joe said, continuing his tour as if he'd never been interrupted by a weed. "As you can see, we have a modern padlock on the door for when the museum is closed, to discourage vandals and vagrants. During open hours, we remove the lock to make sure an overly enthusiastic game doesn't result in someone getting locked in."

"I see you have removable chain link in front of the wagons," Mrs. Shiregrove said, with more enthusiasm than the committee chair. She had always supported the museum, buying two dozen Masque Ball tickets each year and doling them out as special favors. She also wrote large checks at Christmas. Her family money had seeded the grant fund.

Later today, she'd ride in a flower-filled open carriage representing the Garden Club in the parade.

The president of the Garden Club was the third member of the committee. She (Dusty could never remember her name) echoed Mrs. Shiregrove in everything.

"Yes. We bring out some of the less fragile exhibits for special events, like the parade today. Your carriage, Mrs. Shiregrove, is usually housed here but is now being cleaned and decorated for the festivities. Children especially love the replica covered wagon. They learn more about life in pioneer times crawling over it, becoming involved in the exhibits, than simply reading about it in textbooks," Joe replied. He looked a little sweaty in his good suit. More from nerves than the mild early morning temperatures.

Dusty longed to exchange her professional garb for a sundress like Thistle's and retreat to her dim basement where even above normal mid-August temperatures rarely penetrated.

In ten minutes she'd have to change to a calico gown, petticoats, and a clean apron. But she wouldn't wear a corset.

And she wouldn't have to deal with outsiders who judged her. Like Dr. Johnson-Butler.

Thistle beckoned urgently from the far side of the barn. She looked a bit angry, with determined mischief in the set of her chin and the flow of her hair as she flung her head back. Dusty faded out of view of the grant committee . . . again. Joe didn't really need her. He dealt with the business side of managing the museum all the time. Dusty's job as assistant curator was to take notes and keep her mouth shut.

"You have a visitor." Thistle pointed toward a tall, blond man standing on the porch reading a bronze plaque with details of the house's construction and historical significance.

"Isn't that Phelma Jo's new assistant?" Dusty asked, adjusting her glasses upward. She watched the man carefully, admiring the fluid grace of his hands as he caressed the doorknob.

"Yeah. He reminds me of someone," Thistle replied. Her gaze remained fixed on the man.

"Maybe you saw someone like him on TV."

"No. I don't watch TV. I've seen him before. I just can't seem to flutter my wings right to trigger a memory."

"I'll go see what he wants. M'Velle and Meggie aren't here yet." Dusty checked her watch. Still ten minutes to official parade gathering and another two hours to opening the museum. The girls weren't late. He was very early.

"Let me get that for you," Dusty called as she hastened over to the main building. And, gratefully, away from the grant committee.

"I'm sorry, I thought you opened at nine thirty instead of ten," Haywood said. He stepped away from the door just enough to let Dusty get to the lock.

She fumbled her wad of keys out of her pocket, dropped them, bent to pick them up, bumped heads with Haywood, who also reached to retrieve them, and they both came up laughing. She held the end of one key. He clutched the covered wagon medallion keychain.

"I . . . I . . . I'm sorry." Dusty dropped her eyes as a blush spread across her neck and face. "Actually, we're opening late today because of the parade." She gestured toward the horse-drawn pumper wagon pulling into line. The volunteer fire department manned the antique, all dressed in old-fashioned uniforms of blue shirts, buff knickers, tall boots, suspenders, and huge hats.

"Don't be sorry," he whispered. "You're too pretty to be sorry about anything."

"Huh?"

"May I?" he asked, nodding toward the disputed keys.

"Um . . . I really should. My responsibility," Dusty stammered, wishing she could look away from his charming smile and the brightness of his golden-brown eyes.

Finally, she forced herself to unlock the front door and step into the crowded parlor—at least that's what the first curator had named the front room. Originally, it had been the only room in the log cabin. A century of occupation had led to expansion up and out. The loft became a full second story within twenty years of construction, then multiple additions to the back and sides—also two stories signified growing prosperity. But the original log walls remained in the parlor. The resto-

ration committee had stripped off the half-rotten panel-
ing and wallpaper to reveal the sturdy logs when they
moved the house before World War II.

"This is really interesting," Haywood said stooping to
examine the workings of a spinning wheel. "Can you
work this?" he asked, straightening up.

"Not well. I know the principles, but I've never taken
the time to really learn spinning or any of the needle
crafts so popular and necessary in previous centuries."

"Too bad. I find the process fascinating to watch.
From a tangle of fiber comes the thread that makes a
garment. Sort of like a spider spinning a web of silk."

Something about his phrasing sounded odd, and
oddly familiar at the same time.

"A spider spinning a web of silk," he repeated.

"I presume you've come about tickets for the Masque
Ball?" Dusty said.

"Tickets? Ms. Nelson told me I should fetch an official invitation." A frown creased his brow.

"Apparently Phelma Jo doesn't realize this is our
largest fund-raiser of the year. We sell tickets to anyone
who will buy them. Our email invitations are really just
a reminder of the date of the Ball and that preorders
help us pay for music, food, and advertising."

"Oh. I'm sorry about the misunderstanding. How
much are the tickets?" He pulled an oxblood leather
checkbook out of his breast pocket."

"Fifty dollars per couple," she said flatly. As nice as this
man looked, his tweed sport coat, that fit him beautifully,
looked a bit dated and his shoes were worn and scuffed.
He might not have enough money to pay for the tickets,
and Phelma Jo wasn't likely to reimburse him. Everyone
in town knew that she collected money and property,
rarely parting with it; a legacy from her childhood.

And now that she had money, she didn't fix her rab-
bity overbite. Keeping her teeth flawed reminded one
and all of how she'd been mistreated as a child and why
the world owed her. What they owed her, Dusty could

never figure out, just that she and Dick were expected to feel less than human because their parents could afford braces for both of them. And they had two parents.

No one had ever heard what happened to Phelma Jo's father. Her mother had moved to town, a single, teenaged mother, when still pregnant with Phelma Jo.

"Any single tickets available?" Haywood asked, his smile returning and aimed right at Dusty.

"Um. Not usually. Surely you can come up with a date for the evening."

"I'm new in town. Don't know many people outside the office. I suppose you've had a date booked up for months."

"Ah, not really. I'm usually so busy organizing I don't think about a date."

His smile blazed brighter. "Good, then I'll take three couples' tickets and you can be my date. And you can be my date. That is if you want to go with me?" His smile fell just a bit.

"I . . . we don't know each other . . ." Dusty's face flamed, and the pressure in her chest squeezed the breath out of her. She couldn't look at him. And she couldn't look away.

His eyes captured her gaze. She thought she saw sparkles around the edges of him.

"Miss Carrick, would you do me the honor of having dinner with me tonight? That new Greek place on Main Street looks interesting, and I hate dining alone. We can get to know each other better before the Ball."

"That would be nice." Did she honestly say that? Her heart beat so loudly she couldn't hear her own thoughts, let alone her words.

Could this be the date that would really work because she'd accepted it herself without someone arranging it for her?

"Pick you up at six thirty?" He tilted his head so that a stray shaft of sunlight struck his hair and turned it to molten gold.

"Six thirty is good. Meet me here?"

"You're reluctant to tell me where you live."

"Um . . . I get off at six thirty." Finally, she broke eye contact and stared at her shoes. The dried water droplets marring the black polish appeared to fascinate her.

He lifted her chin with a finger and smiled. The entire room seemed brighter, full of life and color. "Six thirty," he whispered, almost conspiratorially.

"Come into the office, and I'll get you those tickets." Reluctantly, she turned away to lead him through the maze of rooms to the last addition on the house.

"Here," she handed him the three tickets a few moments later. The close confines of Joe's office suddenly felt too small and private. Airless.

Haywood curled his fingers around her hand instead of taking the three heavy card stock tickets with a unique art deco logo and embossed and gilded printing; collectors' items in themselves.

"I look forward to tonight," he whispered.

The sound of voices and footsteps in the front room startled Dusty away from his mesmerizing eyes.

"I'll see you out front at six thirty," she replied, pressing her behind into the sharp edge of the desk.

"Yes. You got the check?"

She nodded, holding up the flimsy paper.

"Good. Who are those people anyway? Important, I'm guessing."

"Grant committee. We desperately need a heat pump to keep the artifacts at a constant temperature and humidity."

"Oh. Well, then. I guess I'd best get out of your way. Ms. Nelson is expecting me back at the office."

"Don't let her work you too hard. It's Saturday."

"Don't worry. I won't." He paused a moment, gazing into the near distance at something only he could see. "I won't. I know when she's trying to take advantage of my good humor." He backed out of the room, blowing her a kiss at the last moment.

Eleven

THISTLE GRABBED A PAPER CUP full of water off one of the long tables set up along the street side of the park. She downed it in one gulp and immediately felt better. She reached for a second cup.

"Hey, those are for the parade participants," an older woman with a bad perm in her black-and-gray hair yelled from the other end of the table.

Thistle wandered through the increasing bustle and chaos of the parade preparations toward the museum. Maybe Dusty would have more water. Halfway to the deep porch, she heard the distinctive wail of a frightened child. She followed her instincts to befriend the little one and push away the fears. That's all children needed at times like these, a friend to remind them they weren't alone.

She halted when she spotted Joe Newberry crouching in front of his two daughters. He'd shed his suit jacket and tie. Other than that, he looked entirely too modern for the costumes worn by most of the parade participants—which seemed to be most of the town. What was the point of a parade if there was no one left to watch?

Both girls wore long dresses with cloth bonnets, like most of the women gathering around the assembly of horse-drawn wagons, and flatbed trucks, all decorated and signed with various organizations.

"Now, girls, we talked about this. Mrs. Ledbetter, the story lady from the library, is going to walk with you in the parade. You'll be right beside the horses pulling the covered wagon. You like horses."

Thistle glanced back at the huge brown beasts flicking their ears in curiosity and apprehension at the noise, the heat, and the bugs—actually a large swarm of yellow Pixies. Must be Dandelions. She'd be scared of those horses, too, with their huge stamping feet and long snapping teeth. The flowers decorating their collars and harness didn't make them any less scary.

"I like ponies, not horses. Pink ponies with wings," Sharon, the older of Joe's daughters, whined. She thrust out her lower lip in a pout.

"I never heard of a pink pony before," Thistle said, approaching the girls cautiously. She hummed a bright tune in the back of her throat, *dum dee dee do dum dum*. No need to add to their upset. "But I've seen a couple with wings." Not really a lie if you considered robins and varied thrushes as Pixie ponies.

"You haven't?" Both girls stared up at her in wonder.

"Nope. Never." Thistle shook her head. She increased the volume and speed of her tune.

"Don't you watch cartoons?" Sharon asked, more boldly than before.

"Not lately."

"Um, girls, you could tell Miss Thistle about the pink ponies while you walk in the parade," Joe suggested cautiously as he stood back up and turned to face her. "I'm sure Mrs. Ledbetter would like to hear about it, too."

Please help, he mouthed to Thistle when his back was turned to the girls.

"Don't wanna walk. It's too hot!" Suzie protested. Her chin quivered in preparation for more tears.

"Could we ride in the wagon?" Thistle asked.

"Historically, very few people, even small children, rode in covered wagons on the Oregon Trail . . ." Joe said. It sounded like the automatic response of a teacher.

"But this is 'Pioneer Days Festival' not the Oregon

Trail. Let's see if your Auntie Dusty will let us ride in the front of the wagon. We can wave to all the people, and you can tell me about the pink ponies with wings." Thistle offered her hands to the girls. *Dum dee dee do dum dum.*

They each slipped hot and sweaty palms into her own, already trusting her as a friend who would never harm them. They began humming along with her.

"You'll need a costume, Miss Thistle," Joe called after them.

"Auntie Dusty will take care of it," Sharon replied, keeping her hand in Thistle's.

Twenty minutes later, the covered wagon lurched forward to lead the parade. A big white ribbon with a pleated rosette at the top proclaimed third prize.

"We should have won first place," Thistle grumbled as she plucked the calico gown away from her sweating body. At least the cloth bonnet shaded her eyes. Dusty had given her several bottles of water to carry in the wagon with the girls.

"I bet we would have won if they'd let us have pink ponies instead of big brown horses," Sharon said. She leaned forward on the plank seat to better see the horses.

Thistle settled more comfortably on the seat. She half turned to the right and waved at Dusty where she stood on the museum porch. The girls waved, too.

The horses settled into a smoother gait as they rounded a corner on the long winding pathway through the residences and then toward downtown. "Look! There's Mrs. Swenson, my teacher," Sharon called, waving wildly. Her sister joined her as they enthusiastically found more and more people they recognized. Thistle waved, too, enjoying the party atmosphere that had taken over the town.

Normally, when the parade filled the town with noise and strange people, Thistle's tribe of Pixies took refuge in the shady secret places within The Ten Acre Wood.

They had plenty of work to do blurring paths and snapping ferns against the shins of all the extra children who sought treasures there. Thistle had even switched some of the signs identifying plants for the nature trail showing a lowly dandelion as a towering giant cedar.

She giggled and waved some more.

A blur of movement whizzed around the horses' heads and zoomed up and over the top of the canvas wagon cover. She squinted against the sun glare to pick out details. A jaunty blue Pixie led a ragged group of mixed followers, some Dandelions, of course, with a Daisy and an Aster and some other pinks and yellows that spread out too far away to identify.

"Chicory!" she called to the leader of the mob.

He and his followers kept right on flying past her. They hadn't seen her at all. They hadn't heard her.

The Pixies were as blind and deaf to her as most adults were to Pixies. To them, she didn't exist at all.

Her music died in her throat.

※

Chase paced the blocks around the museum, trying to look like a cop on patrol. The parade had come and gone with minimal traffic snarls and only a few pranks—though he'd like to know where those eighth-grade boys got illegal fireworks. The carnival rides were now in full swing up at the community college. That's where he should be right now.

He wasn't sure why he needed to keep an eye on Dusty and Thistle. He just didn't like that Haywood Wheatland fellow sniffing around. He was back, after an early morning visit.

Chase watched as Dusty escorted him out of the building and stood a moment conversing on the long shady porch. Chase heard snatches of conversation about the parade and which businesses stayed open during Festival.

Chase's gut twisted as Dusty flashed the newcomer a

smile bright enough to rival the blazing sun on this heat-drenched day.

When had Dusty ever smiled at a virtual stranger? She barely raised her eyes to people she knew!

Haywood Wheatland was trouble. Chase knew it. Why didn't anyone else see it?

But if Wheatland drew Dusty out of her shyness, gave her someone to trust, someone who wouldn't belittle and judge her . . . maybe he was a good guy.

But if he broke her heart, he'd drive her deeper into her basement solitude.

"If you hurt my friends, Mr. Smooth and Handsome, I'll see you rot in a hell of your own making," he swore.

Then Chase paced some more, looking at houses for signs of something off kilter.

All he could think about was Dusty and that man.

"Dispatch, this is Sergeant Norton, patch me through to records," he said quietly into his shoulder radio.

"Sure, sweetie, what's you need?" Mabel asked. "You know that I know more about this town than what's in the official papers." Anyone but the seventy-something, supposedly-retired dispatcher would get into deep trouble for gossiping and calling everyone by suggestive endearments. Trouble was, she'd been around so long the department wasn't sure they could operate without her.

She'd anchored the police department since God was a pup. He guessed that by now she didn't know what to do with herself anywhere but anchoring reception and dispatch. Except putter in her garden growing the most magnificent roses in the county.

Funny, he'd never actually seen Mabel Gardiner work in her garden. She was always down at the police station behind City Hall.

And she knew where all the bodies were buried, who had secrets, and where everyone was at any given time. She had to have a legion of spies.

"I know, Mabel. But this is about that new guy work-

ing for Phelma Jo." Chase had to smile at finally coming
up with a question she couldn't answer.

"Haywood Wheatland. Heard about him. Not much
on his resume, but he knows how to make Phelma Jo
smile. That's a wonder in itself," she came back at him.
"That child was born angry."

Damn, the woman did know something records
couldn't tell him.

No wonder Haywood Wheatland could charm Dusty,
easy pickings compared to dragging a smile out of
Phelma Jo.

"How'd you know about his résumé?"

"I have my ways, boy. Phelma Jo keeps her private
files private, but I know a few tricks she doesn't. He
claims he graduated from that tech college in Portland
and knows tricks with office management software. Saw
his handle on a search of some city rules and regs regarding parks and recreation this morning, so I guess he
knows his way around the Internet. What else you
need?"

"Have the interns in records come up with anything
on that full background check? I want to know everything about him right down to his shoe size." Judging by
the scruffy loafers the man wore this morning, Chase
guessed a nine narrow. Haywood looked big and im-
pressive, but standing next to petite Dusty as he exited
the museum, he stood only half a head taller than her.
That put him about five-nine. Five-ten tops.

What kind of wiry muscles did he hide under that
thrift-store-reject tweed sport jacket?

A flicker of purple near the first rank of trees in The
Ten Acre Wood drew Chase's attention.

"Mabel?" Chase opened his radio again. "Anything
show up on that deep background on Thistle Down?"

Mabel coughed long and hard. "Sorry, sweetie, I swallowed down the wrong throat. Who'd you say?"

"Thistle Down. The woman I brought in yesterday
morning for dancing naked in Memorial Fountain."

"Um, Thistle . . . Thistle. . . . Thistle. Oh, yes, the dark-haired lady with purple eyes. Nope, nothing on her. No driver's license or Social Security number under that name. No hits on three fingerprint databases. Signing off until I hear from records on that other check."

No comments, no speculation, nothing. Very unusual for Mabel to cut him off rather than gossip a bit.

Chase's shoulder mike crackled. "That high school gal summering down in records says she should have something for you by twoish," Mabel said. She sounded wary, almost uncertain.

Definitely unusual.

"I'm walking a sweep of the neighborhood on the ridge, Mabel, checking on some of the elderly, make sure they've got fans and water. Not all of them got to their porches to watch the parade. I'll make sure they're okay. Don't want to have any of them succumb to heat stroke." Chase turned his back on the museum.

Dusty retreated inside, and Haywood walked off whistling something jaunty and hauntingly familiar.

Damn, now Chase had an earworm of that tune, and he couldn't remember the words.

Dum dee dee do dum dum.

A burst of static on his shoulder mike interrupted the almost combination of three words in the song.

"Sergeant Norton. What do you have for me, Mabel?" That was quick.

"Get over to Mrs. Spencer's on Fifth and Oak. Just got word of a break-in in progress."

"On my way." Chase ran like he had a football under his arm, the goal post in sight, and fullbacks closing in from each side.

Mrs. Spencer hadn't watched the parade.

Twelve

THE NOISE AND CROWDS from the parade had dispersed. Dusty retreated inside the museum. Dick went off to do something he called work. That left Thistle alone, tired, hungry, and thirsty. She wandered back toward Dusty's house, wishing she could just spread her wings and fly.

A laughing golden Pixie she didn't recognize circled her head. At least he could see her.

"Go away. I'm not one of you anymore," she cried, batting him away, much as she'd seen humans do to the Dandelions who got too close.

"And you never will be again," golden boy taunted her. He flipped in midair and zoomed straight for her head, grabbing at a few tendrils of black hair. "Who ever heard of a black-and-pink Pixie. Looks diseased to me!"

Thistle slapped at her head where the pulled hairs stung her scalp. "Who are you? You're bigger than most Pixies." She squinted her eyes a bit to catch a glimpse of his aura.

Red-and-orange flames encircled his yellow, green, and brown life energy.

"You're part Faery!" she gasped. She'd heard stories of such strange creatures. Myths of bizarre matings that took place before the Faeries went underhill. The half-breeds were bigger than either their Pixie or Faery parents, with more potent magic than a Pixie but less than a Faery.

That was long, long ago. Before Thistle was born. This

jeering fellow looked too young to have come from the before times.

"You don't exist. You can't exist!"

"Neither do you!" He flew off, zipping in wild circles and loops, showing off the magnificent wings formed from splayed grain stalks.

"Lost. I'm lost to Pixie and lost to myself," she cried.

Her stomach growled and her throat grew sour with thirst. She bent in front of a rhododendron no one had bothered to deadhead. The flower stamens still held their loads of pollen. A nice Pixie meal.

"Eew!" she spat out the sour grit. "That's not what pollen is supposed to taste like." Hastily, she sought a few drops of dew to rinse her mouth.

Nothing! The morning had grown too late and too hot. All the plants and gardens looked dry and sere. Ah, there on the side lawn of the big old house, a hose curled around a rack. A quick flick of the tap and she'd have a drink before trudging back to Dusty's home.

A curtain flicked in the widow of a house across the street.

Thistle felt eyes following her every move as she stumbled while rising from her crouch. Damn, she'd depended upon her wings to right her and they weren't there anymore.

"So, I'm as big and lumpy as a human. I need to be careful about trespassing and being seen. I can't flit about, as unnoticeable as a dragonfly." A tear welled up in her eye. She dashed it aside. That just made her thirstier.

So, she walked a few steps farther down the sidewalk until the itchy crawlies along her spine quieted. Her next step went sideways (where she tripped again with the shift in balance), on the other side of the overgrown rhododendron, onto the scraggly grass of the big old house with peeling gray paint and a sagging porch.

The tap didn't twist easily. She tugged at it with both hands. Rust flaked off as she shoved it one quarter of a turn. Water gurgled lazily through the coils of the hose, leaking out of slits in the worn rubber. She captured a few drops with her fingertip and sucked the moisture greedily.

It tasted warm and acidic. A closer look revealed more rust in the water.

A dog howled from the shaded window above her.

"What's up, boy?" she asked the graying muzzle that pushed aside the slats of the covering blinds.

Extreme distress gushed from the animal. *Help us*.

"I didn't quite get that, Horace. That is your name, right?" When she was a Pixie, she could converse with all the dogs and cats. But she avoided the cats. They were mean alien monsters bent on murder. She knew them all intimately. Not this one.

Another whimper, this time in agreement. *Help us*.

"Um, I'm not supposed to come inside without an invitation, you know. Pixie Law. Human law, for that matter, too."

Horace howled again.

"Okay, I guess that's an invitation. Are the doors locked?"

Horace didn't know.

Thistle rose on tiptoe and peeked through the tiny opening Horace had left between the slats. His muzzle still poked through, his whines becoming more urgent.

A bloated leg covered in a thick opaque stocking with a hole in the toe lay on the floor unmoving.

Thistle ran to the front door and knocked. She pounded her fist against the solid wooden barrier. The only sound of stirring that answered her was Horace's claws on the other side. Mrs. Nosey across the street might object if Thistle waltzed into a stranger's house through the front door. Was that a good or bad thing?

Thistle tried the doorknob. It remained solid, unyielding.

She jumped off the broad porch and ran along the side of the house toward the back. More signs of neglect here in the weeds running riot through the rose beds.

"Wonder if the rose pollen will taste any better than rhododendron?" she mused. "Or has my tongue changed now that I'm big?" She shook her head and proceeded through the sagging wooden gate. She had to help the old lady Horace companioned. The gate hung crookedly, no longer able to close completely or latch.

"I know something's wrong, Horace," she said to the dog who paced her progress from window to window.

The door of the screened-in porch also sagged so that the latch didn't work. Thistle pulled it open with little resistance. She stepped into the shadowed room lined with more screen than wall. "Heaps of discarded furniture and a fine sanctuary for spiderwebs," she mused. It reminded her of a hollow log Pixies had abandoned to beetles and ants when it began to crumble in the winter rain and no longer sheltered the tribe. "If Horace weren't inside begging me to come in, I'd think this house abandoned for a long, long time."

The back door, however, had a sturdy lock. Rusty, but still firmly engaged.

Horace began barking, his anxiety now filled with hope. Human or Pixie, Thistle couldn't abandon him.

"If I were still a Pixie, I'd just fly through the keyhole. Keyhole. Hmmm, what does it look like inside?" Thistle closed her eyes trying to remember what keyholes looked like from the inside.

Blackness surrounded her memory. "Faery snot!" she cursed.

Horace barked louder.

"Okay, okay, I'm coming. If I only had a little Pixie dust left . . . Well, I did yesterday morning. Let's see if I can find any more." This time when she closed her eyes, Thistle placed her fingertip over the hole and blew with her breath and her mind.

Bright sparkles erupted out of the hole, encasing her hand in warm tingles.

"I am going to be in so much trouble if Alder ever finds out I did this." Without thinking further, she twisted the knob, felt the lock give way, and pushed the door open.

Horace jumped against her, paws landing heavily on her chest. His golden fur looked oily and matted. He smelled strongly of dog in need of a bath. Then he bounced away dashing for the nearest bush in the yard. He lifted his leg and poised there seemingly forever.

Thistle took one step inside. Waves and waves of hot air poured over her, leeching her energy. She nearly dropped to her knees in exhaustion. Not knowing what else to do, she crawled through the kitchen to the sink, then hauled herself up to the drainboard. This tap worked easily. But the water flowed warmly over her hand. She splashed some on her face and felt better. A tall glass stood upside down in a plastic drainer. She filled it drank down one glassful, refilled it, and walked slowly inward, taking an occasional sip.

Horace trudged back in and led the way. She followed him and the smell of sour bread rising. Not good. Not good at all.

In the front parlor, a tiny old woman, not much taller than Dusty, but much stouter, lay sprawled on the floor beneath the window.

"Oh, dear. We need help, Horace."

Help us.

"What's that number people shout when they are in trouble? What is it?" She racked her memory and came up blank. She had to call someone. Who?

An old black phone sat on a lamp table at the end of the sofa. Thistle grabbed the receiver as she'd seen humans do for as long as she had befriended them. There on the base in big red letters she saw 911 and a red cross.

"Let's hope that's right." She dialed the three numbers, waiting a long time for the rotary to return to its original position in between.

"911, do you need police, medical, or fire?

"Um . . ."

"Stop! What are you doing?" Chase yelled from the

archway to the kitchen. He stood, feet braced, a wicked-looking pistol held in both hands, menace written all over his face.

"Help us!" Thistle shouted, pointing with the hand that still held the glass of water. Liquid spilled and splashed all over the old woman. She stirred in the slight relief.

Suddenly, the heat, the exhaustion from throwing Pixie dust, and the smell robbed Thistle of all her strength.

She gave in to the need to lie down. Right here. Right now.

Chase stood with his mouth hanging open as Thistle wavered, shimmering in and out of view. The outline of wings in the shape of thistle leaves sprouted across her back as she collapsed. Her skin took on a decidedly lavender tone. Deep-purple highlights shone in her black hair.

Then the heat made everything in the room look off kilter.

He shook his head free of the illusion and took a good look around, assessing the situation. As he'd been trained to do. He plucked the receiver out of Thistle's hand and briskly ordered an ambulance and a cruiser.

Then he found the thermostat and turned it off. Next to it, he found the ceiling fan switch and flicked it on. Mrs. Spencer must have mixed them up. What else could he do?

Windows. Cross ventilation. One by one, he unlatched and raised as many windows as he could reach behind more overstuffed chairs, bookcases, knickknack tables, and just piles of stuff. He opened the front door as well, after releasing two deadbolts, a security chain, and the normal knob lock.

Why all this security and leave the back door open? He'd looked. Thistle hadn't forced her entry.

The dog began licking moisture off Mrs. Spencer's face. How long had he been locked inside with her? He didn't seem to be in much better condition than the woman who had taught fourth grade to nearly everyone in town.

He grabbed the glass, returned to the kitchen, and filled it. The first lot went into the dog's dish beside the fridge. The second glass he dribbled on Mrs. Spencer's brow and wrists.

Thistle stirred, too, as the fan stirred up enough of a breeze to lighten the air.

He watched as the light glinted off the heat aura that looked like wings, then dissolved as she pushed herself up to a sitting position. Her skin remained very pale and lavender tinged.

"Get yourself some water in the kitchen. I hear the ambulance coming," he ordered. When she'd slumped through to the kitchen, he shook his head again. "It's the heat. Has to be the heat. I did not see Pixie wings. I really didn't."

Horace licked his hand. His golden eyes told Chase he was lying to himself.

Dick would laugh himself silly at Chase's lack of belief in the face of this evidence.

Thirteen

DICK LEANED HIS HEAD BACK against the wall where he sat in the utilitarian chairs of the community college's free clinic waiting room. He always had to wait for his appointments to review the drug samples the volunteer physicians dispensed and to explain the new pills his company needed him to get them to try.

Nurse Edwards appeared at the door to the inner sanctum. Dick started to rise, grabbing his case along the way. But she beckoned the teen with the bloody elbow and forearm instead. "Skateboarding without pads again, Josh?" she quipped.

Dick settled back into his chair, squirming to find a more comfortable position. Yeah, he had an appointment, but patients came before pharmaceutical salesmen.

At least no one else had come in for the last half hour. Maybe he really would get to see the doctor on duty soon. In preparation, he pulled up a spreadsheet on his netbook showing all the samples he'd left here in the past six months and the ones he'd retrieved because they expired before anyone got around to prescribing them.

He couldn't concentrate. Images of Thistle in her purple-flowered sundress dancing in his arms last night kept morphing into his faulty memory of the girl with purple hair he'd kissed . . . oh, so many years ago.

And then there was the annoying buzz of Chicory, the blue Pixie at the nursery. His tune clashed with Thistle's.

Had he imagined the entire episode? He didn't think so. The logical, science-trained portion of his mind told him Pixies didn't exist. And they certainly didn't grow to human size, losing their wings, their magic, and their purple skin.

The woman he and Dusty had taken in had to be a con artist, just like Chase insisted.

And yet . . .

He didn't want her to be.

"I know better," he muttered, applying himself to the spreadsheet, marking items nearing expiration and others that turned over rapidly.

An ambulance wailed in the near distance.

Uh-oh. Dick stood to peer out the high window of the clinic. The siren came closer. Only the one siren, no police cruisers or fire trucks beforehand.

Dick stepped closer to the window. Sure enough, the white-and-red vehicle screeched to a halt in the covered drive adjacent to the clinic. An EMT thrust the vehicle's double doors open with extreme haste, letting them slam against the side panels. Another uniformed attendant hastened from the front to assist with the gurney.

Part of Dick needed to run out and check the swinging IV to make sure it didn't come loose from the patient's arm. "I'm not on duty," he reminded himself.

He did what he could, running around the corner and slamming the automatic open button on the sliding door. Then he pushed it open faster than the programming wanted him to.

"Thanks, Dick," the EMT said as he passed, pushing the gurney.

"Mike, is . . . is that Mrs. Spencer?" Dick asked. "Our fourth grade teacher?"

"Yeah. Heat stroke. Her dog alerted a passerby who broke in and called 911. If she hadn't turned off the heat and dribbled water on her brow and opened windows, we might not have been in time." Then Mike was past Dick and into the tiny emergency room attached to the clinic.

"Looks like I'll be here a while," Dick sighed and returned to his computer.

Another flurry of movement at the clinic front door broke his limited concentration. A police cruiser had pulled in behind the ambulance.

A flash of purple, then the door came open. Chase, red-faced and sweating, dragged a protesting Thistle by the hand. She dug in her heels and leaned backward. She'd changed from her parade costume, back into the rumpled sundress.

Chase compensated for her resistance with a mighty thrust worthy of a shot put Olympian, propelling the woman forward against the receptionist's counter.

"What's wrong?" Dick jumped up and examined Thistle's wrist for signs of bruising, or dislocation.

She yanked her hand back and used it to rub her midriff, further creasing the cotton dress he'd bought her yesterday.

"I got word of a break-in at Mrs. Spencer's. Found this one administering rudimentary first aid," Chase said, not in the least apologetic for his rough treatment. "I don't know if I should book her, or thank her. First, I need the doc to check her out, make sure she's okay. She collapsed from the heat. Seemed very listless and tired until I got her to drink some water."

"I didn't break in. The back door was unlocked, and the dog told me his lady needed help," Thistle insisted. She turned her eyes up to Dick, imploring him to believe her.

"You talked to the dog?" Dick wanted to give in to her silent plea for help and understanding.

"Actually, he talked to me, but I couldn't understand much. Mostly he howled and whined. I peeked through the window and saw the lady on the floor. I knocked on the front door. Horace led me from window to window until I found the back door unlatched. She's going to be okay, isn't she?"

All three of them looked to the receptionist for information.

"We all had Mrs. Spencer for a teacher at some point, but patient privacy prevails. I can't tell you anything more than that she's alive," the forty-something woman said. Janet Boland, according to her name plaque, with artful gray streaks highlighting her brown hair, nodded at them and then said, "Damn computer. It's frozen and won't let me access any files."

"Last I heard, Mrs. Spencer had moved to Salem to be with her daughter." Dick leaned over the counter, trying to pick out words and phrases on the computer screen. "Try control/alt/delete."

"I did, and it won't work. I'll have to manually power off and reboot."

Dick checked his netbook. It scrolled automatically through his open database, from top to bottom, then bottom to top.

He shook his head and turned it off.

Ms. Boland gave up on her computer and fell into easy gossip mode. "Apparently, the daughter wanted to put down Mrs. Spencer's dog. Too much trouble. He's almost as ancient as Mrs. Spencer and has bladder control problems."

"Horace only has a problem when no one remembers to let him out," Thistle insisted.

"Who told you the dog's name?" Dick asked, surprised and delighted.

"Not Mrs. Spencer. She was unconscious when I got there. EMTs said she'd been out for quite a while," Chase added.

"Horace told me," Thistle said. She rolled her eyes as if everyone talked to dogs and understood them.

"Wait a minute. You said you didn't understand what the dog said."

"Well, I got a few thoughts. Everyone knows their own name and how to communicate it. And he said 'help us.' I knew I had to get in and do something." She shrugged.

Dick's gaze met Chase's over the top of Thistle's head. Neither understood precisely what was going on.

Dick had an idea, but it warred with everything he'd been taught.

"The daughter called us this morning to let us know Mrs. Spencer had moved back home yesterday. She wanted us to be aware that the old lady was alone," Janet Boland added. "I hate to see these old folks come in to emergency like that when all they need is a friend."

Thistle stilled. Her eyes flicked right and left, seeking something, a connection. Then she dropped her gaze to her feet. "I know how to be a friend. It's what Pixies do best. We offer friendship to anyone who can see us as Pixies and not just dragonflies." She shot Chase a wicked glance.

"Can I go now? Dusty says I have to find a job and move out. But I don't know what I can do, or where to go." Fat tears welled up in Thistle's eyes.

"My sister is heartless," Dick said, offering Thistle his clean handkerchief.

"Sounds to me like she's practical and cautious," Chase sniffed.

"Wait a minute." Dick needed to think—and think fast. "We've got a lot of old folks living on the ridge in those ancient houses with outdated plumbing and no air-conditioning. Many of them live alone. In this heat they need someone to check on them, make sure they drink enough water, turn on the fans instead of the heat, let the pets out. What if a bunch of people chipped in and paid Thistle to do that?"

"Loaves and Fishes does a lot of that," Ms. Boland said. A note of caution drew the words out.

"But not all of them sign up for Meals on Wheels. Like Mrs. Spencer. She was a proud old lady, wouldn't take charity. Said she didn't need it," Chase mused. "And those volunteers only come once a day, and not always on weekends. They are volunteers, after all, and there are only so many of them."

"I bet they don't stick around to make sure the folks eat or drink," Dick expanded on the topic. "Or let the dogs out."

"I've got a patrol officer checking the neighborhood now," Chase said. His fingers tapped a rhythmic pattern on his utility belt, a sure sign that he was thinking as fast and furiously as Dick. "But I haven't the budget to do it all day every day. Especially with Festival in full swing and someone selling illegal firecrackers to teens. You might have a good idea, Dick. At least until the heat breaks. Come winter, we'll have a similar problem. Making sure furnaces work and don't spill carbon monoxide."

Thistle looked around sniffing the air. "Ten degrees cooler tomorrow and the next day. But no rain in sight. And the third day the temperatures go back up into the nineties again, with higher humidity."

"We wouldn't be able to pay her much. And someone would have to take her around, introduce her to everyone, including the neighbors," Dick thought out loud. His gaze met Chase's again.

"Dusty could do that. She takes library books to the old folks; she could introduce and *vouch for* your friend," Ms. Boland suggested.

"I suppose. Funny how Dusty will sit and talk to those old folks but hides from people her own age."

"Maybe the elders are so grateful for company, they make her feel welcome and don't judge her if she has a smudge of dirt on her nose, or she says something awkward," Thistle said. "Maybe she collects stories about olden times from them. They don't get bored talking about the past."

"I'll make up a list of candidates," Ms. Boland said. "And I'll chip in ten bucks a week."

"Wh . . . what about Dusty telling me to move out?" Thistle asked on a sniff.

"I'll talk to my little sister. As far as I'm concerned, you should stay with us. We're right in the middle of the district you need to patrol."

"Thank you. I know how to be a friend. I can do this. You can trust me to be a friend to these people." Thistle placed her hand on his chest and looked up at him with deep purple eyes full of gratitude and . . . and something Dick couldn't quite define.

His heart melted, and logic flew out the window. He knew those eyes. He'd seen that expression before . . . The day he wiped her wings free of the dog drool Chase had used to glue them together.

Chase turned away from Dick in embarrassment. This-tle was looking at him in awe, as if he was a superhero.

That was his friend, Dick. Defender of the innocent, protector of the vulnerable. Who was it had first given him that nickname?

Chase thought it was his youngest sister Ginny who'd first used the phrase. How many years ago?

Their sophomore year in high school. Spring term . . .

Chase threw his book bag onto the bench seat of the booth in the far back corner of Norton's Family Diner, the booth Mom reserved for Chase and his friends after school. He and his sisters had to come here and do homework right after school. That was the rule. This wasn't football or wrestling season, so he'd jogged down from school as soon as the final bell rang at the end of eighth period. He had to jog everywhere to keep in shape.

"Mom, can I have a Coke?" he called into the back.

"Help yourself, dear. And fix glasses for your sisters," his mother leaned out the order window from the kitchen.

The smell of hot grease for fries and grilled burgers made his stomach growl. "The girls aren't here yet. Ginny has play practice and Lynette wants to watch cheerleading practice so that she can learn some moves and try out in the fall," he said, explaining their absence. "Can I have a burger?" he asked hopefully as he pulled the lever on the soft drink machine and watched the brown liquid foam on top.

"Your dad's cleaning the grill. It will take a while to

bring it up to temperature again. How about a piece of pie. I think there's still some fresh apple." His mother ducked back into the kitchen.

Chase studied the pies in the rack. The apple was almost gone. Maybe he should save that for Dick; it was his favorite, and he hadn't been too happy lately, what with Dusty in the hospital and all. "I'll have the lemon meringue," he said to his mother.

He'd barely settled at the table with his math book when Dick slumped through the door. He dragged his book bag on the floor and practically fell across the bench seat.

Mom saw him coming and placed the last piece of apple pie in front of him along with a tall glass of milk. His mother's rule.

"How was school today?" she asked them both.

"Biology's a bunch of crap," Chase spat. His text sat in the bottom of his bag, practically accusing him of neglect.

"No, it's not. It's the best class I've got," Dick responded, perking up a bit. He took a big bite of pie. "It's World History that's too boring for words, and Dusty's too sick to help me with it." His fork sank back to his plate, and he looked like his pie tasted bad, but he was too polite to spit it out.

"Any news about your sister?" Mom sat down next to Chase and leaned across the table toward Dick. She patted his hand.

Chase suddenly felt all warm and fuzzy, sort of like when he made a touchdown in the first quarter of his first junior varsity football game. His mom was the best, letting the kids hang out here after school, making sure they got snacks—often without paying for them—and just being a good mom to all of them.

Especially now that Dick's folks spent so much time at the hospital with Dusty.

Ginny and Lynette burst through the front door in a clatter of laughter and banging books. Five other kids, mostly juniors, followed them and took a seat across the way. At thirteen, his sister Lynette was just beginning to show signs of growing up. Chase worried about her and the rough boys in her class. He knew what guys thought of girls. She wasn't safe. He'd have to have a word with some of them, prove to them they didn't want to mess with her, or they'd have to mess with him. Ginny was eleven and still very much a little girl. She spent a lot of time with Dusty, despite the two-year difference in their ages. At least she had until Dusty went to the hospital nearly a month ago.

The girls went about fixing their own snacks. They wanted the chocolate cake instead of pie. Too sweet by half for Chase, especially with the Coke.

"How's Dusty?" Ginny asked right off, like she did every day.

Dick kept his face down and didn't answer. If Chase didn't know better, he'd think Dick was crying.

He wiped his face and looked out the window at another troop of kids aiming for the front door. These were seniors, and the entire crowd orbited them, hoping for a crumb of wisdom or a brief glance of notice.

"What is it, dear? Maybe we can help," Mom said to Dick while keeping an eye on the newcomers.

"No one can help. Dusty's got leukemia. It's a kind of cancer." Dick gulped his milk, his Adam's apple bobbing suspiciously fast as he drank.

"Leukemia. That can be bad." Mom sat back a bit. "Depends on the kind of leukemia. There's one that I've heard has a really good recovery rate, if they catch it early."

"Th . . . that's what the doctors told my folks. They caught it early. They can treat it with chemo. But they want to wait until they have a bone marrow donor lined up for afterward. If they can't get a perfect match, they don't know if she'll get better or not, even with chemo. 'Cause the chemo destroys her marrow and her immune system. She can't live long . . ."

"I'll donate," Chase said. Why had he volunteered so fast? Dusty was okay, for a girl. Really smart about some things, but just so little, five years younger than him. Last time he'd seen her, she'd looked pale as a ghost and had no energy or sense of humor or anything.

"Doesn't work like that, I'm afraid, Chase," Mom said. She hugged him tight. "But it was really good of you to offer."

"The doctors said I was the best chance of a match," Dick said quietly. "But it's still only a chance."

"When will you know?" Chase asked. He could see how much Dick was hurting. Chase felt a tightness in his chest, too. He wanted to help. He really did. He just didn't know how.

"I'm having a blood test tomorrow," Dick said. "Since I'm fifteen now, they don't see a problem in taking my marrow if it matches. Little kids sometimes have a problem donating 'cause their bones aren't big enough."

"Why?" Chase asked.

"Do your biology homework and you might find out!" Dick grinned at him. "I'll help you with it. I'm doing an extra credit report on the DNA of siblings because of Dusty and me being a donor and all."

"You sound like you want to be a doctor," Lynette said. She made goo-goo eyes at Dick. She'd had a crush on him for a couple of weeks now. Chase wasn't sure he liked that. If she and Dick started to really like each other, he might have to hit Dick if he got too fresh with his sister.

"I made up my mind this morning," Dick said, lifting his head proudly. "I'm going to be a doctor. And I'll find a cure for leukemia so that no other little kid has to be as sick as my sister."

"Protecting little kids, that's . . . that's like a superhero," Ginny said. She stared at Dick with the same awestruck look as Lynette.

Oh, crap. Now Chase had two sisters falling all over themselves to get Dick's attention.

But the description of Dick as a superhero had stuck, for a while at least. And Chase had a hard time living up to it. That was why he'd majored in criminal justice and joined the local police force. To compete as best he could with Dick's image as a superhero.

Good thing neither of Chase's sisters had followed through with their crush on Dick. Lynette had gone off to college in Spokane and married a classmate—a computer nerd who'd developed a specialized database for farmers and ranchers and made a lot of money. They had two kids now and lived on a small farm near Spokane. Ginny had a degree in restaurant management and still worked at the diner, planning on taking it over when the folks retired. She was dating the son of their landlord. He hoped she genuinely liked him and wasn't doing it "for the business."

Chase knew that if he ever got up the nerve to ask Dusty out on a real date, he'd be thinking of more important things than business.

Maybe he should stop by the museum later and make sure she got home okay. She'd be tired after a long day and the parade and all. She'd forget to eat.

Sounded like a good excuse to get takeout and surprise her.

Fourteen

"**D**USTY, YOU HAVE TO COME OUT of that corner," M'velle insisted. She stood, frowning down, with feet planted and hands on hips.

Dusty peeked up at her, keeping her head on her knees and her arms wrapped around her legs. And her butt firmly planted on the floor. "I . . . I can't."

She'd gotten as far as changing from her sweaty calico costume back into her navy skirt and an ice-blue shell. Then her knees had wobbled and her tummy roiled in uncertainty.

And fear. Her hands shook and sweat poured down her back and under her arms. "What if . . . what if . . . ?"

"Nonsense. You can get up. And you will. You have a date with that handsome man in half an hour," M'velle insisted.

"I can't do it. I can't go out with him."

"Why ever not? He's buying you dinner at that awesome new restaurant downtown. Even if you decide you don't like him, you'll get a free meal out of it," Meggie added, entering the museum employee lounge.

"But . . . but . . . what if he doesn't like me?" Dusty shivered in fear. She needed more information. Where was Thistle and her endless stream of gossip when Dusty needed her?

Ages ago, when Dick had first started dating, Thistle would come to her room and tell her all about the girl, from the color of her lipstick to the brand of toothpaste she didn't use and should.

Thistle's gossip was unerring. She and Dusty predicted how long each romance would last. Thistle was always right.

So Dusty should cancel the date with Hay because Thistle felt "funny" around him. Shouldn't she? But "feeling funny" didn't add up to a snorty laugh, or shopaholic habits, or high maintenance "pay attention to me" attitudes, or a refusal to go to Norton's after the school dance because it was too inexpensive or low class.

Neither Thistle nor Dusty knew anything about the man other than his handsome face and glorious smile. At least he brushed his teeth. He had to in order to maintain those brilliant teeth.

"So what if he doesn't like you? You'll get a free meal out of it," M'Velle confirmed.

"And you'll never know if you like him, or if he likes you, unless you go out with him," Meggie said. "Here, take a sip of this. It will help. I promise." She held out a miniature bottle filled with amber liquid.

"What is that?" Dusty lifted her head enough to peer suspiciously at the bottle.

"Scotch. I found it in Mr. Newberry's bottom desk drawer." Meggie unscrewed the cap and offered the bottle to Dusty.

"How do you know it will help?" Dusty asked. She kept her hands firmly clamped around her legs. "You aren't old enough to drink scotch."

"That's what my dad says. He calls it Dutch courage. Though I guess it should be Scottish courage." Meggie pried Dusty's fingers open enough to slip the bottle behind them. "It's dusty, so Mr. Newberry has had it hidden for a long time. He shouldn't miss it from the back of the bottom desk drawer."

"So how did you know to look there?" Dusty asked, pushing her panic aside long enough to act like the adult. Maybe the scotch would give her enough . . . false courage to stand up and go home. She couldn't sit here all night quaking in fear, her knees too watery to hold her up.

Mom was due to call tonight. Again. She'd be worried if Dusty didn't answer the phone.

She took one cautious sip, holding the liquor in her mouth a moment before she could force herself to swallow. A hint of flowers lingered where the scotch touched her tongue. Warmth crept outward.

Then she let the liquid slide down her throat. It hit her stomach with explosive force, burning all the way back up to her mouth. Her eyes opened wide with surprise, and her mouth gaped, trying to breathe flame.

And miraculously that hint of flowers returned as a gentle reminder of the wonders of the drink.

Feeling returned to her cramped knees, and her hands stopped shaking. She took another sip with only slightly less spectacular results.

"I could get used to this."

"Don't." M'velle crouched before her, placing one hand over the bottle so Dusty couldn't drink again. "It's dangerous to rely on it. Good only in emergencies. That's what Mr. Newberry used it for, but hasn't needed it in a long time. Now this is an emergency. Can you stand up?"

Dusty nodded.

The girls each got a hand beneath one of her elbows and heaved her upward. Dusty swayed, leaning heavily against Meggie, the taller and stronger of the girls. Her head spun. But she kept the tiny bottle inside her fierce grip.

"Now that you are willing to listen," M'velle demanded her attention. "You need to go on this date, Dusty. If you don't go tonight, then you'll never have the courage to go again. You'll be left with your mom's lame and unsuitable fix ups. None of them have worked. This one might."

"You'll wind up a withered stick of an old maid before you're twenty-six," Meggie added.

"No, Dusty, you don't have to do this," Joe said from the doorway. He still wore his calico shirt and canvas pants from the parade. He looked tired and worried. "You don't have to do anything you don't want to." He walked toward her on silent, careful steps. "I'll take you home. You and me and the girls can make popcorn and watch an old movie. You don't need this other guy."

"No, Joe. The girls are right. I have to do this." Dusty pulled herself up straight, balancing on her own two feet. Her head remained clamped to her shoulders. She looked at the scotch bottle with disdain and a curious longing. Time to put it aside, along with her childish fears.

Memories of her flying dream returned with gentle but persistent jolts. She held the sensation of carefree soaring firmly in her heart.

She'd told Thistle she had to grow up. The time had long passed when Dusty needed to take her own advice.

"We'll do popcorn and a movie another night. Maybe tomorrow. I think they're replaying *Mary Poppins*."

"Dusty, I. . . ." Joe reached a hand toward her, then dropped it. "Never mind. Do what you have to do."

"If I don't go out with Haywood Wheatland tonight, I'll never go anywhere other than the basement or home, for the rest of my life." She repeated the girls' words. Then she patted his shoulder and thrust the bottle of booze into his hand, closing his fingers around it.

She whispered. "I don't need any more of this. And I don't think you do either." Then she marched toward the bathroom to wash her face and tidy her hair.

"Here," Meggie thrust something else into her hand. "This color of lipstick and blush will look really good on you."

"Thanks." Meggie had helped her pick out her date outfit, and provided makeup. Just as well as Phelma Jo would have. If she could ever again consider Phelma Jo a friend.

Phelma Jo hid behind her menu as Haywood Wheatland and Dusty Carrick walked into the tiny restaurant tucked between a furniture store and a florist on Main Street. He touched Dusty's back in an intimate gesture that suggested a long relationship. They looked at each other, not at any of the other patrons, including Phelma Jo. Hay didn't even acknowledge her presence, though she'd orchestrated the entire evening for him.

Heat flashed across Phelma Jo's face while her gut turned to ice. She gulped her iced tea.

Hay held a chair for Dusty and helped her scoot closer to their tiny round table at the center of the dining room. Three other tables and six booths along the walls filled the space. The single waiter barely had room to negotiate between, carrying his heavy tray over the top of his head.

Phelma Jo remembered her own humiliation when a waiter had spilled an entire pitcher of beer on her the other night. She wished ardently that this one, the husband of the chef and joint owner, would dump a plateful of messy tomato dishes on Dusty's head.

The evening was out of her control and she hated the helplessness of just sitting and watching.

However, the entire meal passed uneventfully. Haywood told elaborate and preposterous stories. Dusty laughed. She positively sparkled. Dusty! The woman barely spoke to anyone and here she looked as lovely, happy, and *vivacious* as any normal teenager out to impress a date.

What was going on here?

Jealousy ate at Phelma Jo, turning her dinner to a heavy lump. She needed Hay to lean across the table and dab at a stray drop of honey from the baklava with his napkin on *her* mouth, not Dusty's.

His hand lingered a bit too long. Their eyes met and probed each other too deeply. He looked like he wanted to kiss Dusty right then and there. In public.

That degree of intimacy was above and beyond the

call. Hay worked for Phelma Jo. He was supposed to woo Dusty, keep her occupied while Phelma Jo completed her business, not fall in love with her.

Then, finally, as Haywood signaled for the check, his gaze caught Phelma Jo's. He nodded ever so slightly and smiled.

A secret smile just between the two of them. She had nothing to fear. Their plans continued on track. He was just following orders.

Phelma Jo took a last bite of her own baklava and signaled for her check.

"Not so fast, PJ," the Thistle creature said, plunking herself down opposite Phelma Jo. She wore a different sundress from yesterday. This one had big splashes of hot-pink flowers with lots of green ferns scattered through the cotton print. She smelled of lavender soap and shampoo.

The way Phelma Jo had wanted to smell when she was little.

All of a sudden a memory grabbed her and took her back to the school counselor's office. He talked gently about her need to bathe more often. Phelma Jo tried to keep her mouth shut, too humiliated to admit why she avoided the bathtub.

The counselor persisted, worming his way under her defenses, taking control of the interview until she blurted out how she wouldn't take off her clothes because her mother's boyfriend watched and drooled, and then he touched her. Sometimes until she screamed.

And her mother snored away in the bedroom too drunk to care.

That was when Phelma Jo learned to manipulate and control her life by how much she revealed and when. By holding back, dribbling bits and pieces, she made the counselor's horror grow. Made her story more believable. Got herself into foster care where she could take a bath in safety.

"Excuse me, I don't have to talk to you," Phelma Jo looked Thistle in the eye, daring her to say more.

"Don't chew your lower lip, PJ, it makes you look like a rabbit. Bad habit left over from when you were thirteen and state funds wouldn't pay for you to get braces."

"I'm not listening to you. Now leave me alone." Panic nibbled at her belly. She was losing control over the situation.

"I'll go away soon. So listen closely. Dusty is my friend. I thought I'd better tell you that I won't let you pull any more nasty tricks on her," Thistle said.

"What . . . how . . . ? You don't know what you're talking about. And neither do I." Phelma Jo covered her surprise at the woman's audacity with wounded dignity. "Dusty is the one who pulls nasty tricks on her *friends*."

"Not the way I heard it. And you do know what I'm talking about. I just thought I'd give you fair warning. Trick for trick. I'm protecting Dusty."

"Very well. If you insist. But who will protect The Ten Acre Wood?" Phelma Jo arched an eyebrow. She threw a twenty onto the table and left without waiting for Dusty and Hay to exit first.

Fifteen

"**I**'M NOT ON DUTY," DUSTY CALLED to the two retired schoolteachers who worked the museum on Sunday afternoon. She tripped lightly through the maze of rooms, smiling at the few guests. Intense sunlight took on a softer quality as it filtered through the windows. She paused a moment to admire the bright colors in the braided rag rug on the floor of the parlor and the crazy quilt hanging on the wall.

She kept thinking about the easy camaraderie she had shared with Hay last night, how his funny stories made the Greek food more tasty, how the touch of his hand on hers sent shivers of delight from her fingers to her toes to her heart.

Eventually she yanked herself back to reality and headed for the basement; not to hide, but to finish the neglected piecing together of broken pottery fragments.

Dusty didn't bother turning on the lights over the stairs. She skipped down them lightly with easy familiarity. As her feet touched the cement foundation floor, she reached overhead for the light chain. An incandescent yellow glow flooded the area. She noticed the shadowed grime for the first time.

How could she have spent so much of her adult life down here hiding from sunlight? And from life?

Instead of heading directly to the potsherds spread out over the left-hand plank counter covered in white cloth that wasn't really white, she made her way through a maze of packing barrels, sifters, magnification light boards, and other analysis equipment for the set-tub and cleaning supplies beneath one of the few high windows. She grabbed a spray bottle of cleaner and some rags, then turned to survey the full basement. Where to start?

Everywhere. She started at the sink, thinking to move outward from there.

Before she could scrub more than one side of the deep square set-tub, her cell phone vibrated in the pocket of her denim skirt. Absently, she grabbed it and flipped it open without checking the caller ID.

"Dusty? Is that you? You sound so far away," Mom said.

"Hi, Mom. I'm in the basement. Not much signal." Dusty set aside her cleaning supplies and moved to the next counter beneath a slightly larger window, hoping for better reception.

"Where else would you be on your day off?" Mom said soothingly. "I hope you're having a lovely time making up stories about the people who used the artifacts you work with."

Dusty smiled in memory of the Indian princess and the Russian pirate who gave her that decorated ceramic pot. Daydreams and what ifs. She now had a lovely date with Hay to occupy her thoughts.

"Sorry I missed your call last night. I had a date," Dusty said, half afraid that if she spoke the words aloud her wonderful evening would evaporate just like her dream of flying with freedom and self-confidence.

"That's nice, dear. Dick told me that you and he went out with Chase and another girl. Did you have a nice time?"

What? Mom had confused the days. Not hard for her to do when at home with the calendar on her phone, her computer, and the kitchen wall, let alone 6,000 miles away.

She hadn't even asked about the Garden Club's entry in the parade.

Dusty decided right then and there to keep her amazing happiness a secret a little while longer; to hold it close and cherish it before someone could dash it into more slivers than the blasted Russian pot on the other counter.

"Yeah, Mom, we had a wonderful time. Did you know Chase does a really graceful two-step?"

"That doesn't surprise me, dear. Who is this new girl Dick dated?"

"Um . . . er . . . she's not really new. Someone we met in grade school who just came back into town. You wouldn't know her. She moved away a long time ago."

"You'd be surprised whom I know, Dusty. I was very active with the other parents back then. And I taught high school English until we started your homeschooling. Then I took over the Masque Ball and met literally everyone in town. Which reminds me, did that boy I recommended call you? How are you doing with the organizing? Do you need me to call anyone or email them? You know, I think maybe your father and I should just come home early. I wouldn't want you to become overburdened by the Ball. Your health is so fragile. You should enjoy your date and not worry about the Ball."

"Everything is fine, Mom. No glitches, everything on schedule. I just have to organize my own costume, something a little more elaborate than my usual work clothes. Though my pioneer dresses are historically accurate."

"Oh." Mom sounded more than a little disappointed. "Are you eating properly? Did you wash your hands? What about your date with . . ." Static filled the line.

Through the window, Dusty noticed Thistle playing ring around the rosy with a group of small children, including Sharon and Suzie.

"You and Dad have fun. Dick and I are managing on our own quite well."

"Oh."

"Mom, are you okay?"

"Yes. Yes, of course. I'm just not used to having all this free time."

"Then enjoy it, Mom. You've earned this chance to explore Shakespeare as deeply as you can."

"Yes, of course. The play's the thing, and all that. Gotta run, dear. We're seeing a different version of *The Merchant of Venice* tonight. It's set in the mid-Victorian era with steam engines." A bit of enthusiasm returned to Mom's voice.

"Sounds like fun, Mom. Talk to you in a few days. Good-bye."

With a snap, Dusty closed her phone and set back to work humming the tune that had haunted her for two days now, not at all minding that she couldn't put a title or lyrics to it. *Dum dee dee do dum dum.*

"How can she fly without wings?" Thistle asked eyeing the moving pictures on the TV skeptically. She'd watched programs with Dusty and other children over the years, (safely on the other side of the room so the electronics didn't go haywire) mostly cartoons and car crashes. *Mary Poppins* was new to her.

"She's magic," three-year-old Suzie explained with a touch of awe.

"And she's a 'specially good babysitter," Sharon added with her superior six-year-old knowledge. "Like you, Miss Thistle."

I am the best babysitter ever! Thistle thought as she smiled and hugged the girls, one on each side of her on the sofa. A big bowl of popcorn rested in her lap. "I'd like to meet this Mary Poppins. I wonder where she lives."

"A long, long, long way away," Sharon informed her. "The city is called London. See it doesn't look at all like Skene Falls."

"You're right. It looks . . ." she was going to say fake, but that might disappoint the girls. "It looks like a very old city, far, far away."

"I wish Auntie Dusty could watch the movie with us," Suzie sighed. She grabbed a fistful of popcorn and jammed it into her mouth to compensate for the absence of her other friend.

"Auntie Dusty and your dad need some time alone together," Thistle explained. She tried not to squirm and fidget at that glorious bit of matchmaking.

"I don't see why we couldn't go along." Suzie pouted.

"Got your nose!" Thistle grabbed hers between thumb and forefinger, pretending to have stolen it, before Suzie could turn the pout into sniffles.

"No, you don't!" Suzie put her palm up to her face, just to make sure.

They dissolved into a bit of a tickle match, all three of them rolling around the sofa, popcorn flying, *Mary Poppins* nearly forgotten.

"This was a good idea, Dusty," Joe said quietly.

"I'm surprised you trusted Thistle so easily with the girls," she said rather than committing to this being a good idea or not.

This Sunday evening, they had the local, family owned and operated theater nearly to themselves. For the rest of the week, during Festival, the stage in front of the cracked movie screen would serve as a platform for costumèd players to reenact the founding of the town, and a place to crown the high school senior girl as Queen of whatever this year's theme was. Meggie had narrowly missed out on being in the court this year to a cheerleader with a lower GPA and a bigger bustline.

"Thistle has an amazing rapport with the girls. I noticed it when she first showed up at the museum on Friday. And she must be trustworthy, or she wouldn't be staying with you." Joe flashed her a grin and offered her a sip of the giant lemonade with two straws.

Dusty shook her head. She didn't want any of the giant bucket of greasy popcorn covered with fake butter and too much salt either. Joe knew how her stomach rebelled at junk food and too much sugar. He should have stuck with a small unbuttered popcorn and bottled water. They weren't teenagers on a first date, trying to impress each other.

They'd been good friends for a long time.

Joe tried to engage her gaze. He looked more like a sick puppy than an ardent lover.

She pointed to the screen where the test pattern dissolved into an ad for huge boxes of chocolate treats available at the concession stand. The lights dimmed and Dusty leaned back in her chair, wondering what had possessed her to let Joe push their friendship to a date.

Joe was Joe: bland, conservative, and middle-aged. His hair was thinning and his belly hung over his belt a bit. He hadn't changed much at all since she'd first met him eight years ago. But they had a lot in common and never lacked for topics of conversation. They could always discuss history if nothing else.

Not at all like Haywood. The dashingly handsome man excited her. He told wonderful, if improbable, stories. And he made her laugh. When he held her hand, the air seemed to sparkle. Her world narrowed to just the two of them.

The lilting phrases of a popular love song rose through the sound system as the opening aerial shot of Chicago signaled the commencement of the romantic comedy that had been popular last spring and had fallen in the ratings when the summer blockbuster—special effects but no plot or characterization—flicks had filled the first run theaters.

Joe slipped his hand around Dusty's. Then he raised their joined hands and kissed the back of hers.

She fought her gut reaction to jerk her hand away. This was Joe. He was safe. Boring but safe.

"We're friends. More than friends," he said softly.

"Yeah, friends," she replied and settled back into the stiff and uncomfortable seat. Why ruin a good friendship with attempts at passion that wasn't there? At least not for her.

For two hours she did her best to enjoy the movie and ignore the touch of the man beside her. A safe and well-known companion.

Right?

"Thank you, Joe. That was fun," Dusty said as Joe walked her toward his house from his parked car in the driveway. He still held her hand.

Her palm was clammy, but he didn't seem to notice.

"Yes, it was. We should do this more often." He leaned forward.

Okay. This was the moment. Her first adult kiss. What was she supposed to do?

Joe tugged on her hand, bringing her closer as he bent his neck a little to reach her mouth with his.

Dusty closed her eyes and let it happen. A feather-light brush of his lips against her own. Soft. Undemanding. Safe. And gone almost before it started.

That's it? Where's the magic, the starlight, the enthusiasm?

"Come say good night to the girls, Dusty, and then you can take Thistle home. I appreciate you bringing her over here so that I didn't have to pack Suzie and Sharon in and out of the car."

"Yeah. No problem." No nothing.

Sixteen

CHASE WANDERED DOWN the marble halls of City Hall just after dawn on Monday morning. Designed and built before air-conditioning, the one-hundred-fifteen-year-old building held the cold, making it the most comfortable structure in the downtown area during the summer months. Especially this summer.

The more modern police headquarters tacked on behind the City Hall was less substantial and the meager air-conditioning strained to meet the demands of the weather.

Just as Thistle had predicted, today the outside temperatures would only reach the mid eighties. That made the interior of the old building almost cold.

Chase yawned as he approached the clerk of the court's office with his sheaf of citations and warrant requests. She opened her office before anyone else, preferring to work in the morning coolness.

He hated paperwork. He'd much rather be out on patrol, even on a hot day. Saturday night, after the parade and the adventure with Thistle and Mrs. Spencer, he hadn't been able to sleep. The vision of Thistle and her purple skin and Pixie wings haunted him, and then Dick told him Dusty had a date with Haywood Wheatland.

Dusty didn't date. She barely knew how to look a stranger in the eye. So what made the newcomer so special?

Maybe because he was a newcomer and didn't know everything about her, like most folks in town.

Maybe because her mother hadn't arranged the date.

Then last night, Sunday, she'd gone to a movie with Joe Newberry *without* his daughters. A romantic movie.

Two dates in a row after years of none.

So Chase had sat up all night polishing off two weeks' worth of overdue paperwork to keep from wondering whether Dusty had kissed Haywood or not. Then he'd fretted all day and night on Sunday because he couldn't turn in the reports.

He'd pulled appliances at the family diner and scrubbed grease out of the traps behind them.

He'd heard nothing from Dick about the success or failure of Dusty's dates.

He'd resorted to painting the picket fence around his folks' house to burn off frustration. The lavender paint didn't look right. It reminded him too much of Thistle, or purple dragonflies. But that's what his mom wanted.

Ginny had painted the ladies restroom in the diner the same color. Mom needed to do something with the leftover paint. Practical. Ordinary chores. Home, an anchor without questions. But it was mindless work that allowed him to think too vividly of Dusty dating both Haywood Wheatland *and* her boss.

He paused with his hand on the doorknob to the clerk's office. Raised voices within the series of rooms inside caught his attention.

"We can't sell the timber in The Ten Acre Wood," City Councilman George Pepperidge nearly shouted. "It's a city park."

Chase grew rigid in fear. Log off the woods? How could they destroy the haven of every child in Skene Falls for the last six generations? The town would react as if the City Council desecrated holy ground.

Dusty would be devastated. The Ten Acre Wood abutted museum grounds. Her whole life centered on that museum.

Except Saturday night she'd gone out with a stranger who had no interest in her museum.

He could almost understand a date with Joe. They could bore each other all day and half the night arguing about historical trivia.

Chase burst into the office ready to cite ordinances against cutting timber in city parks.

The room was empty. Not even the clerk plucked away at her keyboard. Had everyone gone for coffee at the same time? Before starting work?

The soft susurration of distant voices led him to a heating grate set high against the corridor wall.

A trick of the acoustics with all the echoey marble had channeled a private conversation directly to him.

"I don't care how badly the city needs the money. An offer from an anonymous buyer through a third party, out-of-town lawyer shouldn't even be considered," George Pepperidge continued in outraged tones.

Hmmm, where in the building could the councilman be having this conversation?

Chase threw the stack of papers on the clerk's desk and set off to track him down.

"I'll get this tour group, you finish your lunch, Meggie," Dusty said, swallowing the last of her spinach and feta cheese salad with pita bread.

"Huh?" Meggie dropped forward; the front legs of her chair thudded sharply. "Are you okay, Ms. Carrick? You've been smiling all morning and you haven't retreated to the basement once."

"We're busy. I'm needed up here." She moved into the front room to greet the group of two adults, five teens, and three grade-schoolers. A family with friends. Kids these days rarely went anywhere without friends. Their companions rated higher on their priorities than family.

She remembered when Thistle was her best friend and how special she felt to have the tiny Pixie hide in her hair when Mom and Dad took her places.

Except the hospital for blood tests and scans to make sure the cancer had gone away. Thistle couldn't stand the smell of the place. She acted as if ignoring the possibility of Dusty getting sick again kept it from coming true.

Dusty started the tour with the memorized portion of local history that led to the building of the house. Then she noticed the gazes of the teens glazing over and wandering toward the long rifle on the wall. In three sentences she transitioned to a discussion of the early weapons industry and how each gun was individually made.

"With so many variations in muzzle sizes, the gun owners pretty much had to make their own bullets." She indicated the paraphernalia required to keep the gun cleaned and armed.

"How come the muzzle's so big?" one of the girls asked. "Dad's hunting rifle is about half that size."

Dusty could see in her posture how she imagined holding the weapon and aiming it.

"Buffalo," she answered promptly. "We had buffalo in eastern Oregon in the early years, but they were hunted out quite quickly. With a bore this large, a pioneer could be pretty sure of taking down an angry bear or cougar on the rampage with one shot. If he wanted to put meat on the table, though, he'd use a smaller gauge as the large balls damage too much muscle."

"Wow!" The girls leaned over the ropes separating them from the gun, eager to learn more.

The girls? Usually the guns fascinated the boys. But they were bent over the spinning wheel trying to figure out how it worked. If Dusty wasn't careful, they'd probably try to dismantle it.

"At the end of September we have a black powder rendezvous over at the community college with demonstrations and lessons in loading and shooting these weapons. They also have spinning and weaving and other pioneer crafts . . ."

By the time she concluded the tour in the upstairs bedrooms, she realized she'd actually had fun with the kids. The father had been just as eager. The mother, however, failed to show a spark of interest at anything other than her perfect manicure.

"You are free to wander the grounds. The outside exhibits are well signed. But if you'd like, I can accompany you. Perhaps the boys would like to see what an early jail cell was really like."

She'd never offered to continue a tour beyond the indoor requirements.

Happily, she led the group outside and headed toward the knot garden. Three men standing behind the carriage barn at the edge of the woods caught her attention. She saw their bright yellow hard hats first.

These men weren't interested in the exhibits. They'd set up survey equipment with sighting devices on tripods and were carrying industrial-length tape measures and clipboards.

Dusty stood at the edge of the herb garden, shivering in the heat. The floaty feeling she'd had since Hay had called her this morning before work just to say "hello" sank to her heels, forming a huge magnet that kept her rooted to the ground. She couldn't flee, couldn't think, couldn't answer the question about the silver plant at the center of the garden.

"Are you all right, Miss?" the father asked.

"Please, call the curator," Dusty choked out.

Seconds later, Joe marched out of the museum toward the three interlopers. When he passed Dusty, she gathered enough momentum to creep after him.

"What's going on here?" Joe asked authoritatively. His slender stature seemed to expand with righteous indignation.

"Just doin' my job, buddy," the man with the clipboard said with a shrug.

"This is a city park. Unless you have authorization signed by the parks commissioner . . ."

"I got a work order signed by my boss. That's all I need. These days work is work, I'll take what I can get paid for."

"May I see this supposed work order?" Joe held out his hand.

"Sure, buddy. But don't stand there very long. You're in my way, and I gotta start cutting this timber on Friday."

"Th . . . that's the day before the Masque Ball. It will be ruined!" Dusty found her voice. "We'll have to cancel and give back all the money we've already raised. But we've spent most of it setting up the party." Tears welled up in her eyes.

"I see nothing official from the city on this paper," Joe said, handing back the ordinary looking memo.

"Talk to my boss about that."

"And who is your boss?"

"A voice on the phone from Pixel Industries, Ltd. I'm independent, subcontract out to the big guys." He waved at his assistant at the other end of the tape measure to move slightly to the left.

"I've never heard of Pixel Industries, Ltd."

"Neither had I. But I got a fax with the work order and an advance wired to my bank. Now get out of the way."

"Dusty, go call the police. And the mayor's office," Joe ordered. "We'll find out who and what is behind this. As far as I know there's a law against cutting timber in city parks except for removal of dangerous and damaged trees."

"I'm from Portland. Don't know about your city laws. I just know I got work after a long dry spell of no work." The hard-hatted man returned to his equipment, clearly dismissing Joe and his protests.

He took a sheet of notepaper from one of his compatriots, started recording the figures, paused, and pushed his hard hat to the back of his head. Then he peered closer at the paper, over the tops of his glasses and loosed a long low whistle.

"Holy ef . . . cow! That big oak alone has enough timber to make up for the purchase price. Can't get old growth oak like that anymore. Surprised it's not on the list of heritage trees."

"The Patriarch Oak! No. No. No." Dusty picked up her long costume skirts and ran back inside the museum.

She paused at the head of the stairs to the basement and made the two calls. Then she retreated to the sorting of potsherds she should have been doing instead of gleefully giving tours.

Seventeen

"DUSTY, WILL YOU PLEASE come up here?" Thistle coaxed from the top of the stairs. Faery snot! Why did her friend have to hide underground? Underground robbed Pixies of strength and thought. Going underground was sort of like dying.

Faeries could, and did go underground during the day, only coming out after dark. The cowards! They were hiding from people who didn't believe in them any longer. Dusty was hiding from reality, from herself, from ... everything.

"I never thought you'd be more akin to my mortal enemies, the Faeries, than to the Pixies you love," Thistle muttered.

Cutting down the Patriarch Oak would end the mating rituals of all Pixies. Cutting down The Ten Acre Wood would kill all of Thistle's tribe. She didn't dare think about that. Dusty had to find a way to save the forest. Dusty was the only one who could.

But she hid. Just like a cowardly Faery. Whose side was she on, anyway?

Thistle was too close to the darkness here. The cellar stairs beckoned her with fascinating horror of the terrible things underground would do to her.

"No!" Dusty said. Her voice barely reached Thistle.

"When something scares her, she hides down there for days," M'velle whispered.

"A lot of things scare her," Meggie added. Both girls peered over Thistle's shoulder toward the dark hole where Dusty retreated.

Thistle could understand how her friend found solace and protection in the darkness. Like Thistle once found in the elbow of a spreading branch in the old oak tree.

At the edge of the basement, Thistle only found fear.

"Why don't you go down and get her?" Meggie asked.

"I . . . I can't," Thistle cried. "Pixies can't go below. And I really need Dusty to come up and save The Ten Acre Wood."

"She has to come up on her own. Just like she had to decide to go on that date. Force will only make things worse," M'velle added.

"Dusty, please. I've got to go back to work, and your friends up here are worried about you," Thistle pleaded. *Don't talk about The Ten Acre Wood, or her fears. Talk about things that would make Dusty want to come up on her own.*

"Work? You have a job?" Dusty's voice came closer. "I didn't think you could *do* anything."

Thistle stepped back, grateful for her release from the thrall of the death that awaited her below. "Yes, Dick and Chase invented a job for me. I'm to befriend the old folks and make sure they and their pets have what they need. They said you need to take me around and introduce me to my new friends. They know you and trust you, so they'll trust me too if you say they should."

"That sounds good. You did a good thing for Mrs. Spencer on Saturday. But you won't be needed once this heat wave breaks." The stairs creaked, then stopped. Dusty had come up three risers by Thistle's count. Then no farther.

"I'm also babysitting for Joe on the nights he has lodge meetings or something like that." Thistle stepped back again, bumping into the two teenagers. "That gives you a couple of free evenings a week. But I can't get started without you."

Coaxing Dusty up was sort of like luring a cat into the wetlands. Tantalize it with a flash of wings and confused loop as if lost. Then when she'd caught the wicked beast's attention, fly a little closer to the target. Stop, wait, tease, let it pounce, but make sure it missed. Repeat, until the nasty cat landed up to its chest in icky mud and algae.

The last time Thistle had played that game, she'd won ten gold-and-cream-colored hairs from the cat's tail as her prize. No Pixie had managed more than six hairs before.

If The Ten Acre Wood was destroyed, there'd be no more games with cats, or children. Thistle would have no more family. She'd never be able to return to Pixie.

She took a deep breath, trying to concentrate on her job. Be a friend to Dusty, just like she was a friend to Mrs. Spencer and seven other elderly folks living on the ridge.

Thistle looked at her fingers, wondering if Pixie dust would work underground. Probably not. Without the forest nearby, she had little magic. Using the tiny bit available to her exhausted all of her strength, as badly as going underground. She had nothing but herself. And her few friends, like Dusty.

"What if we called the guy who took her to dinner Saturday night?" Meggie asked. "I bet he could persuade her to come up."

"I called him already, he can't come," M'velle replied.

"Dick says there are a lot of old folks who need help, this coming winter, and even in good weather," Thistle called down to Dusty. She wished the girls would shut up and let her get on with this. "Our elders forget things. They need to be reminded to eat and tend their pets. Some of them need help taking out their garbage and washing their dishes. I can do that. I especially like the part about letting the dogs run and play for a bit. I like dogs. We get along great. I don't like cats. But they pretty much take care of themselves."

"Who's paying you?" Three more steps creaked. Dusty must be almost to the first landing.

"I'm not sure. They said something about a community fund."

"Don't you need training and an insurance bond to do this? Me vouching for you isn't enough." Dusty's voice came clearer now, unmuffled by the death that leaked out of dirt walls underground.

Thistle flashed a smile at the girls. "Dick is taking care of it. But I need you to trust me, Dusty. I'm your friend."

Meggie left to tend to two women wanting a tour. M'Velle stepped back far enough to keep an eye on the front door and still monitor the situation with Dusty.

"Wh . . . what's happening with The Ten Acre Wood?" The creaking stairs said that Dusty retreated; so did the smallness of her voice.

"This is ridiculous," Joe said on a huff coming out of his office. He pushed Thistle aside and trod heavily down the stairs. It sounded like he had to go almost all the way to the bottom. "Dusty, it's time to grow up and come help me."

"Joe . . . I . . . I can't."

"Yes, you can. Dusty, I'm your friend. You know me. I need you upstairs. We've got to sort out this mess with City Hall. But it's Monday and the mayor's office is closed. He always plays golf on Monday. We can't do anything until tomorrow. So you might as well stop hiding and *do* something useful."

"Like . . . like what?"

More stairs creaking, like two people climbing them.

"Like research an alternate venue for the Masque Ball if we can't get a hold put on the timber work. We won't clear as much money if we have to rent something, but we can still have the Ball."

"We won't be able to string Faery lights on the trees."

"Those are Pixie lights," Thistle corrected her. "Faeries are snooty cowards who smell bad. They're afraid to get their wings dirty but think they can run the world by remote control from underhill."

"Pixie lights. Yes. Around the shrubbery and the knot garden, even the covered wagon. We can't have a covered wagon if we go somewhere else," Dusty protested. The creaking on the stairs stopped.

"I bet you can find a place that will have lots of places to string Pixie lights. You're good at researching stuff online," Joe reassured her. The two of them appeared in the dim light, more than halfway up. Joe had a firm grip on Dusty's elbow.

"But they'll cut down the Patriarch Oak. That's a very special tree," Dusty almost cried.

"I know. I've got calls in to the mayor and several members of the City Council as well as the city's lawyer and the police chief. We'll get this straightened out. I promise, Dusty. Hiding won't help. We have to work on this together." Joe patted Dusty's hand and led her farther up the stairs. "This town needs you."

Hot tears welled in Thistle's eyes.

"What's wrong?" M'velle touched Thistle's back in sympathy.

Thistle leaned into the gentle touch. "I failed Dusty. Pixies are supposed to do anything to help their friends. Dusty needed me to go into the basement with her and . . . and I couldn't. Pixies can't go underground."

"Ever think that maybe you need a friend, too? You've got your problems. Dusty has hers. Seems like you should help each other."

"But . . . but humans have never helped Pixies."

"I think they have," M'velle said. "And now Dusty is going to help you by saving The Ten Acre Wood and the Patriarch Oak."

"She's only doing that to help herself." Thistle dashed away the moisture from her eyes. "That's all that humans can do. Help themselves. That's why you need Pixies."

"Maybe so. But in helping herself, she helps you. She helps a whole lot of people who love those woods. Everyone who grew up in this town thinks of those woods as their own personal fantasy land. Good things happen in that bit of forest. Magical things. She helps the whole town maintain a major asset in that park. Trust her. She's your friend."

"Will you be my friend, M'Velle?"

"I already am. You made me laugh when some kids teased me for having dark skin when I was six. I never forgot that. I didn't want to remember you when I grew up, but when you came back to us, I did. You made me believe in Pixies again."

"You always were the smartest, and the kindest in your class. You always kept your gossip to nice things, even about the children who were mean to you."

M'Velle blushed and looked at her shoes. Then she raised her head proudly. "I had you to emulate."

***

"Mabel, you know more about what goes on in Skene Falls than anyone," Chase said. He hoped he made his statement sound admiring. Casually, he perched his left hip on the corner of her desk at the heart of the police station.

She glared at him for intruding on her space.

He remained planted.

"What do you want, Chase?"

Oops, maybe he'd presumed too much. If she called him by name rather than an endearment, she was pissed.

"I overheard part of a conversation. When I went looking for those involved, I found every door in City Hall closed to me."

"Happening a lot around here since Mayor Seth told a few folks semiofficially he's not running for reelection. Haven't had an open election in nigh on thirty years. Lots of people think it's their turn to run things. And they're all plotting behind closed doors."

"Who do you think will win the election in November?" Whoever won would have to deal with an outraged community over the destruction of a favorite park. Good reason to cloak it in anonymity. The offer came through a third-party lawyer out of town. Pretty hard to track that with client-lawyer confidentiality.

"Lots of people throwing their hats into the ring," Mabel hedged.

"Like?"

"George Pepperidge."

"Councilman Pepperidge has been on the Council, what, seven years? He's qualified, about the only councilman who takes his job seriously and actually asks questions rather than rubberstamping the mayor's decisions." Pepperidge had protested the land deal. Who had he protested to?

"This town is old and slow to change. Except there's a lot of new people commuting to Portland. They might want change, bring things up to date," Mabel mumbled.

"Sometimes I think we need an influx of new blood. But I hate to see drastic changes in our traditions," Chase replied. "Like logging off The Ten Acre Wood."

"Heard a rumor that Phelma Jo Nelson had her eye on the mayor's job." Mabel covered her quiet words by taking a sip from her iced lemonade glass. Had she ignored his comment about the park, or diverted his attention?

Chase's eyebrows rose nearly to his hairline. "Phelma Jo has never shown an interest in politics before."

"Except where it interferes with her wheeling and dealing."

"Where'd you hear this rumor, Mabel?"

"Sweetie, if I told you that, I'd lose the power of secrecy. Let's just say I have a tribe of Pixies living in my garden. They spy for me in return for a safe haven. Got it in my will that my two acres and house become a city park when I die so that no one, absolutely no one can destroy my garden or break it up for development," she said on a laugh.

Chills ran down Chase's spine. He'd seen wings surrounding Thistle Saturday just before she passed out. She claimed to be an exiled Pixie. Now Mabel? She pretended she was joking. Was she hiding the truth beneath the outrageous story?

He didn't like this at all.

"Coming from anyone else, I'd think you were lying. Thanks, love. Just one more thing. Who's your favorite judge in town?"

"Johnny Pepperidge. Old George's son." A phone buzzed from the console on her desk. "Skene Falls Police Department, how may I direct your call?" She touched a control and spoke into the headset that seemed implanted in her cap of gray curls, thus ending the conversation.

Eighteen

THREE RAPS ON THE KITCHEN DOOR drew Dick's attention away from the salad he threw together for himself. Thistle and Dusty were still at their jobs.

"Come on in, Chase," he called, continuing to chop green onions.

"Can I use your Internet, Dick?" Chase asked meekly almost before he'd finished entering the long room with up-to-date stainless steel appliances. An antique farm table big enough to seat eight ran down the middle. When the house was built, the owners had servants who cooked elaborate meals here. These days, the room was underutilized.

"Sure. What's up that you can't use your own Internet or the one in your office?" Dick paused in his chopping, wondering if he should add an extra tomato and cucumber to stretch his meal to include his friend.

"Um, I'd rather not have my search traced back to me and the diner wifi is down. Ginny's updating the server or something." Chase closed the door quietly, but only after peeking out and scanning the backyard.

"Sounds interesting. . . ." Dick invited Chase to share his information, as they'd shared most everything since second grade. For the first time he noted that Chase had changed out of his uniform shirt, but not his trousers. And he'd removed his utility belt and weapons. Was he on duty or off?

"I'm not saying anything until I find or, rather, don't

find what I'm looking for." Which meant he was officially on duty, but if he got caught doing something he
shouldn't, he could claim he wasn't.

"O-kay." Dick sought a way to pry something further
out of Chase. "Want some supper?"

"No, thanks. I grabbed a sandwich at the diner on my
way over. Mom says she doesn't see enough of you, and
you need to stop by and catch up soon. I could sure use
some iced tea, though. It may be cooler today, but it's
still damn hot and humid."

"I'll bring it to you. Use the computer in Mom's office. It's got DSL hooked to the modem. All the others
are wireless. Don't know if that makes eavesdropping
easy or not. I know criminals have devices to pirate
wireless phone receivers to make expensive long-distance calls, or tap into conversations about vacation
plans to know when a house will be deserted."

"Always presume someone is listening on cell and
wireless receiver phone calls. Maybe paranoid, but good
advice." Chase nodded agreement with Dick's caution.

Dick turned back to his salad, curiosity burning holes
in the back of his head. He really, really wanted to peer
over Chase's shoulder as he typed in Internet addresses.
Was this a criminal investigation? If so, why not leave it
to Skene Falls' only detective. Maybe that was the problem; the detective was always overworked and didn't
have time for minor problems.

At least Dick hoped this was a minor problem.

He poured a glass of tea from the jug in the fridge,
added a touch of lemon, one sugar (real sugar, not that
agave nectar Dusty used) and three ice cubes. Just the way
Chase liked it. Then he carried it, with a coaster because
Mom would kill him if condensation on the glass marred
the finish on her antique rolltop desk, over to the office off
the kitchen. The square room had been the cook's quarters
when the house was built. In 1888, everyone kept a cook
and a maid, and sometimes a stable man to take care of the
horse and carriage. The carriage house and stable now pro-

vided garage space for his convertible, Dusty's tiny hybrid, Mom's boat of a sedan, and Dad's pickup.

As he moved into the office, Dick tried to figure out where Chase searched on the Internet. The screen on the nineteen-inch flat monitor looked like a Google list of addresses.

"Anything I can do to help?" he asked, peering closely. City government and county offices. Public information. If this was information available to anyone, why the back door secrecy?

"Don't know yet." Chase clicked on the Skene Falls City Council meeting agenda. City law required a posting of their planned topics, so anyone could attend and make comments.

"What are you looking for?" Dick asked.

"I'll know it when I see it. Or don't see it, rather." Chase bent closer to read the small print, moving the mouse to highlight each item.

"What don't you see?"

"Something related to a piece of conversation I overheard but couldn't trace." The mouse hit bottom and moved back to the beginning.

Dick pulled up an extra swivel chair and read each item as the mouse moved down.

"What's that?" he asked on the third to last listing.

"Looks like a cleanup of old statutes." Chase moved down one then back up one. "Why does the Council want to rescind the mayor's authority to sign work contracts for city maintenance?"

"Can you pull up the original ordinance? I've heard rumors that Mayor Seth Johansen is ill and not up to running the city by himself anymore. The Council has just been a rubber stamp for whatever he wanted for as long . . . well, at least since we studied civics in sixth grade," Dick said.

"Mabel thinks he's had a stroke. Apparently, he's leaked a press release to the local paper—should be out on Wednesday—that he's not going to run again, and he officially endorses Phelma Jo. But a bunch of other people are also announcing their candidacy," Chase mused, sitting forward to examine the tiny print.

"PJ? Wow, that's going to be one hot and dirty race."

"At the moment I'm more interested in the council member who put the item on the agenda." Chase highlighted the name of George Pepperidge. "Why would he want to limit the power of the mayor when he's running for the office?"

"Send him an email and ask."

"But I don't want him to know where the question comes from."

"Make up a name and get a quick mail account. Then, as soon as you get an answer, cancel the account." Dick shrugged.

"You mean like you do when you aren't sure if you want to date a girl more than once?" Chase sniggered.

"Yeah." Dick blushed. "So what is this about?"

"You don't want to know."

"Yes, I do!"

"Okay, I overheard George Pepperidge talking to someone about an offer to log off The Ten Acre Wood. The offer came through an anonymous third-party lawyer from out of town. Couldn't find them, just stray words drifting down an old ventilation shaft in City Hall. The place is riddled with redundant and abandoned vents, whispering corners, and other weird acoustics. I need to know who Pepperidge was talking to and where they are hiding the paperwork."

Dick whistled long and low. "That is major. Maybe that's why Pepperidge wants to take contractual authority away from the mayor, to keep him from signing the permit without a vote from the City Council."

"Exactly."

"Email Pepperidge while I think about who else might know." Dick stood up, ready to go back to the kitchen and think while he chopped veggies. "Is it time to alert Tommy Ledbetter down at the *Post*?"

"Not yet. We want a little more than pieces of an overheard conversation before we turn Digger loose." Chase replied.

"How'd he get the nickname Digger? He certainly doesn't do any investigative reporting," Dick chuckled. "He's all gossip and this year's most fashionable hat at the Garden Club." And Dick asleep at the wheel while the volunteer fire department loaded flowers.

"Goes back to grade school." Chase tilted back in the office chair, arms stretched over his head and rotating his neck to relieve tension. "Some girls found him digging for pirate treasure in The Ten Acre Wood."

"We all dug for pirate treasure by the big oak."

"But we didn't get caught. Let's not get caught on this search. Not yet at least."

"Thistle, do you know how to do an Internet search?" Dusty asked as they mounted the steps to the enclosed back porch. They'd had a successful afternoon introducing Thistle to her new friends. Few of the old folks wanted to admit they needed help. They gave in to the idea of Thistle "just checking on them" because of Dusty.

"No," she replied, eyes studying her sandals as if they held all the answers. "Remember how your computer used to go all wild colors and static when I rode the mouse with you?"

"Damn. I was hoping you'd have some ideas about tracking down the people wanting to cut down The Ten Acre Wood." Dusty bit her lip, juggling options.

"Pixies are tied to Earth and Water. Earth gives us an affinity with the metals in computers, but water drowns it. Faeries are tied to Fire and Air. They have an affinity with the signals flying through the Air, but Fire makes them scatter and become useless. Computers don't like any of us."

"Water nurtures Earth and brings forth glorious plants and trees. Air feeds Fire, making it stronger. I wonder if a half-breed could inherit stronger affinity with Earth and Air to overcome Water and Fire. Then they'd be able to handle computers and cell phones," Dusty mused.

"Don't even think about half-breeds! They're monsters out of legends. No one has seen a half-breed since . . . since before the Faeries went underhill. Only one old Faery remained. He took up residence in the Patriarch Oak and pretended to advise and rule Pixies from there. He was too old to breed then. He's gone now. That's why Alder is king. He succeeded the old Faery."

Thistle's eyes crossed like she remembered something but didn't want to talk about it. Then her expression cleared. "I have other sources of information."

"Do I want to know about your sources?" Dusty imagined homeless men sleeping under the bridge or drug addicts hanging out around the back of the liquor store. Chase sometimes talked about gleaning information from such creatures.

"Trust me, if anyone knows about the murdering loggers, I'll find out. But can we eat first? I'm hungry. And thirsty."

"Me, too. It's too hot to cook. Murdering loggers?"

"Yeah, if they cut down The Ten Acre Wood, they'll murder my whole tribe of Pixies."

"Oh."

"Can we have pizza and beer?" Pure joy crossed Thistle's face.

Dusty almost laughed. "Have I created a monster?"

A puzzled frown marred Thistle's pert features. For the first time Dusty noticed how pointed her chin and ears were, making the slight uptilt of her eyes look longer. In low light her face would appear something other than human.

Like a Pixie.

"How about a big green salad with hardboiled eggs?"

"Oh, yes, that sounds delightful." Thistle moved

ahead of Dusty into the kitchen. "I'll tear up the lettuce if you'll boil the eggs. I'm not sure how to turn on the stove yet."

Dusty surveyed the half-made salad on the drainboard and the tray of ice cubes melting in the sink.

"Dick!"

"In here, Dusty," he called from the office.

"Why can't you clean up after yourself?" Dusty kicked off her shoes and ambled toward the blue light that indicated Dick had his nose engrossed in the computer.

"I got interrupted." He leaned forward, blocking the screen from her view. Beside him, Chase typed furiously. Then he moved the mouse and clicked. The screen shifted abruptly. He must have sent an email.

"Typical. If we finish fixing your dinner, can I have the computer after we eat?"

"Sure. I'm done now," Chase said, pushing away from the desk.

"Dusty had a nasty shock at work," Thistle said.

Dusty glared at her, not sure she wanted her brother to know how she'd hidden in the basement rather than face a bad situation.

"Oh? Why didn't you call me?" Dick stood and put his arms around Dusty.

She pulled away from him. "Because you'd immediately go into overprotective mode and hide me away. Joe convinced me I need to do something positive. I can't stop the logging of The Ten Acre Wood by hiding."

Both Dick and Chase froze.

"What do you know about that?" Chase asked. He sounded wary, and . . . and suspicious.

"I know that Tri-County Logging has a contract to start cutting wood on Friday. I saw the work order faxed from Pixel Industries, Ltd."

"Friday!" Chase exploded. He stood up so fast the heavy oak office chair that matched the rolltop desk tipped behind him.

"No wonder Pepperidge wants to rescind the mayor's authority to sign contracts. I bet he's going to push for a vote tomorrow and make it effective immediately," Dick said. He righted the chair and sat at the computer, typing quickly.

"Getting that piece of business taken care of fast is the only way to stop the logging. I wonder why the rush?" Chase bent over Dick's shoulder and pointed to something on the screen.

"If they start cutting on schedule, they'll ruin the Masque Ball," Dusty said quietly. Tears threatened to spill out. She gulped them back.

No more hiding, she reminded herself. Action, she needed action.

"I can't get off work tomorrow to sit in on the Council meeting," Chase said. "Can you go, Dick?"

"I'll rearrange my appointments. What about you, Dusty, can you come? I'm thinking we need bodies, people who will ask questions, a lot of questions."

"I'll send Joe. He's better at asking questions than I am." She backed out of the room, fear burning from her belly to her face. Tracking down shadow corporations on the Internet was something she could do. Speaking in public? Never.

You speak in public every time you give a tour of the museum, her conscience reminded her. The inner voice sounded a lot like Thistle.

Nineteen

THISTLE EASED OUT of the crowded kitchen as soon as she finished washing her salad plate and lemonade glass. Her friends argued noisily about Internet searches, persons of influence, places they could eavesdrop. She didn't really understand what the Internet was, or how to search for things there. Dick and Dusty put a lot of faith in what they could find on that search.

Maybe it was like the garbage dump outside of town. She'd heard from other, more venturesome Pixies that one could find all kinds of wondrous treasures there if you looked long enough and hard enough.

"I'll do a more conventional search. I'll meet up with them later at the Old Mill Bar and report on what I find," she decided as she walked slowly uphill three blocks and then south another five. She'd done a lot of walking today and her feet hurt. If she were still a Pixie, she'd curl up for a nap in the crown of a lush sword fern. "I'm not in Pixie," she reminded herself. "No naps. This is more important than sore feet."

Thistle paused at the middle of a white picket fence that came up to her waist in height. Bountiful roses spilled over the top, filling the neighborhood with their heady fragrance. Pinks and yellows dominated with the occasional coral and variegated red and white. None of them smelled as if they were anything but prideful roses.

Dwarfed by its showier cousins, a little pink wild rose climbed and twined around the fence and arched gateway, competing for light and space to grow upward. It smelled exactly right: sweet, fecund, mature, and wise.

She leaned over the fence a bit, cupping a single blossom and bringing it close to her nose and mouth.

"I know you're in there, Rosie. Come out and talk to me."

The pink petals fluttered, as if a stray breeze had wandered past.

"Rosie, we used to be friends. I need to talk to you."

"Yeah, what of it?" came a disgruntled voice. More movement among the yellow stamens at the heart of the blossom.

"The Patriarch Oak is in danger."

"Not my problem."

"But it is! All the tribes use the Patriarch Oak for mating flights. If that tree falls, it will be the end of Pixie."

"Wrong. It will be the end of your tribe." The petals ruffled again and a tiny snore came from within.

Pursing her lips to keep from shouting her anger, Thistle plucked two of the pink petals and pulled upward. She held the draped skirt of the Pixie by the hem. Rosie hung upside down. She spluttered and spat and kicked to no avail.

"Since time out of mind, all the tribes have used the Patriarch Oak as the center of mating rituals," Thistle insisted. "We of The Ten Acre Wood are merely the caretakers and guardians. That's why the old Faery stayed with us, and not you."

"Yeah, well, have you noticed anyone but your precious King Alder using the oak since he put a crown on his head? Life was better for us all when the ancient Faery still ran things in this part of the world."

Thistle had to think about that.

"And your buddy the king has used it dozens of times. Not just with you or his queen. Though rumor has it *she* hasn't trusted him enough to mate yet. Will you put me down?"

"Say please."

"Okay, okay, okay. Please put me down. I hate flying upside down by myself. Though Alder does make that fun."

Thistle wanted to drop the impertinent gossip. Instead, she drew in a deep breath to master her temper, and dumped Rosie into her open palm.

"Whatever your grievance, I need to know who in the human world wants to destroy The Ten Acre Wood."

"Like I said. That's your problem. This garden is my territory. You can't have it. Even before your ignominious exile, you couldn't come inside the fence without an invitation. The Ten Acre Wood belongs to Alder. No other Pixie can enter without his permission, and that's been mighty rare. Your territory is not my problem." Rosie jumped, spread her wings, and flitted off to the safety of a pink dahlia closer to the old carriage house converted into a cottage at the front of the lot.

Thistle reached to grab her, missed, and nearly fell over the fence. The pointed wooden slats jabbed her middle, fiercely.

"Don't you dare tell those lies about my Alder!" she called after the other Pixie.

He's not your Alder. He never was, Thistle had to remind herself.

"They aren't lies. Ask anyone. Ask Milkweed, the queen who won't mate with your king!" Rosie called back.

Chase stood on the corner of Tenth Street and Maple Drive, watching Thistle talk to a rosebush in Mabel Gardiner's front yard.

Why didn't this surprise him?

He wasn't sure when he'd stopped doubting her story. Not that he truly believed she was a Pixie, only that it was easier to just accept it than to try to find an alternate story that made everything fit.

Like the aura of thistle-leaf-shaped wings growing out of her back when she collapsed.

Now she talked to something fluttery in her hand. He detected faint traces of movement and a high-pitched buzz that might take the shape of words and sentences.

Three days ago, he'd have thought she cradled a pink dragonfly in her hand.

Today? Today he wondered if the green-and-purple dragonfly he'd captured long ago and Dick had set free really was an insect. He'd never found a dragonfly with those colors or that size in any of the bug books he checked out of the library.

Then Thistle reached too far over the fence toward the escaping . . . thing . . . and nearly fell.

He took two steps to see if she was hurt, but she dashed off down Maple toward Skene Falls Boulevard, or SFB in local parlance.

His feet dragged, unwilling to check out Mabel Gardiner's two acres—a standard lot facing the street with a long strip between the backyards of adjacent houses that ran nearly the full length of the block—for signs of Pixies. Part of him really didn't want to know if she'd spoken the truth. He'd rather believe that back lot connecting to the derelict Victorian mansion on Filbert Street was a haven for the homeless and offered privacy for teens to make out under the scraggly apple trees.

If Thistle had spoken the truth, if this Pixie nonsense was real . . .

Dizziness assaulted all of his senses. Colors flashed brighter and more intensely before his eyes. Outlines became crisper and better defined. Talk about upsetting his worldview!

He didn't know how long he stood there, trying not to think about it, but thinking of nothing else, when Haywood Wheatland sauntered up Tenth from the direction of SFB.

Chase did his best to fade into the mongo pine that leaned over the sidewalk.

He needn't have worried. The blond man stopped at the same spot Thistle had. He, too, leaned over and cupped a delicate pink blossom in his hand—a delicate, long-fingered hand that looked too fragile to belong to an athletic man. On careful consideration, Haywood Wheatland appeared a lot more slender and lighter-boned than on first glance. As if he'd puffed himself up the other times Chase had seen him. Or disguised his size by padding his sport coat and adding lifts to his scruffy shoes.

Chase shook his head and closed his eyes, trying to clear it of the multiple images layered one atop another.

When he looked again at Haywood, the man seemed normal, just as tall and robust as he should be.

"Rosie," he called into the bank of prize-winning roses. "Rosie, my beloved, where are you?"

A pink bug darted out of a showy flower near the house. It flew from bush to flower to tree branch in short, hesitant bursts of energy, pausing at each point as if to rest. Or search for intruders other than Haywood Wheatland.

"Ah, Rosie, sweetheart, there you are." Haywood held out his palm and the pink bug alighted on it. Its green wings, shaped like rose leaves, rubbed together in a decidedly flirtatious preening.

Then that high-pitched buzz invaded Chase's head again.

He turned sharply away from the scene. He had too much to do and too much to think about to linger. Digger was expecting him, and then he'd meet up with Dick and Dusty and Thistle at the Old Mill.

But he couldn't get the thought of *Pixies* out of his head.

Twenty

THISTLE GRABBED AT THE SMELLY and furry thing Dick plopped on top of her head. He grinned hugely at his joke. She wrinkled her nose and tried not to spit at the ugly lump.

She'd only just stepped across the threshold of the Old Mill Bar and Grill; not even enough time to absorb the smells of spilled beer, sweaty bodies, grilling meat, and . . . and an emotion she guessed was fatigue or wariness. Or both.

"Relax, it's just a coonskin cap. And it's fake fur, not the real thing," he said, spreading the lump out and exposing the striped tail. He wore one, too, the tail hanging over his left ear at a jaunty angle.

"Why would anyone want to wear such a thing?" Then she noticed almost everyone in the bar wore similar headgear.

"It's coonskin cap night," Dick explained, taking her elbow and guiding her to a small table in the back corner. Dusty and Chase already sat there, pouring beer into tall frosty glasses from a pitcher. They, too, wore the fuzzy hats with the tail trailing down their backs.

"What does that mean?" Thistle asked, still fingering the obnoxious lump.

"If everyone at your table wears a coonskin cap, then the drinks are two for one. It's a Festival tradition," Chase said. He looked grumpy, eyes watching the crowd, shifting from group to group. "Actually, it's a tradition whenever the owner gets bored."

Thistle remembered the dozens of furry blobs hanging on the wall the last time she was here, Friday night. She looked above Chase's head. Only a few hats remained on the wall.

"A lot of people have their own hats," Dusty explained. "The management keeps a stock on hand for the rest of us."

"Put the hat on, and I'll go get another pitcher," Dick said, placing the hat on her head for her. He bounced away.

"He's in a good mood," Thistle commented. "Did he find out anything?"

"We just got here. Thought we'd wait for you to exchange information," Dusty said. She held her glass in both hands, not drinking.

Chase only sipped his own drink.

"What's the matter?" Thistle asked quietly.

"Lots of things," Chase replied.

Both Thistle and Dusty raised their eyebrows questioningly. Interesting, Thistle noted, how they'd begun to use similar gestures and expressions after only a few days of living together. Or had the similarities happened when Thistle was Dusty's only friend?

"Phelma Jo's not wearing a cap," Chase observed.

Both Thistle and Dusty turned to look. Sure enough, Phelma Jo and Haywood Wheatland sat at a table with the mayor and Councilman Smith. None of them participated in the community nonsense.

Dusty frowned, then looked away hurriedly. "They must be working," she said, as if needing to justify Haywood's presence.

"I'd like to hear what they're saying," Chase said, rising from his chair.

"Not you." Dusty placed a hand on his arm to keep him in place. "You represent the law, even if you are off duty. You get too close, and Phelma Jo will shut up."

They both looked pointedly at Thistle. She shrugged and pushed her chair back. "Gathering gossip is a Pixie duty . . . and thrill." She bowed formally, as if she was still four inches tall and had wings. Her cap fell off. She left it where it was.

Thistle worked her way around the room slowly, glass in hand. She nodded to people she'd seen in the parade, and the families of her new friends. Snatches of conversations reached her.

"Wish it would rain." "Been a long hot summer." "Forests are set to burn at the next lightning strike." "Who needs a new cell phone tower? It's ugly and spoiling my view of the mountain." "Too hot to take the kids to the carnival." "Had to run off some teens I didn't recognize." "That new discount store they're building up on the hill will kill the merchants downtown." "They had firecrackers and matches." "Spray painted gang logos on the produce warehouse down by the tracks." "Damn cell phone won't work."

All grumbles. No delight or excitement over the Festival. Thistle frowned. Pressure in the air made her uneasy. Trouble. She knew trouble was coming. And soon.

A wiggle of blue on the top shelf behind the bar caught her attention. Chicory sat between two bottles on the edge of the shelf surveying the entire room. His hat sat askew and his wings sagged. He was drunk on beer fumes, and probably some honey he'd stolen from the kitchen.

His report back to Rosie or Mabel, whoever nabbed him first, would be garbled at best.

From the way he kept moving his head back and forth, pointedly not letting his gaze rest on Thistle, she knew he'd seen her. Just like he'd probably seen her during the parade. Either Rosie, his queen, or Mabel, his boss, had ordered him not to acknowledge Thistle now that she'd been exiled from Pixie.

Thistle was betting those orders came from Rosie.

"Thistle, where are you going?" Dick asked, grabbing her arm.

"Huh?" She looked around and found herself with one foot inside and one out. A quick look at the people told her she'd passed through only half of the room. She turned to Dick and smiled. "It's stuffy in here. I thought I'd get some air."

Deliberately, she stepped back inside and aimed toward the table where Phelma Jo presided. A heartbeat later, she was back with Dusty and Chase on the opposite side of the room without knowing how she got there.

Something strange was going on. Why couldn't she get close to Phelma Jo?

She had Saturday night at the restaurant. What was different tonight?

Haywood Wheatland.

She squinted her eyes to check his aura. All she could see was drifting beer fumes, smoke from the kitchens, and the overlapping energies of the other three people at his table. Nothing from him at all.

Before she could voice a concern to Dusty, the entire building shook, followed by a whoosh of air and a deafening *kaboom*!

Thistle swayed. The room went fuzzy.

"Thistle, what's wrong. Are you okay?" Dick asked anxiously.

"Explosion at the new cell phone tower on the hill. It took out a bunch of construction equipment when it fell," the bartender called over the unnatural hush in the bar. He waved his normal phone. "No cell signal anywhere in town. Chase, they need you down at the station. Dick, the EMTs are rolling and want you on board."

"Damn, that's the second attack on the cell tower. Only half complete and vandalism has put completion behind by three months," Chase muttered.

"Explosion. Fire and Air. This is Faery work. Faeries making trouble," Thistle breathed. Her vision cleared.

"Go, Chase. Go, Dick. Thistle and I will be okay," Dusty reassured them. "Do what you have to do. We'll talk later."

As the men dashed out the door, a blue blur followed them. Chicory would get answers, even if Rosie wouldn't part with them.

"Did you get any sleep at all last night?" Dusty whispered to Dick as she slid into the folding chair beside him in the Council Chamber of City Hall. Thistle sat on the other side of Dick, dutifully studying a few printed paragraphs Dusty had helped her prepare.

"A couple of hours. No serious injuries at the explosion site. Just some peripheral damage to the hearing of people in the closest houses. Mostly, we EMTs worked on the fire fighters trying to contain the flames. Some smoke inhalation and minor burns. General cell phone signals should be back up and running by now."

Dusty checked his skin color and the clarity of his eyes. She hadn't heard him come in last night. But here he was, freshly showered, in a crisply pressed suit, looking bright-eyed and enthusiastic.

"You really thrive on emergency medicine, don't you, Dick."

"Yeah. I'd make a great ER doc, but I was a lousy med student. Can't do one without the other." Dick grinned at her.

"So you compromise, volunteering with the fire department while raking in the bucks as a pharmaceutical rep."

"You got it. So why are you here? I thought you were going to send Joe," he asked casually.

"Joe couldn't make it," Dusty whispered, brandishing her own printed pages. "He . . . he sent a statement." She held out the two closely typed pages to Dick.

"I'll read it for you." He patted Dusty's hand in reassurance.

She relaxed, easing her hot feet out of her white flats.

"I think Dusty needs to read it," Thistle said under her breath. Her eyes darted about, weighing and assessing. "You already have your statement to read, Dick. And I have mine."

"I don't know." Dick looked directly at Dusty. "If you don't want to . . ."

"I think she has to," Chase added, taking the seat beside Dusty. He looked pale and hollow-eyed. Obviously running on less sleep than Dick. "I'm on coffee break if anyone asks. How close to the end of the agenda are we?"

"One more item until the one we are concerned about," Dick replied. "Dusty doesn't have to do anything she doesn't feel comfortable with."

"She represents the museum. They have an official concern with the logging off of the park. The rest of us are just private citizens," Chase said. He carried firm authority in his voice and his posture despite his fatigue.

Dusty flushed, breaking out in a sweat despite the fans, the cold marble walls, and the lightness of her sundress. "I . . . I can't."

"Yes, you can, Dusty," Chase insisted. "No one will judge you. They will judge the words that Joe wrote. Trust me. I'm your friend and I won't lie to you." He took her hand in his. "I'll be right here. Just pretend you are reading that statement to me. Don't look at the mayor or the Council. Just at the paper and me."

He sounded so calm and reassuring, Dusty forgot her fears for a moment.

"What did Joe find out?" Thistle asked.

"Judge Pepperidge says until he sees the paperwork authorizing the logging, all he can do is put a forty-eight-hour halt on all work, to give the city and the timber company time to come up with proof this isn't illegal. But if anyone comes up with a contract signed by the mayor, he can't do anything."

"What happens if no papers show up after forty-eight hours?" Dick asked.

Dusty shrugged. "I don't know. Joe is trying to get a face-to-face meeting with the judge, or the guy in the hard hat, or the lawyer who issued the work order. No one is talking to him or to each other."

"That we know of," Chase mused. "Hush, we're up next."

Councilman Pepperidge read the proposal to rescind

contractual authority by the mayor. Dusty dismissed the legalese in the speech, too worried about her upcoming session with reading aloud her own document. She hadn't given an oral report since fourth grade, just before her bout with cancer and subsequent homeschooling.

She gave tours to strangers and school groups every day.

That was material she knew inside out, upside down, and backward. She could do a tour in her sleep.

She knew the arguments in the statement she'd helped Joe write equally as well.

"This is preposterous!" Mayor Seth Johansen shouted. "You all gave me the power to sign work orders and contracts to end the bickering, posturing, and indecision that plagues the Council. Nothing got done before you signed off that authority, and nothing will get done if you take it away from me. Toilets will remain plugged in public buildings, parking meters won't get fixed. Potholes won't get filled. You didn't want to have to *work* at the job you got elected to and paid for."

"Excuse me, Mr. Mayor," George Pepperidge interrupted the tirade. "That power was granted to you twenty-five years ago, by a different City Council, with a different agenda. And now we feel that we should have a greater say in the management of the city." He kept his voice calm and rational.

The mayor, however, turned beet red, breathed shallowly, and drooled a bit.

Dick half stood, as if to rush to the mayor's side and begin CPR.

"This meeting is adjourned." The mayor pounded his gavel and pushed his chair back from the long table.

"Excuse me, Mr. Mayor. There is an issue pertinent to the measure still on the floor." Dick finished standing and addressed the Council as a whole.

"No measure is still on the floor. I have adjourned the meeting."

"No, sir. According to the rules of order, the Council

has to vote that they have finished the daily business before you can adjourn," Dusty found herself saying. "You have to follow the rules of order."

"Who are you people?" the mayor asked suspiciously.

"Benedict Carrick, sir," Dick replied.

"Juliet Worthington's boy? Didn't she marry that teacher person, never thought any good would come of that relationship."

"My parents are still married after thirty-two years and still happy. Sir," he added the last a bit belatedly. "And there is the issue of who signed the work order allowing Pixel Industries, Ltd to log off The Ten Acre Wood," Dick continued as if he hadn't been interrupted. "The Ten Acre Wood is a city park, the timber is protected from cutting by city ordinance."

"The park is special to everyone in town, enhancing the city, granting necessary recreation, and preventing serious erosion of the fragile soil on the ridge." Thistle jumped up and recited her own piece. Not once did she look at her paper.

Chase nudged Dusty's side with his elbow. "Your turn. Read the paper to me, not to the Council."

Gathering as much calm and dignity as she could, Dusty stood, adjusted her glasses, and began reading the words Joe had set forth for her. Her heart pounded loudly. Sweat dripped from her brow, making her glasses slide to the tip of her nose. Two minutes later, she shifted to the second page, unaware of anything she'd said.

But she got through it. She presented all of Joe's logical arguments in order, without failing him. "Respectfully submitted by Joseph Newberry, Curator of the Skene County Historical Museum, and staff." She dropped back into her chair the second the last syllable left her mouth.

Chase took her hand again and kissed the back of it. "Good job."

She couldn't help smiling at him, and the warm tingles that crawled up her arm from where his lips had touched her.

Chaos erupted around the room. All Dusty heard was, "You can't cut down The Ten Acre Wood!" repeated again and again. The acoustics picked up the words and reverberated them around and around, again and again.

Thistle sat and covered her ears against the noise, whimpering slightly.

A bit of sparkling light caught Dusty's attention. By the time her eyes focused on the blur of movement, she saw only the slender back of a man in a gold-and-tan sport coat exiting the hall behind the mayor's dais. A bit of the shimmering haze clung to the mayor's head.

"Ahem," Mayor Seth cleared his throat. The marble walls picked up the sound and sent it around the room loud enough to cut through the noise. "Such a proposal has come to my attention. The purchase price of the timber is enough to keep the free clinic open for another year and to rehire three of the five teachers we had to let go due to the current budget crisis. This is something I must consider seriously."

Dusty sat in stunned silence.

"Why weren't we told that the clinic is closing?" Dick asked. "It's part of the community college. Nursing students get most of their clinic hours required for graduation there. All the people who have lost jobs and, therefore, their health insurance depend upon that clinic."

"The college provides less than half the funds required to keep the clinic open," Mayor Seth said with a sneer. "I was told last week that the state budget can no longer fund the rest. Our area is growing. We aren't an isolated community anymore. Other hospitals and clinics are within easy commuting distance and along mass transit lines. That is enough on the subject. This meeting is adjourned." He pounded the gavel once more, rose slowly, took up his three-legged cane, and stumped out of the room.

Twenty-one

❦

PHELMA JO NELSON READ THE NOTE that Haywood placed in her hands, not on her desk.

"Free clinic closing January 1 or before."

Interesting. Haywood had been back and forth between the office and City Hall half a dozen times today. This was the first tidbit of news to intrigue her. Especially since the receptionist from the free clinic sat in front of her.

She schooled her face to make it look like she listened intently while her mind wandered to daydreams of the look on Dusty Carrick's face when her precious fund-raising Ball was ruined.

"As you can see, we need donations from the entire community." Janet Boland finally finished her shpiel.

"Donations look good on a resume," Haywood whispered to Phelma Jo, finally settling behind her left shoulder. "The elderly in this town represent a strong voting contingent come November," he added so quietly Phelma Jo had to strain to hear him.

She glanced at the note again and read the second line of handwritten text. A bigger idea popped into Phelma Jo's head.

"You need more than just a few donations now, Ms. Boland. You need a nonprofit corporation with a continuing stream of donations."

"You are right, Phelma Jo," Ms. Boland said. "The problem of seniors needing a little extra help will continue and get severe again with the first cold snap and

snowstorm. But this is a new project. We only have the
resources to start small and temporary. It all came about
because of Mrs. Spencer's collapse—you do remember
Mrs. Spencer from fourth grade, don't you?—and that
new girl, Thistle Down. She needs a job and this is something she can do. Actually it's something she's good at.
She saved Mrs. Spencer's life. Her intervention might
very well save several other valuable voters." So she had
heard Haywood's comment.

Beside her, Phelma Jo felt Haywood stiffen. Hastily,
he wrote a note and passed it to her, keeping his hands
below the desk level. "Remind this lady that the clinic is
closing, and she'd make a better employee than
Thistle."

Phelma Jo already had that in hand.

"Ms. Boland, I have the staff and resources to set this
up. Leave it in my hands." Phelma Jo smiled her
dismissal.

"We need donations now, not six months from now
when the paperwork for incorporation clears," Janet
insisted.

"So you do." Phelma Jo retrieved her personal checkbook in its oxblood leather cover from the desk drawer
and scrawled numbers and a signature.

Haywood fidgeted nervously. What was with the man
today? One of the reasons she'd hired him was his calm
reassurance.

As she put the final flourish on her signature, Phelma
Jo's field of vision seemed to narrow. Darkness encroached from the sides.

She raised her head a moment in alarm. Sparkles replaced the darkness, pretty sparkles in wonderful autumnal colors of gold and green and russet.

"Since the clinic will be closing soon, I suggest we set
this corporation up so that you will take the job of
checking on the seniors, Ms. Boland. You are much more
qualified than Thistle Down. Much easier to obtain a
bond on your honesty and integrity. Especially since she

has a criminal record under another name. Something to do with gang violence and vandalism."

"The clinic is closing?" Janet seemed to wilt. Her mouth gaped in stunned astonishment. She might not have heard the second statement after the shock of the first. "They can't do that to the community. Why weren't the employees told first?"

"Not my decision. I just heard about it. But if I were you, I'd start checking my options. In this town there aren't many." Phelma Jo ripped the check off the pad and handed it to the woman with great satisfaction. "There, that should get things rolling."

Janet Boland took the paper without even looking at it as she stumbled out of the office.

"Haywood, get on that nonprofit setup."

"Certainly, Phelma Jo. I'll make sure you are listed as primary trustee and registered agent. You can list this charity at the top of your good works in the mayoral campaign literature. It will look as if the whole thing was your idea."

"And put Ms. Boland's name as the sole employee."

"Already done. The Carricks will get no credit for this, and Thistle Down will be unemployed, homeless, and probably in jail by nightfall."

"When did you learn to read, Thistle?" Dick asked when they left the City Council meeting together.

Dusty and Chase wandered off together in animated conversation.

Several things today were hanging at in Dick's mind. He addressed the first of them to the woman walking beside him.

"I've always been able to read some. Just not well," she said, looking away with a blush.

"The Pixie I knew as a child couldn't read, had no need to." Was that disappointment, suspicion, or anger rising up to nearly choke him?

"It's something we all have to learn eventually," she said, still not looking directly at him. "Dusty taught me a lot more than street signs could. She had nothing better to do with her time while she was sick. And she was so lonely being homeschooled that teaching me basic reading and numbers helped her pass the time. Kept her mind active when she was too tired to do her own schoolwork."

"Oh . . . I thought . . . I don't know what to think."

"I truly am a Pixie in exile. I am, Dick. You were the first to believe me. Why don't you now?" Then she turned those fabulous purple eyes up to him. Moisture made bright drops on her lashes that caught the overhead lights and turned to sparkling crystals.

He stumbled on the smooth marble floor. He wanted to fall deeply into those eyes, allow his soul to merge with hers. He wanted all the hopes and promises she held out to him.

"You told me that Pixies can't read."

"I was young then. I hadn't ventured much beyond The Ten Acre Wood. But later, when I did, Alder showed me street signs and how to puzzle out the symbols so they meant something. I knew all the streets and the stop signs, and even when to cross on a green light." She nibbled on her lip. "Then Dusty taught me more. I know that her museum is the Skene County Historical Museum, and that I landed in Memorial Fountain—named because it's dedicated to the men from Skene Falls who died during World War I. I know this because I *read* the signs and I understand them. Just as I read the paper you gave me last night. What did you think when you wrote out my statement? That Dusty would make me memorize it."

"I don't know. Maybe I thought you'd bring it to me and I'd help. But then the explosion happened, and I didn't think anymore." Hope blossomed inside Dick, soothing a bit of the irritation.

"Dusty found the paper on the computer desk when

we got home. It had my name on it, so she gave it to me. I read it over and over and over until I knew it and could speak it without hesitation because you needed me to be strong and confident when I said it. Dusty helped me with some of the bigger words, but I read most of it by myself, because I needed to help you, be your friend."

"I . . . um . . ." How did he express his doubts?

"You can't sign that contract! You'll ruin this town if you do," a strange voice hissed around them; distant but still clear and precise. Obviously spoken loudly, with vehemence, muted by distance and mazes of walls and vents between them and the voice.

"I'll be saving this town if I do."

"Who said that?" Dick asked.

"Where did he say that?" Thistle added to his question.

They both looked around. The big room was empty, all the exit doors closed to keep the natural air-conditioning inside.

"If you were still a Pixie, how would you find the speakers?" Dick asked quietly, so that his words wouldn't carry as clearly as the other man's.

Thistle pointed to a small grate up near the ten-foot-high ceiling.

"Chase said this place was full of redundant ventilation shafts and whispering corners," Dick mused.

"I think I can follow the sounds," Thistle said.

"How? You're too big to fit inside."

"Because I've done it before. I know the path of that shaft. Come on." She grabbed his hand and led him to the exit right under the grating.

The strength of her grip tingled all the way to his shoulder. A sense of well-being and purpose filled him. The muted light seemed to sparkle with life and energy.

Enthusiastically, he matched her running pace as they headed up a nearly forgotten staircase full of spiderwebs and dust that made him sneeze. His footsteps creaked on the aging wooden risers. He kept his left hand tight on the banister in case something gave way. Thistle still claimed possession of his right hand.

She bounced lightly up each step hardly making a sound or raising a puff of dust.

Thistle paused at the first landing. She looked up, pressing her ear against the wall. Then, on a giggle, she pointed to the next grating. Dick guessed that it was placed directly above the one in the ground-floor meeting room.

"Onward and upward," he said, and sneezed.

"Shush." She placed a finger on her lips, then touched his own with the same finger.

He kissed the finger. Instinct or impulse?

She smiled, then set forth again, moving up the next set of steps. She kept her gaze on the internal wall. But she kept flicking pleased glances toward him.

He couldn't watch anything but her, the way her hips swayed beneath the draped skirt of her green-and-white outfit, the way her slender feet barely caressed each step, the luster of her hair, even in this dim and forgotten back stairwell. She seemed to float. Or fly.

The close air made him a bit dizzy. He thought he saw double leaf-shaped wings across her back. And had her skin turned faintly lavender?

He closed his eyes and shook his head briefly. If her capillaries were very close to the skin and suffused with blood, her naturally pale face would take on more color, he told himself. When he looked again, all seemed normal. Just a trick of the light and the windowless stairwell on a hot and humid day.

God, he wished it would rain.

"Here," Thistle whispered. She stood with her ear pressed close to a steel fire door.

Dick noticed that she kept a few careful inches between herself and the metal. Her hand reached for the door lever, but she jerked it back as if burned.

"Is that a not-so-subtle way of saying a gentleman should always open a door for a lady?" He tried the latch. It refused to budge. He jiggled it a bit. It still resisted pressure.

"We're locked out. And that's a major violation of fire codes," he muttered, standing back a bit and surveying the door from all angles, as if that would give him some clues for getting through it.

"Let me try something," Thistle said quietly. She swallowed deeply and pressed her finger close to the tiny key slit in the handle.

Suddenly the entire stairwell filled with sparkling lights, dancing and arcing in magnificent whorls and spirals.

Dick's mouth opened. "Is that Pixie dust?"

"I . . . I . . . help," Thistle moaned. Her arm flexed again and again as she tried to remove her finger from the lock.

"What?" Dick hung back, uncertain what he needed to do.

"Help me. The iron . . ." Thistle slumped, her finger still stuck to the metal. The bright starbursts moved faster, more frantic and erratic in their patterns as they faded.

"Huh?" Dick caught her around the waist, then gently grabbed her wrist and pulled. Her hand came away with a popping sound.

The whirling, colored pinpoints of light vanished. Thistle collapsed against him, head lolling on his shoulder.

He held her tightly, too worried about her paler than usual face and rapid but shallow breathing to relish the close contact.

After a moment she stirred, eyelashes fluttering as if awakening from a deep sleep. "Thank you."

"What do you need?"

"Water." Her voice sound weak and scratchy.

"Down we go, then. I know where the water fountain is on the ground floor. Can you walk?"

"I . . . I think so." She broke away from him and took one step. Her knees buckled.

He caught her as she slid toward the edge of the steps. "Um, maybe you should sit. I'll go find you a bottle of water." He guided her onto the first step and sat beside her.

"Don't leave me alone." She clung to his suit jacket lapels with new intensity.

"Never." He looked into her deep purple eyes, losing his concentration in their luminosity. "Thistle," he breathed.

"Dick." She looked up at him, mouth slightly parted.

A new awareness wrapped them in an isolation bubble. Nothing existed but the flowery scent of her skin, the warmth of her body pressed against him, and the tingles of excitement bubbling in his veins.

As if drawn together by magnets, he lowered his mouth to hers as she reached up to him. The first touch invited more. He deepened the kiss. They melted together. As she opened her mouth to accept him, he forgot where he ended and she began. The lines of *self* dissolved.

Gradually they withdrew, lingering here, renewing there. Until finally he remembered to breathe. Still she clung to him.

He wasn't sure he could stand on his own.

"If you'd just hold me up a while. That little bit of magic drained me terribly." She rested her forehead on his chest.

"Magic, huh? That kiss was magic." He lifted her chin with his finger and coaxed her into another softer, more tender kiss.

She withdrew before he did and looked at the door, puzzled.

"Pixie dust should open any lock. I've never met resistance like that, no matter how much iron was in the lock."

"What would do that?" He brought them both up to their feet again, pinning her to his side with an arm around her waist.

"Another Pixie locked it."

"Another Pixie?" Dick needed to sit again. The world spun crazily for a moment. Logic and preconceived notions crashed against her words like matter and antimatter in a supercollider.

"Another Pixie is working against us."

"Who?" He looked around the stairwell half expecting to see a tiny being flitting about, laughing at their antics. He blushed that their kiss might have been observed.

"If I knew who, I'd know how to counter it. If I was still a Pixie." She studied her fingers.

"I think you're still a Pixie, just a little disoriented. That sparkling dust wasn't normal."

"It's just a trick. Not real magic. Not like enticing clouds our way and tickling them until they spill rain like laughter."

"You can do that?"

"Silly, not anymore. I'm human now. I have limits. But that other Pixie doesn't. He's got more power than a Pixie should have." She paled again. "The magic tasted . . . hot like fire. Like Faery magic, not Pixie tricks."

"Well we aren't going to find out anything trapped in this stairwell. We need to get you outside and find you something to drink." He dropped a kiss on her nose and gently led her downstairs and back into reality.

Twenty-two

❦

"**I**DID IT, JOE. I READ THE ENTIRE statement
you wrote, and I only stumbled once," Dusty announced as she skidded into her boss' office.

He looked up from the stacks of paperwork on his
desk with bleak eyes, rimmed in red and shadowed with
black smudges beneath. "Did it do any good?"

He didn't sound hopeful.

"I don't know. Everyone listened, but the mayor explained how the money from the sale of the timber would
save the clinic and replace some of the teachers."

"Crap." Joe buried his hands in his face. "I just wish I
knew who is behind this and why they are in such a
damned hurry."

"I don't know. I wish I did. I almost think it's a ven-
detta against the museum, trying to get us to cancel the
Ball."

"We need that fund-raiser. Grants are drying up,
school field trips are getting fewer, so admission fees are
down. We just don't have enough income to keep this
place running without the money from the Masque Ball."

"The grant committee . . . ?"

"Haven't heard back from their inspection yet. Oh,
Dusty, I don't know what to do."

"You'll figure it out, Joe. You always do." She reached
across the desk to clasp his hand. He returned her grip
with a light squeeze as he rose and came around the
desk without releasing her.

"Thanks. It would help if you'd marry me . . ." He

stood too close, pressing his body against hers, lowering his head, ready to claim a kiss.

"No, Joe." She stepped away from him. Alarm built pressure in her chest. He meant it this time. She was sure. All she felt was a sense of being trapped in this room with him. "You are just tired and alone, and lonely. Me marrying you won't help this financial crisis." She retreated toward the door, nearly tripping over a stack of books on the floor.

"But you'd help the lonely part. I'd cope better. The girls love you. The courts . . ." He followed her.

Her breathing became panicky. The room was too small. He left no space between them. "Joe, you and Monica are going to have to work out custody on your own. Outside of court. Talk to the social workers at child welfare. Monica deserted them when they were tiny and needed a mom most. She might be better able to cope now, but you are the only real parent they know. Talk to Monica and work out a fair visitation. When you've done that, you can talk to me again about marriage. Not before."

Dusty held her head high and turned to go, masking the quivering fear in her belly. She had to face the real possibility that he might be serious and she had to examine her own feelings, her own need to hide from the emotional and physical intimacies of marriage.

For once she resisted the urge to run down to the basement and hide. Instead she took up residence behind her computer screen and started searching the Internet. She had to find an alternate venue for the Masque Ball. Now. The likelihood of stopping or delaying the logging of The Ten Acre Wood looked highly unlikely.

Half an hour later she slapped the desk beside the keyboard. "Dammit, we moved the Ball from all of these rental locations because they are too small and expensive!"

"Ms. Carrick?" Meggie asked from the doorway. "Are you all right?"

"Yes, of course, Meggie. I'm just upset."

"I don't think I've ever heard you curse before. Not even the time the four year old went potty on the upstairs carpet."

"Oh."

"I had an idea when I started filling out an application for the community college," Meggie said hesitantly, almost as if embarrassed to let Dusty know she applied or that she might have an idea beyond makeup and fashion. "Maybe if we offered them a percentage of the take, they'd let us hold the Ball on campus. They've got a really nice arboretum and rose garden for the botany and forestry students to practice on. And I think there's a cement circle there for the dancers."

Dusty felt like smacking her head against the desk. "Why didn't I think of that?"

"Because you're stressed." Meggie shrugged. "There's another tour group gathering. I'll take it while you make some phone calls." She dashed off to the front of the museum.

Just as Dusty reached for the phone, it rang. She stared at it a moment as if an alien being interrupted her train of thought. Should she answer it or get Joe to call the college on the other line?

The insistent jangle stopped abruptly.

"Ms. Carrick, Mr. Wheatland wants to talk to you," M'velle called from somewhere in the maze of rooms.

Dusty bit her lip in hesitation. So much easier to let social contacts slide around her than deal with life. Then she reached for the receiver, determined to break a lifetime of habits that led to greater and greater isolation.

"Good afternoon, Hay." She smiled while she spoke, a trick a college professor encouraged her to try. It worked. She really was pleased to hear from him.

"I hate to do this, but I'm afraid I'll be a little late picking you up this evening. I'm stuck at the office until seven. I'll understand if you want to cancel our date." He sounded anxious and sad.

Relief warred with disappointment. She really had enjoyed her date with Hay. They had a lot of common interests. Especially the history of the town.

"Seven is fine. Why not pick me up at home instead of the museum."

"You trust me enough to give me your address?" His voice brightened with surprise and delight.

"Of course." She rattled off the address and phone number. "What did you have in mind?"

"Hot dogs from a street vendor and a walk along the river promenade. I want to see some of the pioneer landmarks we talked about last time. Wear comfortable shoes."

Hot Dogs? Nonorganic, processed meat from dubious sources? She remembered the smell of the grilling staple of the American diet and her mouth watered. She didn't have to make a regular habit of eating them, but she should try them at least once. In the name of research, of course.

"If we start at seven, we only have about an hour of daylight."

"Oh. Well, then, we'll just have to finish off the tour another night. I really want to see you again. As often as you'll put up with me."

"I'd like that."

⚜

"Idiot," Chase admonished himself. "I could have walked Dusty back to the museum, maybe held her hand the whole way. Maybe asked her out." A couple of weeks ago that might have felt like a strange thing to want to do: date his best friend's sister. Not today.

What had changed?

When had he begun to love her as more than his best friend's sister?

He knew the instant. After nearly a year of treatment and isolation, the doctors declared Dusty cured. But her parents, and Dick, had the ingrained habit of obsessive hygiene and natural diet. Chase was allowed into the house, but only after removing shoes and washing his hands thoroughly. His sisters had given up trying to meet Mrs. Carrick's exacting specifications. Chase still tried. He and Dick were in the living room ... excuse me, parlor ... horsing around, practicing wrestling moves.

Dusty sat in the bowed window seat beneath the turret. She stared emptily out the rain-streaked panes of glass holding a pink jewelry box with a ballerina that twirled to a tinny and repetitive bit of music. She wound it up again and again until the noise grated on Chase's nerves and made him angry.

He grabbed the box from her. She lunged to regain it, lost her balance, and fell.

Chase dropped the box to catch her. His stockinged feet slid on the hardwood floor, and he missed. A bruise appeared on her knees almost immediately. Guilt flashed through him. Tenderly he picked her up and carried her to the kitchen so that Dick could apply ice and treat her like a precious jewel.

That's what she was, a precious jewel who needed protection.

But, dammit, she also needed to learn to stand up for herself. If she'd yelled at him or cried that he'd destroyed her treasured music box, he'd have gotten over it. But no, she forgave him and tucked the box away beneath the window seat, never to be taken out again.

Chase paced the police department offices, avoiding the ubiquitous paperwork and the ache in his chest for depriving Dusty of something special.

Through the high window of his own cubicle, he caught a glimpse of Haywood Wheatland. The blond stranger walked rapidly away from the City Hall portion of the antique courthouse building along Main Street toward First Avenue, all the while talking into a cell phone. Phelma Jo, his boss, had her offices on the river side of First near the Amtrak station. A big glass-and-steel, ostentatiously modern building shaped like the prow of a ship thrusting its nose, or snubbing it, into downtown. The first four floors of the monstrosity held offices for a dozen or more high-end businesses. Phelma Jo had the entire fifth floor. Then four floors of pricey condos with Phelma Jo's penthouse on the tenth.

Her errand boy undoubtedly ran back and forth between the office and the courthouse a dozen times a day, keenly observing everything for Phelma Jo. Gathering gossip like Mabel's Pixies?

Jealousy raged in Chase's chest, as if a vacuum sucked all the air out of him and left the heavy machine pressing against his rib cage.

"You're why I'm suddenly obsessed with Dusty. I always thought she'd be there waiting for me when she was ready to notice me. Now I'm not so sure."

Chase dropped so heavily into his swivel chair it spun around to face the whiteboard covered in notes and profiles of recent unsolved crimes. The only thing that caught his attention was a checklist of places he'd looked at to determine ownership of Pixel Industries, Ltd.

In the hasty scrawl he liked to call handwriting, the word Pixel looked like a misspelling of Pixie.

A vivid image of Haywood Wheatland calling a pink bug "sweetheart" and "beloved" flashed before his mind's eye.

Haywood Wheatland worked for Phelma Jo.

Phelma Jo had a reputation for underhanded, borderline illegal real estate transactions. Chase had never dug up evidence of blackmail when people sold prime properties to her at about half market value and hightailed it out of town. Lack of evidence didn't mean she was innocent. Lack of evidence didn't remove suspicion.

He logged on to the Internet and started searching some databases. He had three days to get a court order to stop the logging. He hoped it was enough time.

-»-

Phelma Jo tapped her foot, waiting for Haywood Wheatland to return from the courthouse. He'd dashed back there seconds after Ms. Boland left with her donation check. Something about following up with the mayor . . . ?

Damn, the man couldn't sit still. He flitted about with an intense urgency that left Phelma Jo unsettled and irritated.

Why couldn't she control him? She'd already divorced two men who slipped through her net of seduction, lies, and manipulation designed to keep them firmly under her thumb. If Hay continued on this course of independence, she'd have to fire him.

Never again would she allow any man to hurt her like her mother's boyfriend had. He was bigger and stronger than Phelma Jo. She was just a child. Automatic obedience was expected of her. Disobedience was met with punishment: either the back of her mother's hand across her face, or the boyfriend touching her in ways no adult man should touch a child.

The day the school counselor had called the police and children's services, she'd vowed that never again would any man of her acquaintance do anything she did not dictate.

"Well?" she asked when Haywood finally returned during the lunch hour. He happily whistled a tune she almost remembered.

Damn. Now she'd have an earworm of that tune until she figured out where she'd heard it before.

Dum dee dee do dum dum.

"Well what?" he returned, acting surprised she had questions about the morning's proceedings.

"What happened at the City Council meeting?" She hadn't dared show up.

"The mayor dismissed the challenge to his authority to sign work orders."

"Sit down and stop pacing. I'm getting whiplash trying to follow you."

He perched on the edge of a chair, ready to bounce up again as soon as he could. "Dick and Dusty had prepared statements. Thistle said something meaningless. That policeman was hanging around. I need to spend more time with Dusty to counter his influence." He looked entirely too happy.

"You are supposed to break Dusty's heart, not fall in love with her." Phelma Jo narrowed her focus, watching for any telltale signs that her new employee defied her.

"The only way for me to get to Thistle is through Dusty," he said nonchalantly while surreptitiously checking his watch. His glance barely lingered on the timepiece long enough to register the numbers on the display. He bounced up and began circling the room like a demented collie trying to herd her into the center.

"As long as we get what *I* want."

"You want to run for mayor in November. Don't worry. I'll put you in a favorable position."

"I hired you because you guaranteed me I'd win the election."

"I guaranteed I'd remove your primary opposition, Dick and Dusty Carrick. If they campaign against you, you don't have a chance. Don't worry, they won't be able to say a word against you come November."

"And what do you get out of it?"

"The demise of my enemies. Same as you."

Twenty-three

DUSTY STARED AT HER computer screen until her vision blurred and doubled. Without really thinking about it, she closed her eyes and dropped her head onto her crossed arms.

Suddenly she was ten years old again and bouncing around the backyard, running from rose to dahlia to lavender, smelling deeply of their fresh fragrance. Her legs stretched and her feet landed lightly. She pushed herself harder, taking longer strides, twirling with joy. She panted and a stitch grabbed her side. She didn't care.

She danced outside for the glory of dancing again.

The doctors had told her and Mom that the cancer was in remission. With care, she could grow up normal. No reason now to sit quietly while everyone at school played and ran and danced. Dick didn't need to hang around her all the time protecting and taking care of her as if he was a nurse or something. She'd had enough of nurses and uniformed aides wearing face masks during the months and months of chemo.

A flurry of movement among the herbs around the big old maple tree alerted her that she was no longer alone.

"Thistle?" she called into the trees, pausing to catch her breath. "Thistle, where are you?"

Dusty took one cautious step toward the shadows cast by the maple's interlaced branches. A stray shaft of sunlight shone brightly like an amethyst glinting in the shop window down on Main Street. Mom had promised her a gem like that when she was old enough. Whenever that was. Dusty wanted it now because it reminded her of the tiny Pixie who flitted in through the hole in the screen of her bedroom window, who sat with her and told her all the neighborhood gossip when she was too exhausted to read, or play computer games, or . . . move.

Dusty followed the flicker of purple-and-green motion. She walked slowly, careful not to trip on the garden hose Dick had left out, or sudden dips in the lawn. Mom would kill her if she fell and got bruised or scraped again. Or if she stained her new skirt. Why did moms always make you dress up to go to the doctor?

"Thistle?" Dusty called again. She'd lost track of the purple flashes as clouds covered the weak sunshine.

Raindrops evaporated from the leaves as the sun peaked out again, making the air shimmer.

Dusty tasted the word. Evaporated. She liked the sound of it. Vapor, at the center. Mysterious mists. Hints of menace. But Thistle would protect her.

At last she found a frond of a silver fern bouncing as happily as she was.

A bright giggle enticed Dusty to take a few more steps among the silvery plants of Mom's special garden. She watched very carefully to make sure she avoided the muddy spots. The giggle came again, a little closer.

"Oh, no, you don't, Thistle. I know your tricks. I'm not getting muddy today."

"Spoilsport." Thistle landed on Dusty's shoulder. "You went away in the car this morning. You never leave the house unless it's something special. And now you are dancing in the backyard. What's up?"

"Do you remember that I've been really, really sick?" Thistle forgot a lot of things and Dusty had to remind her often.

Thistle frowned and cocked her head a moment. Then she flashed a smile and ruffled her wings. "Of course I remember. I'm not like other Pixies who forget a friend. I've stayed by you the whole time, keeping you company."

"The cancer is gone. The bone marrow transplant from Dick worked. It's like a miracle. I can run and dance and play as much as I want." Dusty spread her arms and spun in place. She loved the way the trees seemed to twist with her. The world titled and looked different. Awesome.

Her left foot caught on something. The world swung the opposite way as the ground came rushing up to meet her, face first.

Sharp pain spread through her chest and stole her breath.

Tears came to Dusty's eyes. "Ouch!" she cried. A scrape on her knee started bleeding. A lot.

"Don't cry, Dusty. I hate it when you cry. It makes me feel horrible, too."

"It's bleeding. Worse than when Phelma Jo pushed me down and I got an infection and then I got cancer."

"Phelma Jo didn't give you the infection, the cancer did. Dick told me so."

"But she was so dirty and smelly. She hadn't had a bath in like weeks!"

"Silly, you did her a favor by calling her Stinky Butt. The counselor called her in, and now she's with a foster family who are taking good care of her." Thistle erupted in laughter, flying complicated swirls and loops. "I made you trip because you really didn't want to. I figured you needed some fun."

"You needed fun. Not me. Now my new skirt is all dirty." Dusty pulled her knees under her and slowly got up, checking for any signs of infection or bruising. The blood on her knee had already turned into sticky blobs that didn't drip. She'd need a good wash and a Band-Aid to cover the bruise. But maybe, just maybe, she wouldn't get sick again.

"See? No damage. The skirt will wash. I wouldn't hurt you. You're my best friend." Thistle giggled like delicate Christmas bells. "Maybe your mom will let you have one of those bandages with pink hearts on them."

"Is that why you haven't played tricks on me for so long? You were afraid of hurting me?"

"Yes." Thistle quieted and sat still on the bow of her fern frond. "Pixie tricks are supposed to teach people not to take themselves so seriously. We don't hurt people on purpose." She bounced up, wings beating furiously as she darted around the backyard. "What game shall we play? You haven't forgotten how to play games, have you?"

"No, I haven't forgotten. I've made up lots of new games and written stories about them. Mom says they are really good stories."

"Baseball games and tag are so lame," Thistle said.

"Let's pretend I'm a princess and you've come to rescue me from a dragon."

"After you wash your knee."

"As soon as Mom sees it, she'll make me go to bed and drink that awful herb tea."

"Then we won't tell her. We'll sneak in and take care of it ourselves."

Voices intruded on Dusty's memory dream. For a minute she thought Dick and Chase had invaded her private game in the backyard. Not as good as The Ten Acre Wood, but better than alone in her bedroom.

Then she recognized the voice of the grant committee chairman. "I'm sorry, Mr. Newberry. I really can't justify signing off on your grant application. There are just too many unknowns with the parkland. Who knows if the city and county will allow this museum to exist with the budget crunch and the logging off of the park. The money they spend on this place will be much better used by the clinic and the school district."

The dragon of her games had captured her before Thistle could rescue her.

No grant. No Ball. The museum would go bankrupt within six months. A year at most. Her heart sank. She needed to curl in on herself in a fetal ball and hide again.

No. She was done hiding. She had to do something.

Who was the dragon out to destroy the museum?

She had to find out and soon.

The museum and The Ten Acre Wood were treasured by nearly everyone in town. A lot of community activities centered around the park and pioneer buildings.

Maybe she should start looking at people who had moved here recently.

Her fingers froze on the keyboard.

Thistle bounced up the stairs of her friend Mrs. Jennings' house feeling as if her wings were back, helping her float several toe lengths above the sagging wooden risers.

She touched her mouth delicately with one fingertip, awestruck with the tenderness that lingered from Dick's kiss. As she brushed their swollen fullness, she lived again the wonder of his heartfelt caress.

In her mind's eye, she saw herself flitting from branch to branch up to the top of the Patriarch Oak. Bright green leaves and budding acorns trembled in anticipation with her as she followed her mate upward. Her heart felt too big for her chest, and her eyes watered with joy. This was what true love felt like. Not the momentary passion with Alder. Not the broken promises of a Pixie with delusions of grandeur.

In a daze of wonder, she joined Mrs. Jennings in her living room, noting the comfortable temperature and the whir of an air conditioner. "Did you eat your lunch?" she asked brightly.

"It doesn't taste right. I think them folks what brings it are trying to poison me," the old woman said. She pushed aside her walker with the lunch tray set across the top. Her water glass jiggled and tilted.

Thistle dashed to catch it before it spilled. "Now, now, Mrs. Jennings, no one wants to hurt you. We want to help you so that you can stay in your home rather than go to a care center," Thistle parroted the words the nice lady from the clinic had told her to say.

"Hmf, if you send me there, you might as well take me out and shoot me. That's where old folks go to die."

Thistle couldn't hold back a laugh. "You aren't old, and you aren't about to die." She sniffed just to make sure. She found no trace of Death in or around the house.

"Damn straight I ain't old. Not yet leastways. My daddy didn't kick the bucket till he was ninety-three. And he didn't go easy. He fought and wrestled with Death for nigh on three years."

Thistle busied herself picking up stray pieces of paper where the woman had dropped them on the floor. She stacked them neatly on the coffee table for Mrs. Jennings' son to sort through when he came tomorrow or the next day.

"And how old was your mother when she passed?" Thistle asked idly. She frowned at the congealed mass of the meal on the tray. Could she make the microwave work to reheat it?

"Mama only made it to ninety-two. Her heart gave out."

"I'm sorry to hear that. You must have been heart-broken to lose her." Thistle picked up the tray with the meal. What could she do to make it taste better?

"Turn on the TV, girl. It's time for my game shows. I'm ninety-five, you know, and not as spry as I used to be."

"Ninety-five? Is that all?" Thistle fished the TV remote out of a side pouch on Mrs. Jennings' chair and handed the gadget to the feisty woman. It wouldn't work if Thistle hit the power button.

"Just dump that awful mess in the garbage and make me an egg salad sandwich." The old woman's gaze riveted on the bright colors, spinning wheel, and applause on the television.

"You remind me of someone," Mrs. Jennings said absently as Thistle made her way toward the kitchen.

"Oh?"

"Yeah, I had an invisible playmate when I was a kid. I called her Thistle 'cause she had purple skin and barbed green wings, just like a thistle. Never had the heart to pull thistles out of my garden even though everyone told me they were weeds."

Thistle stopped short. "Mavis. Your given name is Mavis, and you lived one block away toward the setting sun and two blocks on the uphill road. There's a spindly stand of lilacs separating your yard from the neighbor's across the back."

"Those lilacs ain't so spindly no more. They growed so big my son has to whack 'em back almost by half at the end of every summer. How'd you know that? You ain't but twenty-five or so. Why, I'll eat that god-awful mess of a lunch if you're a day over twenty-six."

Thistle plunked the tray back on the walker. "Actually, I'm twenty-seven. Or I will be at the Equinox," she half lied.

Her chin trembled with sadness, and moisture gathered at the corners of her eyes.

Pixies could live forever if angry little girls didn't put them in jars with wolf spiders, or cars squished them, or someone cut down their tribal territory.

Humans grew old and cranky like Mrs. Jennings. Any joy Thistle might find with Dick would be short. He'd never fly up to the top of the Patriarch Oak with her. They'd never be able to . . .

"Do you need anything else, Mrs. Jennings? I think the heat is getting to me. I have a headache. I need to go home now." Home to Pixie before her heart broke so completely she'd never recover.

Dick whistled a jaunty little tune he almost remembered the words to. Something about chiming bells and little Pixies. *Dum dee dee do dum dum.*

Pixies. Like Thistle.

He stopped short in the middle of the sidewalk between his car and a group of medical offices.

Thistle and that amazing kiss. For a few minutes this morning he felt like he'd been transported to heaven floating on a sparkling cloud of many wondrous colors.

A cloud of Pixie dust. If Thistle could shoot Pixie dust into a lock, then she was still a Pixie. She'd never be fully human.

He wavered over to a bench beside a tree that overhung the office building, shading it from the glare of a too bright, too hot sun.

"You look the same today as you did sixteen years ago when you kissed me the first time, Thistle. You haven't aged a day. Do Pixies ever grow old and die?"

His bright daydreams of marrying Thistle, having children with her, growing old together, crumbled to dull, gray ashes.

Twenty-four

✿

THISTLE WANDERED AIMLESSLY toward Dick and Dusty's house. Somehow she didn't have the heart or the will to return to the old house that held so many good memories.

Her tummy growled with hunger and her throat ached from thirst. And from crying.

Somehow, without knowing quite how, she found herself on the block behind Mabel's house. A narrow footpath ran between two old houses, small ones. The space between the immaculate dwellings looked wider than normal and the path appeared well used. She followed it idly into a long strip of wild land that ran between the houses on Mabel's street and the one at the beginning of the path.

She stepped onto the pounded dirt where thistles encroached. The jagged leaves left her alone, but a creeping blackberry vine snagged her leg. As she bent to gently untangle it, soft male voices reached her.

She froze in place.

"You did good, bringing down that cell phone tower," Haywood Wheatland chuckled.

"That was awesome!" a younger voice replied. It cracked on the last syllable, climbing upward into a child's range.

Young, just beginning to reach for manhood.

She crept forward, one small step in front of the other until the path opened up into a meadow dotted with goldenrod and Lamb's Tail shrubs. Across the open space, beside the iron gate that led from Mabel's back-yard into the wild strip sat Haywood Wheatland on an overgrown park bench. Five youths leaned against the bench or stumps or sprawled on the ground in a semi-circle around him.

"And here's your reward for bringing down the eye-sore of poisonous steel," Haywood said. He held out his hand, revealing five brown lumps. The scent of chocolate rose from the warmth of his skin.

"Eeww! Looks like cat poop. I'm not going to eat that crap," one of the boys said. He looked to be the largest of the group, taller by half a head and broader in the shoulder with just a hint of beard shadow on his chin and upper lip. His voice remained deep and secure.

"These are different chocolates. Special chocolates. Once you've tasted these, you won't settle for what your mother puts into cookies," Hay replied in a soothing voice. A bit of gold began to glow around his head. "These will take you on a wilder ride than when we went inside the computer and played your war games for real." He smiled secretly.

"Cool, man!" a boy from the middle of the pack and the age group said, reaching eagerly for his treat.

"And when the chocolate and mushroom are fully into your mind, you and I will try something new. Maybe we'll stop all the carnival rides at the same time, and make the Ferris wheel topple."

"More awesome than the cell tower coming down right on top of all those bulldozers?" the leader asked.

Thistle gasped. She needed to stop this. She needed to warn Dusty.

Quickly, she turned to run away.

The pesky blackberry snaked out across the path and tripped her.

Her face met the ground. With an aching groan, she tried to get up, only to find herself trapped by more prickly vines and a rock bigger than her fist flying through the air directly toward her head.

Two hours later she staggered back to her bed, too dazed and sore to remember what she needed to do, or why.

"Do you see the curving pile of rotting lumber?" Dusty pointed to one of the biggest disappointments in her life. The dissolving artifact rested on an island in the middle of the river, just below the main waterfall. The sun was close to sinking behind the ridge, and only a few shafts of light made the wood look like anything more than a shadowy lump.

As thick and undissolving as the lump of hot dog and white bread bun she'd eaten half of while they walked the promenade. She couldn't tell him that, though. He'd been so proud of ordering from the colorful food wagons that sprang up along Main Street during Festival week.

"I think I see it. My distance vision isn't wonderful," Hay said, squinting in the direction she pointed. He put his arm around Dusty and snugged her up against his side as if that would help him see.

Her awareness of the few people out walking the promenade faded. As the sun sank, fewer and fewer people ventured this far away from the lights on Main Street. The explosion on the hill that had delayed not only completion of the cell tower, but the beginning of construction on the discount store, had them spooked. They weren't willing to risk the dark just to catch a bit of cool, moist air after the long, hot day.

"There's not a lot left, but that's the original water wheel that powered the woolen mill," Dusty said, concentrating on what she knew, the history that she was passionate about.

"The mill that employs half the town?"

"Yes. The wheel was built in 1846, before Oregon became a territory of the U.S. As part of my Master's degree, I wrote a grant to dismantle the wheel and rebuild and restore it up at the museum. I actually got the grant, but the current owners of the mill, who have corporate offices in Louisiana, wouldn't give permission for structural engineers to go in and assess the wheel and the plans to dismantle it. They prefer to allow an important artifact of our heritage to rot."

"Too bad. It would have made a nice addition to the exhibits," he said. But he wasn't gazing at the wheel any more. He was looking at her.

She returned his gaze, amazed that she could talk so freely with him. She'd never met anyone who made her feel as comfortable as he did.

They were alone, with only the muted rush of water over the thirty-foot drop in the river, an occasional sleepy chirp of a bird and the hum of evening insects.

"Dusty, I . . . I should tell you that our mothers were roommates in college. They asked me to call you, ask you to the Masque Ball."

"Oh." Her world fell flat.

"I didn't want to call you. I've had some pretty disastrous blind dates and didn't want a repeat. But then I met you, and I knew we could have something special. I'm glad we got to know each other without the false expectations of our mothers hanging over us."

"I'm glad, too. If I'd known about our mothers' connection, I probably would have turned you down.

"And now?"

"Now? If the offer is still open, I'd like to go to the Ball with you."

He lowered his mouth to hers, capturing a tentative kiss.

Startled, she drew back, still within the circle of his arm around her waist.

"I'm sorry. Did I frighten you?" he breathed.

"No, I . . ." She bit her lip. What did she say? She had only the one experience with Joe. Hay's kiss was different, exciting, and scary.

Wonderfully scary, indeed.

"Dusty, I had no intention of falling in love with you."

"Silly, we've only known each other a couple of days."

"I feel like I've known you all my life. Or maybe you are the one I've been searching for since the beginning of time."

"I . . . I've never met anyone like you before." She bit her lip in indecision.

"Do you believe in love at first sight?"

"I believe in lust at first sight that can grow into love." At least that's what she'd always told herself when she outgrew the teen romance books she devoured when she was sixteen. She'd repeated the mantra with each failed date arranged by her family when the total lack of passion, or even interest guaranteed there would be no second date.

"Then believe in this." He captured her mouth again with his, enticing her into a response with gentle flicks of his tongue.

Dusty became malleable clay under his brilliant ministrations. She experienced new flares from belly to head that left her dizzy. Simmers of longing from his mobile mouth on hers glowed deep within her. Her arms crept around his neck, and she rose on tiptoe to bring them closer together.

Her knees turned to pudding. She clung to him even as she pulled her mouth free long enough to breathe.

"Relax, my darling. Trust me," he whispered. "I'll never hurt you."

"Promise?"

"Promise." He kissed her again.

Her world exploded into myriad bright colors rivaling the last rays of the sun shooting above the ridge and sparkling across the river.

Chase scrubbed his eyes free of grit and looked up from his concentrated, fine-print reading. The little digital display on the bottom right of his computer screen read ten fifty two PM. God, he'd been searching and tracing link to link for the whole day and half the night.

But he'd found what he needed. There it was, in black and white, the incorporation papers for Pixel, Industries, Ltd. Signed by none other than Phelma Jo Nelson herself as CEO and sole stockholder. The date beside her signature was less than a week old.

The job order for the independent logger was dated three days later.

"Someone's in a hurry," he muttered. "Looks to me like she's timed it deliberately to interfere with the Masque Ball."

He stretched his back and arms, grateful for the release and cracking after so many hours hunched over his desk.

He saved the screen and printed out a copy. Then he stood and popped the kinks out of his knees.

"I need a walk. Or better yet an hour in the gym." He felt flabby and weak. "The price of getting promoted to sergeant. Too much paperwork and not enough exercise."

He walked a few steps, checked on the printer. It spat out the third of fifteen pages. He paced once around the desk, then out the door to the main corridor of the station. All the doors were closed. The gentle hum of powered-down technology greeted him. Nothing else. Not even the murmur of voices.

His route took him out to the lobby and past the dispatch desk.

"Don't you ever go home, Mabel?" he asked as he came abreast of her.

She shrugged and shook her tightly permed gray hair that had hints of blue and pink streaked through it.

Sort of like Thistle's black hair had deep purple highlights.

Then he remembered the pink bug flitting around Mabel's front yard that paused and talked to first Thistle and then Haywood. Or rather Thistle and Haywood conversed with the bug. Chase hadn't heard any replies. Maybe he'd watched from too far away.

Maybe he'd imagined the entire episode.

He didn't think so.

"All the officers and my relief watch are out on patrol. Had three fistfights outside the liquor store and two inside the Old Mill Bar. I'm needed here to help process the paperwork," she said.

"How many in lockup?" Chase asked, feeling guilty. He should have been out on the streets enforcing calm when the unrelenting heat stretched nerves taut and frayed tempers.

"Only the three who were too drunk to walk home." She chuckled. "Del Payton hosed down the others to cool them off and sober them up."

"So why don't you go home now that the excitement is over?"

"What's to go home for?" Mabel asked. She sounded a bit sleepy, her words almost slurred.

"You need to go home and tend to your army of Pixies who spy around town for you." He threw back the line she'd given him about her source of gossip.

That hit home. Mabel reared back in her chair startled. Her mouth gaped. "How'd you know?"

She must be tired not to have a fast comeback cloaked in endearments.

"You told me."

"But no one believes. Not anymore."

"I didn't used to. But I saw some things that have no other explanation. And I believe." He did. Strangely he did.

A huge weight seemed to lift from his shoulders, leaving him light and free and full of renewed energy.

"Bless you, boy. I'm glad. So, when I die, you can have the house and the yard and the Pixies. Someone needs to take care of them. Don't trust the Parks Department since the hullabaloo over The Ten Acre Wood." Her words came slower and sort of blended into each other.

"You're never going to die, Mabel. I don't think this town can run on its own without you." He scanned her for signs of illness. Skin a little pale but not gray, no blue tinge on her lips or fingernails, so her heart still beat strongly. Her curls were crisp and freshly washed. Maybe she was just a little tired.

"You'd be surprised." Mabel yawned hugely. "I'm going to switch everything over to the county dispatch now. They'll ring me at home, as well as the chief, if anything important goes down between now and the morning crew."

"Want me to drive you home, Mabel?" Chase didn't like the way she gave in to the idea of going home so easily.

"That would be lovely, sweetheart. Mind if I play with the radio on the drive? I've got this annoyingly vague tune running through my head, and I'm trying to figure out what it is." She hummed a phrase. *Dum dee dee do, dum dum*. It was the same tune he had been hearing. Now it ran through his head louder and more persistent than ever. Something about honey sweeter than wine? No, that was something else. Similar, not the same. Spring flowers and May wine. That was it.

"It sounds sort of like the tune you get from one of those musical jewelry boxes; you know, the kind with the twirling ballerina," Mabel mused, still slurring her words a bit.

That thought almost stabbed Chase in the heart.

Dusty's music box, the one he'd broken so long ago. The doctors had made her give up the ballet lessons she loved. She'd had to miss her first solo in the dance recital, never got to wear the silly little pink tutu and tiara. She played the music box over and over and over until it near drove him crazy.

And he broke it.

Dick said she still had the box.

That tune, something with delicate chimes? *Dum dee dee do dum dum*," he hummed the phrase again. "I can almost hear tiny voices singing in the distance . . ."

Maybe Dusty had never quite forgiven him for the broken music box. Maybe that was why she was dating Haywood Wheatland. She couldn't see Chase as anything but the bully who'd broken her favorite treasure.

"Let me grab some papers out of my office. Then I'll drive you home," he said, urging Mabel to close down her desk. He had an idea and wanted to get started immediately.

"Papers that print out might make it easier to request an injunction against the loggers?" Mabel gathered her purse and sweater. "Heard the mayor stonewalled Joe Newberry's request."

"Yeah." If he saved Dusty's Masque Ball, the first one she'd organized by herself and, in doing so, saved The Ten Acre Wood and Thistle's homeland, maybe Dusty would forgive him for that damn music box. What if he bought her a new one?

Nope. He needed to do something better to prove he had always been Dusty's friend and wanted to be more.

"I've also got to find a way to right some old wrongs."

"Here's Judge Pepperidge's home phone number. My spies tell me he's a night owl and never goes to bed before midnight." Mabel handed him a small piece of paper she'd already written out.

"I'm looking forward to meeting your spies."

"Oh, you will, sooner than you think. Bring honey to my little tea party Saturday afternoon before the Ball. They'll love you forever, and that's an honor and a tremendous responsibility."

"The responsibility of friendship."

"Glad to know you recognize that. Not everyone does these days."

Twenty-five

🌿

CHASE SAT STIFFLY in a straight-backed maple chair at Mabel's kitchen table. "Are you sure this is the right thing to do?" he asked nervously.

"It was your idea. Run with your first instinct," she replied, keeping her gaze fixed on pouring two fingers of scotch into a cut-glass tumbler. No more, no less. She lifted the glass to the light and gazed into the amber liquid with fondness, or admiration, or possibly lust. While the scotch captured her attention, Chase examined the label on the bottle.

He let loose a low whistle. "Twenty-year-old single malt. What's the occasion?"

"Drink this," Mabel ordered, plunking the tumbler on her round kitchen table in front of Chase. "You're going to need it."

"I'm tired, it's late. I think I need coffee more than booze."

"Drink it. It will help. I promise."

"Yes, ma'am." Chase lifted the glass, passing it slowly beneath his nose. The bouquet wafted upward, caressing his senses and inviting him to partake. He sipped just enough to coat his tongue, holding the precious liquid in his mouth a moment, letting the peaty smoke fill him. Then he swallowed, appreciating the burn and the rebound that smelled of thistle blossoms, heather, and cold ocean waters.

He had to open his mouth to let the heat escape.

"Oh, yeah. That's the good stuff." He savored the flavors bursting through his senses a moment. "Like I said, what's the occasion? Must be something special," he said when he regained control over his voice.

"Just drink it down."

No one in Skene Falls dared say "no" to Mabel when she planted her hands on her hips and stuck her chin out like a pugnacious pit bull.

Chase had an instant flashback to Julia, the big red mastiff he'd raised as a child. The dog whose drool provided the ropey glue he used to stick a dragonfly's wings together. Only it wasn't a dragonfly.

By all accounts, he was supposed to believe the purple bug was actually Thistle in Pixie form.

He didn't want to examine that thought too closely. He downed another slug of the scotch.

"Good. You're ready." Mabel nodded once, then she walked quietly over to the window on the other side of the nook. The sash window was already open to catch any stray breeze in the hot, humid night. She pushed the bottom of the screen out a bit and whistled three quick notes.

Seconds later a blue blob crawled under the frame and wriggled onto the sill.

"I'm drunk," Chase murmured, rubbing his eyes with both hands.

"You didn't have enough scotch to get drunk," a tiny voice said. Or did it sing? Definitely a hint of jingle bells underneath the words. *Dum dum do do dee dee dum.*

A different blasted earworm tune.

"Yeah, I'm real, all right, and we've got to put up with each other 'cause Mabel says so."

"I do not see a little man four inches tall wearing blue breeches and a hat made of blue blossoms."

"The name's Chicory. And the flower's as much a part of me as your badge and gun are to you."

That made Chase pause a moment and look more closely at the Pixie standing in front of him, hands on hips, glowering disapproval. Chicory fluttered his green wings and rose above the table a few inches.

"Why am I not running away and screaming in disbelief?"

"Because deep in your heart you always knew we were real."

The scotch in Chase's belly threatened to come up. It didn't taste nearly as good the second time around.

"Oh, stop trying to make sense out of Pixies and reality. You two need to figure out how to fix something. Neither one of you can do it alone," Mabel reminded them.

"Well, his fat fingers sure can't fit inside," Chicory sneered.

"How can a Pixie know anything about mechanics?" Chase returned.

"Like I said, neither one of you can do it alone. Now make your peace and get to work. You don't have all night," Mabel insisted. "And, Chicory, you'll need gloves of some sort, there's metal involved."

"Looks like copper, not iron. I'll be okay," he replied.

"I have a feeling it's going to take all night and then some." Chase eyed the Pixie skeptically. "I'm not even sure he's really here."

"Oh, yeah?" Chicory flew up and dive-bombed, taking a nip at the tip of Chase's nose as he passed.

"Ouch! You bit me!" Chase rubbed the stinging bump.

"You bet I did. And you taste like sour sweat and greasy hamburgers. Convinced I'm real yet?"

"Maybe."

"So get to work. Sun comes up before six. You haven't a lot of time. I'm going to bed." Mabel stomped away, letting the swinging door swish back and forth in her wake.

Dusty wandered through the kitchen and dining room two hours before her usual rising time. Dawn crept around the edges of the trees on the east side of the house.

She hummed a sprightly little tune full of chimes and dancing notes.

Dum dee dee do dum dum.

She skipped to the tune, trying out a few remembered steps from her childhood ballet classes.

Despite the impending doom of The Ten Acre Wood and the ruination of her Masque Ball fund-raiser, she couldn't help smiling in remembrance of Hay's kisses last night. So different, more interesting, and much more exciting than Joe's lackluster attempts to woo her.

The tune hit a sour note in her head. Samuel Johnson-Butler, PhD. had decided to cancel the museum's grant. No appeal. He was the absolute dictator of the committee.

Three days to come up with a drastic solution. If only Mrs. Shiregrove had come with him, she could have offered possibilities and alternatives, like matching funds.

Matching funds.

Mrs. Shiregrove lived on a five-acre estate filled with wonderfully landscaped gardens between the house and the horse pastures. Gardens that would look magical with Pixie lights strung around the hedges, with the dense perfume of roses spreading through the dry air.

Dusty reached for the phone and caught a glimpse of the red digital numerals on the stove. "Damn, it's only five thirty. She won't be up."

"Who won't be up?" Thistle asked on a yawn. Her footsteps sounded heavy and hesitant on the back stairs. She rubbed the back of her head and winced at something tender.

"Mrs. Shiregrove. What are you doing up so early? What hurts?" She reached to examine the back of her friend's head.

Thistle shied away. "That hurts!"

"Why?"

"I don't know." She gazed into the distance, looking as if she searched her memory, or the trees in the backyard for the source. "I couldn't sleep." Thistle kept her head down, her thick black tresses flowing forward to hide her face.

That was a trick Dusty had used often as a child and a teen until she decided she wanted a wash-and-go hair-cut last year.

"There's a bump on the back of your head. I bet it's bruised. What happened, Thistle?"

She shrugged and put the kettle on for tea. "I ache all over. Like maybe I'm getting that period thing you told me about."

"You were so happy yesterday at the City Council meeting."

"That was yesterday. Today I think I've grown up."

"I'm sorry. Sometimes we need to retain a bit of our childhood attitudes and perspectives. You've given us all a different way of looking at things."

"Being a Pixie is easier than being human."

"You're needed here now. Since you came back into my life, I've laughed more than I have in ages. I've stopped hiding in the basement so much, and I really have started looking at life a little differently." Memories of how Hay made her blood bubble like champagne sent lovely heat to her cheeks.

Thistle flashed a small smile that almost reached her eyes. "Then I've been a good friend to you."

"Yes, you have." Dusty reached over and hugged Thistle, something she'd never done with anyone since her days of chemo when any touch hurt like fire and in-vited germs to invade her compromised immune system. This felt good. Special. Different from the way she felt when Hay held her, but still important.

"So why are *you* up so early?"

"Lots of reasons. But I may have figured out a way to save the museum, if not The Ten Acre Wood."

"Woodland Pixies don't change to garden Pixies overnight. What will my tribe do if we lose the trees? How will we launch our mating flights if they chop down the Patriarch Oak?" Thistle looked ready to cry.

"I don't have an answer for that. But if woodland Pixies can make do with a garden, they're welcome to the rest of the museum grounds. Maybe they can make a better winter shelter in the carriage shed than in a hollowed-out log."

"Let's eat breakfast and then go talk to Mrs. Shiregrove about your ideas. I have it on good authority that she's an early riser. She likes to feed and groom her horses herself." Thistle hugged Dusty back with a hint of laughter back in her voice. Laughter that chimed and started up that haunting little tune again.

Dum dee dee do dum dum.

"The Patriarch Oak . . ." Dusty mused. "That's the key to this whole thing. Someone said something just the other day. I don't remember who or what, just that it's important."

"Think back, slowly, picture the oak and the words that make you think of it," Thistle coached.

"Patriarch. A big part of our history. Our heritage. That's it!"

"What?" Thistle looked up with eyes wide and luminous. Wild swirls of color seemed to sparkle within their purple depths.

"Heritage trees! They're special. If we can get the Patriarch Oak named a heritage tree, then it's safe. No one, not even Phelma Jo and the mayor, can touch it. How old do you think it is? If I can find documentation that something important happened there more than one hundred years ago, then the state will protect it until it falls down on its own."

"How fast can you make that happen?" Thistle sounded breathless with excitement.

"I'll find out on the laptop while we have breakfast."

"Can we have oatmeal?" Thistle asked, taking the singing teakettle off the burner and wincing at the noise.

"I was thinking of cold cereal. It's going to be hot again today, and I didn't feel like heating up the stove more than I have to."

"That's okay. It will only be ninety-eight today instead of one hundred-two."

"Only."

Just then, the doorbell rang.

"Who would that be at this hour?" Dusty asked, making her way to the front hall. She stood back a few steps and peered through the beveled glass oval in the top center of the door. She caught a distorted glimpse of Chase: tall, blond hair cut short, wearing the blue uniform that took his Nordic good looks and made him distinguished and authoritative.

She opened the door and peered out, leaving the security chain on, making sure her eyes hadn't deceived her. "Chase? Why didn't you come to the kitchen? You never use the front door."

"I . . . um, Dusty, the occasion seemed a little more formal and special." He engaged her glance with a sheepish grin.

Then she noted the dark circles under his eyes, the shadow of unshaven beard, and the wrinkles in his shirt. He looked like he hadn't slept at all.

"Come in and have some tea and breakfast with Thistle and me." She slid the chain off and opened the door wide in invitation.

"This needs to be said just to you. And if you want to throw me out afterward, that's fine. If you aren't furious with me, then a cup of coffee would be wonderful. But I need to do this now." He stepped in beside her, hands held behind his back.

"What's going on, Chase?" He frightened her a bit. Gone was her brother's joking friend, the comfortable companion of her youth. Here was a strong man, all grown up, determined, and as solid as a brick wall.

Dependable, a small niggling voice tickled the back of her mind. *Trustworthy*.

"First off, I owe you a long overdue apology."

"You do?"

"For breaking your music box."

"Oh, that. I haven't thought about that in a long time." But she had. Every time she passed the bay window in the living room, she thought about the pink box with the twirling ballerina that danced no more and sat silent inside the window seat, hidden from the world but not from her memory.

"But you never quite forgave me for breaking it. You said you did, but I could see the pain in your eyes."

"Oh." So many of her emotions had changed and surged over the last week she didn't know what she truly felt anymore.

"So, I sneaked in by the back door last night about midnight. You should lock that door by the way, Skene Falls isn't the safe-haven small town it used to be."

"Why did you sneak in after we were all in bed?" The fine hairs on her arms and nape bristled with a sense of violation. "You don't live here, Chase. I don't care how good a friend you are to Dick, this is not your home."

"No, it's not. And I'm sorry. But I felt this was important enough you might overlook me overstepping the bounds of politeness for the sake of friendship." He shifted uncomfortably and brought out what he'd been hiding behind his back.

The childishly pink, broken music box.

"What?" She didn't know what to think, how to react. Only that the sense of violation grew even stronger.

"I fixed it. Took me all night with a lot of help from Mabel's friend. But I got it working again. And now you can dance and twirl to the strains of *Für Elise* again, just like you did before . . . before the cancer and chemo stole the sparkle from your eyes."

Dusty took the box delicately from Chase. "Thank you. I'll treasure it even more now that you fixed it just for me." Dusty's heart swelled, and a tiny crack in it healed. A tear of gratitude touched the corner of her eye.

He opened the lid while she held the sides and the little pink dancer began spinning in place on one leg.

Only the tune no longer chimed the notes of Beethoven. It played the sprightly *dum dee dee do dum dum* of the tune that had haunted her half the night.

"What?" Chase looked at the box as if she held an alien being. "It played *Für Elise* ten minutes ago when I left Mabel's house."

Behind them, Thistle giggled. "That's my song. It's Pixie music. Pixie magic."

Dusty held her breath. For a few moments, time seemed to stop, and her balance firmed up as if she'd teetered on the edge for a long time and only now found her center. With Chase close beside her, where he belonged.

"She really is a Pixie," Dusty said in awe.

"Told you so," Thistle sounded hurt.

"I'm sorry I ever doubted you, my friend."

"Friends. Now we're all friends again. Let's eat." Thistle bounced back into the kitchen, happy and light again.

"Friends," Chase said as he bent and kissed Dusty's cheek.

Twenty-six

❧

DICK WANDERED DOWN TO THE KITCHEN; the smell of fresh coffee brewing enticed him to keep his eyes open.

On the last step he paused, unsure how to react to Chase being here so early—or was that late?—sitting next to Dusty. She had that stupid broken music box sitting right beside her bowl of oatmeal, one hand stroking the faded pink faux leather affectionately.

Then she opened the lid and let the little dancer spin. Music poured forth. Special music that Dick had begun to think of as Thistle's song though he'd never heard it all the way through before; just snatches of half remembered phrases.

As the entrancing tune came to an end, Dusty looked up at Chase with adoring eyes.

"About time," Dick muttered. "You've been in love with him like forever."

But hadn't she had a date with Haywood Wheatland last night? He wondered where Joe and his daughters fit into the puzzle. Did she even know how attractive she was?

He doubted it. Desdemona Carrick thought about little other than her artifacts and her grant writing to preserve her precious museum.

All that was on the brink of dissolving, so it was good she had Chase to soften the blow.

Chase finished regaling Dusty and Thistle with a story about seeing Thistle converse with a pink Pixie in Mabel's rose garden.

"Confess, Thistle, Mabel's tribe of Pixies are her spies. She gives them sanctuary in her garden in return for information," Chase said. His voice sounded light, but his posture looked aggressive, as if he interrogated a suspect.

"Yes," Thistle replied. "You have to understand that Pixie territories are fiercely defended. There aren't a lot of them left. Possession of The Ten Acre Wood has been an object of jealousy for generations. That's why until recently an old, old, Faery who lived in the Patriarch Oak ruled my tribe. In other tribes the kings always have to marry outside the tribe, to help preserve peace. I guess that's why Alder chose Milkweed from a valley tribe as his queen." She kept her gaze glued to the dregs of tea in her mug.

"Does that have anything to do with why you were exiled?" Dusty asked. She finally stopped her caress of the music box long enough to pat Thistle's hand in comfort.

"Maybe. Sort of." She still didn't look up. But she firmed her chin.

"Don't forget there's another Pixie locking doors in City Hall." Dick found himself saying without thinking. In the glorious aftermath of their kiss, he'd forgotten why Thistle had become so weak and vulnerable and so much more adorable than ever.

"What?" Chase sat up straighter. "What's this about another Pixie in City Hall? That's the same building as the police station and Mabel rarely goes home. She's at the dispatch desk like fourteen hours a day. One of her Pixies could easily play tricks on people all through the warren of abandoned staircases, redundant heating vents, and odd alcoves."

"Thistle, you know Mabel's Pixies. Could one of them have locked the door?" Dick asked on a yawn.

"For Mabel to go out of her way to make sure her tribe will always have that garden is very important." Thistle looked out the window, her eyes focusing on something far away. "Rosie's tribe is one of the few that is really thriving. They have no reason to upset the balance of peace. They have their own territory. They don't need to extend the boundaries to include City Hall."

"Except the Patriarch Oak. They don't have that," Dusty whispered. "Which reminds me. I've got to call M'Velle and have her start researching heritage trees."

Dick told them about following voices up a back staircase only to find the door they needed locked by Pixie magic.

He didn't say anything about how he'd kissed Thistle. She looked up at him at last and nodded a *thank you,* ever so slightly.

She must have come to the same conclusion he had, that they had no future together. She'd go back to Pixie soon, and he'd go back . . . go back to unsatisfying onenight stands because no woman could live up to Thistle.

"Thistle, you once told me that the Patriarch Oak is very special to all the tribes and that responsibility for caring for it makes your tribe more important than all the others combined. Why would any Pixie want to destroy The Ten Acre Wood?" Dusty put forth, returning both her hands to the music box. She pushed aside her half-eaten bowl of cereal in favor of caressing her treasure.

Thistle bit her lip. Her silence stretched beyond hesitation into refusal.

"Thistle, if you know something, now is not the time to keep secrets. We're here to help you, and we will respect your confidence in us." Dick found himself sitting beside her and holding her hand.

I'm not coming on to her. I'm protecting her, taking care of her. But, damn, I wish it could be more.

"The Patriarch Oak is where . . . is where," she gulped. "Is where all Pixies go for a mating flight, the true expression of love and trust. Not all Pixies do it. But kings and queens of a tribe must when they take a mate, as a symbol of the peace treaty their marriage creates."

"Maybe it's someone who's been hurt by Pixies who wants to cut down the oak," Dusty suggested.

"Someone with the fire of Faery in his magic," Thistle whispered. "The Faeries have always looked down upon Pixies. They call us traitors to our own kind because we make friends with humans, risking exposure and something called a witch hunt. We call them cowards because they won't face up to the reality that humans are here to stay, thriving while they build atop our lands. We either have to adapt to them or die."

"Maybe it's because the current king of your tribe won't let anyone use the oak except for him," Chase added, as if he hadn't heard Thistle's last remarks. He tried to pin her with his gaze, but she kept slipping away, hiding behind her black hair.

"How did you know?" Thistle asked quietly. She hadn't removed her hand from Dick's.

He squeezed her fingers in reassurance.

"I half heard your conversation with Rosie. I'm guessing the rest," Chase replied.

"If that's the case, then another tribe might be really pissed off that they can't use the Oak and would rather see it destroyed than let Alder taunt them with his possession of it," Dusty chimed in.

"That's it!" Thistle said with the first show of enthusiasm since the conversation started. Her eyes brightened and she rubbed the back of her head, looking puzzled.

"So we're looking for a Pixie who is influencing the people who bid on the timber in the park," Dick mused. "So, Chase, anyone new in town we should be looking at more carefully?"

"Haywood Wheatland."

Thistle half nodded, then opened her mouth and shook her head, still puzzled about something.

"No!" Dusty gasped. "He wouldn't. He's too kind. He . . . he . . ."

"He also talked to Rosie in Mabel's garden. He called her 'beloved' and 'sweetheart,'" Chase said quietly. He looked as if he wanted to caress Dusty's hands upon the music box.

"No, no, no." Dusty gathered her music box tightly against her chest, eyes closed, and shaking her head in denial. Shutting them all out of her very private misery.

Dick reluctantly let go of Thistle's hand and shifted closer to his sister. He draped an arm around her shoulders and held her tight, weathering together the storm of tears he knew would follow.

"Haywood Wheatland works for Phelma Jo. Her name is on the incorporation papers for Pixel Industries, Ltd," Chase said more firmly. Facts. He laid out the facts as if they weighed more than Dusty's fragile emotions.

"I won't believe that. He . . . he said he loves me. I can't be so wrong about him. I can't. I just can't." Dusty threw the music box back onto the table. It slid across the straight planks where Thistle caught it before it fell to the floor and broke again. Dusty didn't seem to care as she dashed out the back door.

"I'll talk to her," Chase said, rising slowly from his chair.

"No, she needs another woman to talk to now. I know what she's going through." Thistle also headed toward the door.

"No," Dick said firmly. "Either or both of you will only make it worse. I'll let her cry a bit, then I'll talk to her and make her see logic. Just like I always have." Seemed like he still had to protect his sister after all, even if only from herself.

"Um . . . Dick . . . Chase, I think there's something you should know," Thistle said. She looked over her shoulder toward the door where Dusty had disappeared.

"What?" Chase barked, all professional and stern. But he, too, looked toward the back door.

"Last night, I overheard Haywood Wheatland . . ." Thistle spilled the entire story, all the while rubbing the back of her head, wincing occasionally. "I hurt so bad last night I couldn't remember what I was supposed to tell anyone. Talking about Haywood Wheatland made me remember."

"Giving hallucinogenic mushrooms disguised in chocolate to underage kids. That's enough for me to arrest him. I just hope he has a stash on his person, or the kids haven't eaten any yet. I'll need evidence, but an anonymous tip is enough to start a search and ask questions." Chase stood up and straightened his uniform shirt and settled his utility belt around his hips.

"First, you have to tell Dusty," Dick insisted. "She has a right to hear it before you arrest him."

"But . . ."

"Chase, are you in love with her or not?"

Twenty-seven

CHASE SLAMMED OUT THE BACK DOOR of Dick and Dusty's house. He hurt all over. He'd been awake too long. The need to take down a dangerous corrupter of children burned inside him. He needed to hold Dusty in his arms and let her cry out her fears before he could reassure her.

Damn, but he thought Dusty would return his affection for longer than ten minutes once he fixed the stupid music box for her. Didn't she know how hard it was for him to accept help from Pixies? They fit into tiny places and bent broken parts back into shape when his fat fingers just made things worse.

"Okay, Dusty. Time to stop being polite and hash this out," he muttered.

Where would she go? The museum basement, of course.

A tiny blue Pixie sat on the yew hedge that lined the fence. He shook his head and pursed his lips.

"This hurt is older and more primitive than her work at the museum. She's gone to The Ten Acre Wood," Chicory told him.

"You sure about that, buddy?"

"Yeah, I'm sure. I tagged her all the way over there. Do you know how far that is? I'm exhausted. No mere human is worth that much effort."

"Dusty is."

"Then go after her. If you truly love her. Stay here and dither if you don't."

"You're a pest."

"Yeah, but a wise one." Chicory bounced up and dove deep into the yew where Chase couldn't grab him. "Fix this before you take down that half blood, Haywood Wheatland. We'll all be grateful to you when you do." He flew back toward Mabel's house and a well earned rest.

Chase turned his steps toward The Ten Acre Wood. Not that far away, about three blocks, in human terms. Maybe that was a couple of miles to a Pixie. He didn't know. Didn't really care.

He just had to set things straight with Dusty. See where they really stood; see if there was any chance at all.

With each step he found himself stomping harder until he hit the gravel patch at the end of Center Street. Tiny rocks rolled out from under his feet and he just kept marching through the drainage ditch onto the game trail that looked too overgrown for the end of summer when kids had been in and out of here every day for three months.

Two steps farther and he stopped in confusion. The place was dim, too quiet, almost sad. Birds and bugs and Pixies should be buzzing about gathering pollen, capturing the morning dew before it evaporated. Nothing moved. He couldn't even hear the traffic down along the river road.

Sword ferns that bent over the trail drooped. The Oregon grape leaves had lost luster, their clusters of green berries, tiny, hard, and bitter. And sparse. The foxgloves that should stand nearly six feet tall around the edges of the woods had gone to seed long before they reached any taller than his waist.

Something was terribly wrong with The Ten Acre Wood. Like it had lost all of its magic. Its will to survive.

He wanted to say it had been cursed by Faery fire. Preposterous. Or was it?

He crept forward, careful to avoid making any noise.

Some of the dullness lightened in the air as he approached the dried-up pond at the center. He expected a lot of mud with a trickle of a stream meandering toward the waterfall at the cliff edge and the path toward the river. He found hard-baked mud with dandelions and coarse grasses shouldering their way through cracks in the solid barrier. No water at all. No deer tracks. Not even raccoon paw prints.

Aghast, he stopped and stared at the withered landscape. The Patriarch Oak seemed to have retreated behind more scrub hardwoods and weeds. Its leaves sagged beneath the weight of dirt. Very little green peaked through the muddy covering.

A quiet snuffle alerted him to someone else standing nearby.

Dusty stared at the same barren depression he did. She stood beneath a limp vine maple to his left.

"Dusty?"

"It's ruined. Even before the first chain saw fires up, it's ruined!"

"I know. There's a sadness here. A vulnerability." He edged closer to her, needing reassurance that life continued despite the sere landscape.

"The woods know what awaits them," she whispered.

"We can fix this. We have to." He gestured to encompass the entire wood and themselves. "Can we fix what's between us, Dusty?"

"I don't know." She snuffled again.

"Why did you run?"

"It seemed the right thing to do."

"How?"

"You accused Haywood of being behind the plot to destroy The Ten Acre Wood. I was starting to like him. He was the first man I chose to date. It was my decision, not my mother's or Dick's. Just me."

"He seems like a logical suspect. Thistle had some information she shared after you left."

"But . . . but he kissed me. It was magic. I can't be that bad a judge of character. I know I can't!"

Anger sent heat to Chase's head and heart. "When and where have you given yourself the opportunity to learn enough about people in general to judge a man's character?"

He wanted to grab her shoulders and shake her. He got as far as reaching for her.

"What about you, Chase Norton? I thought I knew you. I thought I could trust you."

"I fixed your damn music box!"

"Then you go manufacturing evidence against a man who says he loves me. A man who makes my heart lighter and my toes tingle."

"I didn't manufacture anything. I found evidence that links him to this operation. Thistle watched him give bad mushrooms disguised in chocolate to a bunch of kids, encouraging them to blow up the cell tower and start fires with illegal fireworks. They talked about tipping over the Ferris wheel at the carnival."

"You drew conclusions on bits and pieces of evidence because you can't stand that I like him. Thistle doesn't like him. She hasn't . . . she . . ."

Too angry to speak, he clenched her tight against him and ground his mouth into hers.

She pounded his chest with her fists. Three blows came sharp and fierce and frightened.

He loosened his grip and softened his kiss, tasting, savoring the tenderness of her inexperience. If this was the only time in his life he got to hold her this close, he needed to make the most of it.

Then her fingers spread and clutched his shirt. She rose on tiptoe to come closer.

His blood sang. The world fell away.

And still they kissed, explored, cherished this moment out of time. Nothing existed but the two of them.

They pressed closer. He needed to merge with her body, mind, and soul, become one being, one thought, one life.

He couldn't do it. He couldn't take advantage of her

innocence and inexperience. With a monumental effort, he contented himself with exploring her mouth, her eyes, her neck, with his kisses.

Slowly they relaxed and drew apart.

Chase's hands shook and his knees knocked together.

"What just happened?" he whispered into her hair, too afraid of shattering into a million pieces if he let her go.

"I . . . I don't know."

"Dusty, I . . ."

"This is too much! Too soon." She wrenched away from him and ran, thrashing through the woods. "I don't know who to trust. Who to love."

"Dusty!"

The only reply was the sound of a sapling thwapping against a bigger tree as she thrust it aside in her head-long flight.

Twenty-eight

🌿

"DUSTY, PLEASE COME OUT of the basement and talk to me," Thistle called down the deep black hole into Dusty's lair.

Why did her friend have to hide *down* there?

Dusty mumbled something Thistle couldn't understand.

"I know you feel hurt and betrayed, Dusty. The same thing happened to me. It's why—it's why I'm exiled." Thistle had to swallow hard to get the words around the lump in her throat. Then she swallowed again.

"What?" Dusty appeared at the bottom of the crooked stairs, her face a pale blob in the darkness.

"Please, Dusty, come up. You know I can't go down there."

"Why not?" She came up a few steps, enough for her face to resolve into two huge eyes and a mouth surrounded by shadows.

"Because underground is death to Pixies. Elves and Faeries live underhill, at least during the day, and banished us to the sun when they removed themselves from humanity."

"That's folkloric nonsense."

"So are Pixies." Thistle giggled for the first time in hours. "Want to know what happened between me and Alder? I can almost guarantee it's more embarrassing than your date with Haywood. Some day I'll be able to laugh about it. Not yet, though."

"Is that the beginning of some sage advice?" Dusty moved closer to the light.

Thistle breathed easier and signaled with a hand wave for M'velle and Meggie to back off. She couldn't do anything about Joe trying not to be obvious in his listening. But his office door was open and he read the same page on his computer three times without touching any key to make it move.

"Advice in the form of a long story that I can't tell you while you hide."

"Oh, well, it has to be more interesting than Dick promising to always take care of me. He had the audacity to tell me I didn't need a man of my own, he'd always be there for me. But he can't. He won't. He's my brother, not a potential lover."

"Another good reason for you to take charge of your life and stop hiding."

"Bad habits die hard," Dusty sighed, emerging from the cool depths of the dreaded basement. "You can go back to work, girls," she called, without having to see Meggie and M'Velle hovering around the corner. "But thank you for your concern."

"They're your friends," Thistle whispered. "You can't have too many friends."

"Sometimes I wonder."

A large tour group entered the front door of the museum. "Is this place air-conditioned?" a woman asked, presenting admission tickets to M'velle.

"No, ma'am. It's well designed with deep overhangs and shade trees. We try to keep the place as authentic as possible." She led them off into the parlor.

Meggie greeted the next smaller group and led them upstairs so the tours wouldn't overlap.

"First time I've known those two to jump into tours without protests or at least rolled eyes and huge reluctance to heave themselves out of their chairs." Dusty stared in the direction they'd departed with hands on hips and pursed lips.

"They are learning. Today, they know you and I need to talk, so they've given us the back room." Thistle

looped her arm through Dusty's and led her into the
lounge with its refrigerator, worktable, and blessed
air-conditioning.

Thistle had never thought about the outside temperature in summer. Heat was heat, a fact of life that
couldn't be avoided. In winter, when cold nearly froze
her wings, that was when she sought shelter.

"So tell me why you feel betrayed and why it's worse
than Chase thinking Hay is the culprit behind the logging
order," Dusty ordered while fishing the pitcher of iced tea
out of the refrigerator. "And maybe the instigator in the
recent rash of vandalism. I find it hard to believe. Very
hard to believe. He's sweet and kind." She looked out the
back window toward the cliff and the waterfall.

"Talk, Thistle, or I go back downstairs and try to piece
together that Russian pot found in a Chinook tribal
midden."

"You know about the Patriarch Oak and mating
flights," Thistle said quietly, trying to find a way to say
this so it wouldn't hurt any more than she already did.

"Enlighten me."

Drawing a deep breath, Thistle told her how important a mating flight was, told her about absolute trust.
Told her about how the public display was an announce-
ment of soul mates finding each other.

"Is that why Meggie has convinced all her friends to
call their latest crush Pixie love?"

"She said something about that." Thistle covered the
ache deep in her chest by taking a long sip of tea.

"Who took you to the top of the Patriarch Oak?"
Dusty smoothed her skirts and took a seat across the
long table from Thistle.

"How'd you know?"

"You said you'd been betrayed and that your story
was more embarrassing than mine."

"Alder," Thistle choked out.

"King of your tribe?"

Thistle nodded.

"But don't your kings and queens have to marry outside the tribe to keep the peace?"

"Yes. We hadn't had a true king in our tribe for ever so long. The old Faery in the tree ruled us. So when he finally went away, we didn't know for sure what to do about a treaty or electing a new king or anything. Alder knew. I think he knew the old guy was on the verge of going away and arranged the treaty and the election beforehand, without telling anyone. The Patriarch Oak is supposed to belong to all the tribes. Alder is now refusing to let anyone but himself use it. The other tribes have to make do with their own trees. I thought . . ." She swallowed her pain and blurted the rest. "I thought when he took me up to the top that he meant us to be together always. He took me all the way to the top of the tree at noon, proclaiming to one and all that we were mates. He didn't mean it. He sent for a Princess from the valley tribes to be his mate the next day."

"Ouch."

"Yeah." They sat in silence a moment, each wrapped deep in her own thoughts. The whir of the air conditioner and the soft murmur of voices barely intruded.

"So why'd he exile you?" Dusty finally broke the silence.

"Pixies have treaties with some of the bird flocks. Mostly robins and their cousins, the varied thrushes. We help them find the juiciest worms and they let us ride on them when we have to go long distances."

"And . . .?" Dusty prompted.

"I bribed the varied thrush sent to carry Milkweed to The Ten Acre Wood. He flew the wrong way and led Milkweed and her whole family astray. They were two days late to the wedding." Thistle giggled over that.

"Oh, you are nasty." Dusty smiled, a laugh twitching at the corners of her mouth.

"Alder sure was mad. And I'm told that Milkweed hasn't consented to a mating flight yet."

"Trouble in paradise. If I were Milkweed, I wouldn't trust Alder either. I presume, like most men, you aren't the only one he betrayed."

"Yes. But not all men are as selfish and greedy as he is. Dick . . ."

"Dick is incapable of making a commitment. He hasn't had a relationship last more than a month, ever. Chase isn't much better."

"So what if Haywood is the rogue Pixie trying to cut down The Ten Acre Wood?" Thistle asked gently. She covered Dusty's hand with her own. "I know he bribed a bunch of teens to blow up the cell tower, maybe some of the carnival rides tonight. He's tying them to him with mushrooms."

"I refuse to believe that he could be that devious. He kissed me. And it was glorious. The world sparkled."

Uh-oh. Thistle didn't know if she should suggest an alternative to those colored lights.

"He said he loved me," Dusty insisted.

"Alder said he loved me."

Another long silence.

"I don't know whom to trust. A man I'm very attracted to who says he loves me, or the man I grew up with who has always been a friend. He fixed my music box."

"Don't trust either of them," a new voice said. A high chiming voice that came from the air somewhere close to Dusty's ear.

Thistle searched wildly for the source.

Dusty batted at her ear as if at an annoying insect.

"Hey, watch it, lady! I'm not going to sit around all day and get squashed just because you two are deep into crying over spilled milk. Though, if you spill it on a rhododendron, I'd enjoy lapping it up," a little blue Pixie said.

"Chicory," Thistle said on a long exhale, not sure if she should be annoyed or relieved. "What are you doing here? This is still part of Alder's territory."

"Yeah, yeah, I know, so I'm not sticking around long."

"Chicory." Dusty choked on her tea. She looked pale and a little green around the edges. Her eyes lost focus and threatened to roll upward. As if her mind couldn't quite wrap itself around the reality of the obnoxious blue boy with a cap that looked like an upside-down chicory blossom on his head, knickers and tunic the same shade, and darker blue skin and hair. His blue-green wings stilled their constant flutter as he landed on the table, regarding Dusty with concern.

"So what brings you into dangerous lands?" Thistle prodded the tiny man.

"Mabel sent me."

"Mabel? As in police dispatch Mabel who has an army of Pixie spies?" A little color returned to Dusty's face and her eyes focused firmly on the Pixie.

"Yeah, that Mabel. She says I have to apologize to you, Miss Dusty, for some tricks we played on you, and for spying on you and your boyfriend last night down on the river walk."

"Was that you who made the air sparkle when he kissed me?"

"No. Don't know who threw the Pixie dust. Look, I'm not going to say any more than to warn you to be careful. There could've been some magic enthrallment in that dust. There is more, and less, to Mr. Haywood Wheatland than he says. And he's been known to lie. True Pixies *can't* lie. That's what Faeries do. So just be careful. Chase is one of the good guys. You can trust him. And, again, I apologize on behalf of Mabel's tribe." He executed a formal bow from the waist and set his wings to sweeping rapidly. He rose straight up from the table and aimed for the closed door to the rest of the museum.

Thistle figured he could crawl under the door or slip through the big old-fashioned lock.

"Hey, don't I get an apology?" she asked.

"Mabel didn't say anything about you, exiled one. I think growing big makes it possible for you to lie, too. Mabel just told us to consider Miss Dusty one of ours now. Oh, and I have it on good authority that Mrs. Shiregrove will be home for tea this afternoon and will talk to you." He flitted out before Thistle could call him back again.

Twenty-nine

❧

"THANK YOU FOR SEEING ME on such short notice, Mrs. Shiregrove," Dusty said as she settled in a wicker lawn chair. A grape arbor behind her hostess' imposing mansion shaded them from the grinding heat and humidity. The little bit of relief from stray river breezes didn't reach up here on the third plateau above the Skene River.

"No problem. I prefer to take my afternoon tea with company. What was so important that you left the basement of your precious museum to call on me?"

Dusty blushed. It seemed everyone in town knew how she hid from people among her artifacts and catalogs. Then she mustered her courage to speak, wishing Joe had come to do it for her. "It's about the Masque Ball, ma'am."

"I hope you make a lot of money this year. You're going to need it." Mrs. Shiregrove looked sharply at Dusty.

"Yes, well, I was hoping you could influence the grant committee to match funds for us, since they've denied a flat-out grant."

"That's a possibility." The older woman took a sip of her iced tea, looking out over her extensive grounds rather than at Dusty. "Tell me why the Ball is so important to you. This is the first one you've organized by yourself."

"Only because Mom and Dad are in Stratford-upon-Avon for three months absorbing as much Shakespeare as they can."

"Your mother can be obsessive."

Dusty just smiled.

"So why is the Ball so important to you?"

"Because it gives us the funds to keep the museum open. We are an anchor to the community, an important part of our heritage, part of our identity as a city, and part of the state and region as a whole."

"Commendable. I see you are passionate about the museum."

"That and our local history. How can we possibly move forward if we don't know where we've been?"

"I agree. But I understand even the Ball is in jeopardy, what with the logging off of The Ten Acre Wood. Hate to see that go, but I don't see how to stop a steamroller once it gets started." She paused, her eyes slightly glazed as if she thought long and hard on something important.

"Yes, ma'am. Actually that's why I'm here. We're having trouble finding an alternative venue for the Ball on such short notice."

"Doesn't surprise me," she snorted.

Dusty wondered if Mrs. Shiregrove knew more than she was saying about that.

"Your estate would make a lovely background to the costumes and music and Pixie lights," Dusty whispered, amazed at her audacity.

Mrs. Shiregrove jerked her gaze back to Dusty, forcing her to look directly into her eyes and not the enticing depths of her amber tea. "That it would. Who put that idea into your head, Miss Carrick?"

"I thought of it this morning about six, after the community college turned us down. They wanted seventy-five percent of our gross. We can't afford that. I know it's short notice and an imposition, but I was wondering if we could hold the Ball here? Please, it may be our only hope of saving the museum." The last came out in a rush.

"So you can speak at length about something near and dear to you," Mrs. Shiregrove chuckled.

"Yes, ma'am."

"Oh, don't go all silent and polite on me. I've been waiting a long time for you to get angry enough to stand up for what you believe in."

"The Ball is our major source of funding. Tour admissions only make up a part of it, and those are down this year with the economic crunch. We only had about half as many school field trips this spring as usual, and our high school interns are working for class credit rather than money. The furnace truly needs replacing, or we'll start losing fragile artifacts and artwork to the damp this winter."

"You've convinced me. Actually, some little friends convinced me of it last night. That's why I asked who gave you the idea." She beckoned toward the stand of variegated dahlias across a stretch of lawn. Then she held her palm out.

Dusty didn't see anyone.

"Over here, blindy bat," a tiny voice said.

Dusty looked closely at the orange-and-yellow being standing on the flat of Mrs. Shiregrove's hand.

"You, too?" Dusty asked, feeling all the heat and color draining from her face. "First Mabel and then you?"

"Anyone with an old garden who has been in this town for a long time has them. Only not everyone is willing to acknowledge them. I've known Dahlia here since my husband and I inherited this house from my parents almost forty years ago. She approached me about the Ball last night. Seems that Mabel's friend Chicory mentioned it to her. He courted her for a while but decided he didn't want to move away from all the gossip downtown." She whispered the last in an aside.

"I'm sorry that didn't work out, Dahlia. Chicory is a nice fellow," Dusty said formally.

"Not to worry. I've recently become betrothed to Oregon Grape. But the marriage won't happen unless that self-centered upstart Alder opens the Patriarch Oak to mating flights again. I'm not some frivolous girl who will mate with just anyone. Got to be someone I trust. Someone who's already a friend."

Dusty nearly choked. "I understand, Dahlia. My friends and I are doing all we can to make sure the Patriarch Oak is safe. But we are running out of time."

"Good for you, Miss," Dahlia said. She rose up with a clatter of long wings and lighted on Mrs. Shiregrove's glass of iced tea. After a bit of contortion, she bent double over the rim and sipped at the cold liquid. "Nice and sweet with a hint of lemon. Just the way I like it." She smacked her lips and bent for another sip.

"I know, I do spoil my friends, but they are special."

"Yes, they are, Mrs. Shiregrove."

"So, now that you are properly approved of by the Pixies, I have no choice but to allow the Ball to take place here, if I can't do something about halting or postponing the log off."

"The mayor refused to hear Joe Newberry's petition to stop the logging."

"Seth is an idiot. He's not running for reelection after his latest stroke, so he's not worried about voter opinion."

"I saw in the paper this morning that he's endorsed Phelma Jo Nelson to succeed him," Dusty said quietly.

"Not sure if that's a blessing or a curse. She's organized and efficient, doesn't tolerate fools or liars. She's the only one allowed to lie, cheat, and blackmail," Mrs. Shiregrove snorted in disgust.

Dusty nodded, not knowing how to respond.

"Let me see if I can do something about the log off." She pulled a cell phone from her skirt pocket, one of the smart phones that did everything but dry her hair.

"How can you keep that thing working with Pixies nearby?" Dusty asked.

"Compromise. I tell them everything said and they stay at the other end of the property while I talk." Mrs. Shiregrove laughed as she punched in a number.

"Bill, I've got a news story for you." She listened for a moment.

Dusty held her breath. Bill? As in William? The only William she could think of in the regional media was William Tremaine who anchored the news for a local affiliate of a major television network.

Quickly, Mrs. Shiregrove outlined the situation with The Ten Acre Wood. "Yes, I know it's too late to get a truck and a team out here before tonight's broadcast, but surely you can get the ball rolling."

Another moment of listening.

"Sure, you'll need to talk to Joe Newberry at the museum." She rattled off his cell phone number from memory, as well as Phelma Jo's and the mayor's. "That's right. Call all of them. I love you. Dinner at seven. I've got lasagna in the oven." She closed and pocketed the phone.

"Thank you, ma'am. Thank you very much. Um . . . was that William Tremaine?" Dusty said, eyes wide in wonder.

Mrs. Shiregrove laughed. "Of course it was. I kept my birth name when we married, because he was only a cub reporter and didn't want people thinking he married me for my money. Which he did, of course. But he makes up for it by loving me." She laughed again.

"I'm sure he does. Thank you again, for everything. We all appreciate your generosity. Is there anything I can do about the grant?"

"Besides getting Joe Newberry to resign and taking over his job?"

"What?" Dusty turned hot then cold. The top of her head felt as if it flew off with Dahlia to the other end of the estate. She wanted to flee back to her basement but couldn't move her numb feet.

"That nice Mr. Haywood Wheatland, you know, the young man who works for Phelma Jo now. He said something the other day to Dr. Johnson-Butler that made us ask the Board of Directors for an audit. We haven't found any funds missing, but suspicion lingers.

There are dozens of ways to cover up skimming. Has Mr. Newberry had any unusual expenses of late?"

Dusty barely heard the last part for the roaring in her ears. "I assure you Joe Newberry is honest. I keep the books, not him, and if there is anything funny with the accounts, I suggest you look at the Board of Directors—or the accuser." She gathered her purse and rose to her feet, as tall and as dignified as she knew how to be, not bothering to finish her tea. "Thank you for your time, Mrs. Shiregrove, and all your help and consideration. I'll have my decorating and catering committee chairs contact you directly, just in case we have to move the Ball."

She marched back to her car by way of the gravel path around the side of the home. Her chin wavered, but she wouldn't give in to her emotions. Not yet.

First, she had to find out why Haywood Wheatland would make such a suggestion. Phelma Jo had to have put him up to it. He hadn't been in town long enough to know anything about the museum operation.

Then she was going to spend as much time as necessary going over all the books and the bank statements herself.

"I have reviewed the material you brought me," Judge Pepperidge intoned slowly, never taking his eyes off the sheaf of papers he held. Even with his tie loose and the top button of his dress shirt undone, the white streaks at his temples in sharp contrast to his dark hair, aquiline nose, and chiseled cheeks made him look authoritative and important.

Chase stood at attention in front of the judge's massive desk, designed to clearly separate His Honor from the great unwashed, and lawyers. Chase didn't dare unbend even the slightest. Buck privates in the army facing a wrathful drill sergeant couldn't be more uncomfortable than Chase Norton at that moment. The air-conditioning set at Arctic didn't cool the sweat running down his back.

Tuesday had come and gone before he got this appointment on Wednesday during the lunch hour. He wasn't going to blow it with the slightest unbending that might be interpreted as disrespect.

"You realize that seeking an injunction against a city work order should have come from the DA or at least a City Council member." The judge peered over the top of his reading glasses, making eye contact with Chase for the first time since he'd been summoned to explain himself.

"Begging your pardon, Your Honor, City Ordinance SFCO8795678, November 12, 1932, clearly states that any concerned citizen may seek an injunction against an action they deem harmful or dangerous to their neighborhood," Chase recited.

"I see you've done your homework, Sergeant Norton." The judge rattled the papers as he sat back in his big comfortable chair and swiveled a bit. "We could use more people like you on the force."

"I hope you found my petition interesting and worthy of consideration, sir." Chase's lower back protested his stiff posture. He shuffled his feet, hoping not to draw attention to his discomfort.

"Oh, sit down, Chase. We've known each other since I coached your peewee football team while I was in college."

"Thank you, sir." Chase eased into the closest chair, a straight-backed and uncomfortable one designed to keep petitioners from lingering. The only other option was to drag a softer piece of furniture over to the desk from the far wall. If the judge wanted him to linger, he'd have provided the good chair before Chase got there.

"What made you go looking so closely into this matter, Chase?" the judge asked.

"The speed and the secrecy involved. Pixel Industries, Ltd is offering about ten times the amount of money they can get back from selling the timber, including the massive amount of old growth oak from the Patriarch Oak by the pond. Which should have been designated a heritage tree long ago but wasn't, because people were afraid they wouldn't be allowed to climb it or dig around it for pirate treasure. The money made me wonder why they wanted the timber so badly and why in such a hurry."

"Cutting those trees will make a huge mess of the Masque Ball Saturday night if they start cutting on Friday," Pepperidge mused.

"Precisely, sir. That led me to believe the entire operation was aimed at ruining the Ball, the fund-raiser for the museum. The timber has been there for a long time. Why this year? Why this week?"

"Isn't this the first year Dusty Carrick has taken over the organization from her mother?"

"Yes, sir. And there is only one person in town who might have a grudge against her."

"Phelma Jo Nelson. Wow, that feud goes back a few years." He ran his hands through his hair. "I thought the girls were friends before that. It turned out well afterward since it forced the school authorities to investigate accusations of abuse in Phelma Jo's home. She went into foster care within hours of the incident."

"Because Dusty's injuries got infected and wouldn't heal, she got an early diagnosis of leukemia and was able to have complete remission," Chase added.

"Good outcome all around, and yet the feud persists. Who knows what trauma dominated their minds at the age of nine and ten."

"Yes, sir. I thought Phelma Jo would have forgotten it, especially since she has made such a success of her life, starting from that moment. She has no reason to be jealous of Dusty anymore. But that's her name and her signature on the incorporation papers, which are dated only a few days before the offer to the city was issued to the mayor."

"And it went to the mayor privately, not through regular channels and the City Council. I wonder if Seth would have even told the City Council about it until after the fact."

"I don't know, sir. You know him better than I do. The fact is, this operation does not look aboveboard and should be investigated fully. There isn't time to do that before they start cutting timber unless you issue the injunction." Chase held his breath, hoping he hadn't been too pushy.

"I agree. That's what I told Bill Tremaine a few minutes ago when he called. He's married to Pam Shiregrove, you know."

"Wait a minute, Bill Tremaine? As in William Tremaine, tall guy, white hair, very distinguished, anchors the local news on KRVR?" Chase gulped. Then he had to swallow a couple of times to get around the lump in his throat.

"Go it in one," Judge Pepperidge chuckled. "If anyone could get recalcitrant politicians to act on the threat of negative publicity, he can. Seth will be lucky if he's not run out of town on a rail when Bill gets done with this story. I'm signing this cease and desist order right now, and calling the DA. There may not be anything criminal going on, but I want to find out." He selected a wooden fountain pen from a cup full of similar writing instruments and signed three copies of a form already prepared.

Chase's heart soared. He'd done it. At least he and Bill Tremaine had done it. They'd saved The Ten Acre Wood. Surely Dusty would forgive him for accusing Haywood Wheatland of skullduggery. Especially since it looked like he was guilty.

"I'll let you serve this on Phelma Jo personally. And deal with any reporters hanging around her office. I'll make sure the DA gets a copy, and I'm keeping one locked in my safe to make sure the mayor—or Phelma Jo—doesn't steal it." Judge Pepperidge turned his chair

around so the back of it blocked Chase's view of what
he did at the credenza beneath the window.

"Thank you, sir. I hope to see you Saturday night at
the Ball."

"Wouldn't miss it. I presume you are escorting Dusty
Carrick?" He turned back around, hands now empty,
and peered at Chase over the top of his glasses.

"I hope so, sir."

"Good luck with that. She's worth waiting for."

"Does everyone in town know my business before I
do?"

"That about sums it up. Now get going and deliver
that injunction before Phelma Jo gets impatient and
starts cutting timber before her own deadline."

Thirty

❦

THISTLE TOOK A BREAK from her duties with the old ones who should be revered instead of cast off. Dusty had gone up the hill to visit Mrs. Shiregrove. Dick had appointments in the city. Chase had answered a summons to the courthouse.

She was alone. Time to find some answers. She needed to talk to Alder, who seemed to be at the heart of all the problems besetting her friends.

From Mrs. Jennings' house, she walked two blocks north and then another three west until she faced a seemingly impenetrable wall of trees and undergrowth. The bracken and sword ferns had grown so intertwined they obscured any path that might lurk beneath them. Even the narrow drainage ditch between the graveled shoulder of the rotting road and the ferns looked solidly overgrown.

They drooped with dry dust, looking tired and extremely thirsty. All the life and luster had drained out of them.

No matter. She could find the path. She'd flown along the narrow opening dozens of times a day for as long as she had sought friends among the children playing in the forest.

One step in the center of the ditch and her foot sank deep among the tall grasses, thistles, tansy, and Queen Anne's lace. Most of the plant tops tickled her knees. Except the thistles. Her namesake. Those prickled her arms all the way up to her elbows. She scratched the irritating dots.

Then she paused, wondering if she scratched and annoyed people the way the spines of the plant did. Even as she thought about it, some of the stickers worked their way under her skin, persistent, incapable of being ignored.

She giggled at the thought of how she had worked her way into the lives of Dick and Dusty. Unrelentingly.

But she couldn't let laughter and fun deter her from her task.

She took another step, up this time into the first thicket of bracken and more grass going to seed and thistles flowering, brilliant purple and delicately fragrant. A few of those had begun to fluff white as the seeds worked their way outward from the center. The season marched toward autumn. The days grew shorter.

Surely rain and cooler temperatures had to come soon to give the humans and the plants some relief.

Pixies thrived in summer heat and the cool spring and autumn. Only in deepest winter did they seek shelter, huddling together and sleeping most of the day and night until the days brightened again.

"I must be truly human now if I'm uncomfortable," she mused as perspiration trickled down her back and between her breasts. "The time is long past for me to return to Pixie. Maybe then I won't hurt so bad because I can't let Dick love me."

She took one more step and . . . flew backward, landing on her butt in the rough gravel.

Her hands stung and her back ached. Her senses reeled and darkness crowded in from the sides. She desperately needed to put her head down.

Nothing soft and comfortable showed itself within reach.

"What?" Tears flowed down her cheeks in pain and disappointment. This was the second time she'd been thrown out of Pixie and landed in a humiliating lump.

"You're an exile. You can't go back until Alder says you can go back," a man laughed from behind her.

She twisted around to see who mocked her.

"Haywood Wheatland."

He bowed formally, like a proper Pixie. He stayed a good twenty feet away. Not proper Pixie protocol. He should come to arm's length and wait for an invitation to rub wings.

"Who are you?" she asked, scrambling upward, desperately seeking balance and dignity. Her head took a few heartbeats to catch up with the rest of her. She stumbled and had to plant her feet in a wide stance to stay upright.

"Look closer at your precious Ten Acre Wood, Thistle Down. Look and see what rejects you."

She peered at the line of trees marking the boundary of her tribe's territory. A wall of shimmering energy, much like the aura around frantically flapping Pixie wings swam into view.

"You and only you are the reason for that wall. Now no Pixie can enter or leave The Ten Acre Wood until Alder takes it down. And he won't. Not until Milkweed agrees to a mating flight."

"Maybe he's trying to keep Milkweed from returning to her valley home?"

Haywood gulped, then paused in thought. He finally nodded agreement.

"She's both smart and stupid," Thistle spat.

Haywood cocked his head in question.

"She's smart not to trust Alder. Trusting him to a mating flight is no guarantee he'll be faithful to her afterward."

"You should know."

"Yes. He betrayed me, and probably others."

"Then why is she stupid?"

"If she took the mating flight, the treaty between her tribe and Alder's would stand. She would be queen. A powerful leader of the most important Pixie territory. She could wrest control from him as soon as she exposed his underhanded manipulation of his tribe. Then she could dictate who could use the Patriarch Oak and when."

Thistle vented her anger by brushing dirt and gravel off

her skirt and legs. Jagged bits of rock clung to her, stinging worse than thistle spines. Scrapes burned, and she ached all over. Long scratches and drops of blood trickled down her arms and legs, like the stream trying to gain enough momentum to plunge over the cliff in high summer.

"Granted. Milkweed needs to control the situation," Haywood mused. "That doesn't change anything, though. You are still exiled and powerless. Soon the chain saws will bring down Alder and the Patriarch Oak. Soon he'll have no power, no prestige, no queen, and no territory." He smiled, showing too many pointed yellow teeth the same color as his hair. In the slanted afternoon light he looked like sun-ripened hay ready to ignite into flames if the temperature increased one degree.

Hay? Haywood?

"Stars above and earth below, you're Milkweed's brother!"

"Guilty as charged." He bowed again, laughing. But his mirth sounded harsh and gravelly, not at all bright and chiming like most Pixies.

"You! You're behind the logging," she accused.

"Not me. I signed nothing. Everything is in Phelma Jo's name."

"She hasn't the imagination to think this up. She couldn't see Pixies as a child. She thought we were all dragonflies." So did Chase, but he was learning that life grew beyond logic and the limits of practical explanations.

"The mayor and the lawyers won't believe that," Hay smirked.

"You're from the valley. I bet you learned all about computers and bending rules from the boys you befriended. But how can you get close to anything digital? They go all static . . ." Oh, my. A fiery aura, compatibility with computers, pointy teeth.

He was no ordinary Pixie. She'd bet her wings that he was only half Pixie. Dusty had it right. Half Pixie and half Faery gave him control over all four elements and which ones dominated.

That was why she couldn't get close to him. His Faery blood repelled her, like . . . like magnets or something.

She backed up two steps in fear.

"My boys do love their video games. They learned to like blowing things up from their games. And they love hacking, just to see how far they can get inside other people's computers. I am their faithful friend, learning as much from them as they do from me. Tonight they'll succeed at both their hobbies by taking control over all the computerized carnival rides and then blowing up the Ferris wheel." He almost glowed with pride. Or was that just Faery fire?

"Doesn't it bother you that besides destroying our oldest and grandest tradition, you will break Dusty's heart? You lied to her from the beginning. You said you loved her and then you kissed her. That shreds the first law of Pixie, never to hurt a friend." Thistle clenched her fists. She wanted to hit him, knock him over the cliff, send him back to his traitorous forebears.

But she needed to find Chase, or Dusty, or Dick, someone who could stop the boys from hurting people at the carnival.

"Dusty is my only regret," Hay sighed. "I had not intended to fall in love with her. She is so cute and innocent. Still very much a child in many ways. She tugs at my heartstrings in ways that my betrothed never could. But my engagement to Rosie was negotiated long ago. I will not violate that treaty."

"You truly love Dusty?" Emotions surged and ebbed within Thistle. She didn't know what to think.

"Yes, I love her. I have not lied to her. I do not regret the destruction of your tribe and the Patriarch Oak. I have my orders. Pixies must give way to the greater power of Faeries. Murdering humans are about to destroy our hill in their need to build and expand. A cell phone tower and a *discount store*. It is just too humiliating. They can't even dignify the destruction of our home with a palace or a grand courthouse or something." His face turned ugly with angry distortions, his ears pointing, chin lengthening, eyes extending into an elongated and distorted slant.

He took a deep breath to calm himself, and the alien visage dissolved. "We need a new place to live. Pixies overrun our chosen spot, The Ten Acre Wood. They must go. But I do regret that I must hurt Dusty."

"You lying cheat!" Phelma Jo screamed from the end of the pavement half a block from where they stood.

"It's not like that at all, PJ. She tricked me," Hay protested.

"Don't call me PJ. I hate that."

"He can't be trusted, Phelma Jo," Thistle called and started toward her. Haywood's repulsion sent her into the yard of one of the neighbors. Trespass. She had no permission to walk here. She kept going, doing her best to get closer to Phelma Jo, reason with her. Make her an ally.

Phelma Jo wheeled around and began running.

Hay loosed a long arc of Pixie dust that twinkled and floated.

Thistle caught the brunt of the magic. It rooted her feet to the dirt and gravel, almost as deeply as if she was just another plant.

Only a few flakes touched Phelma Jo. She slowed her hasty retreat, but did not stop.

"Don't make me come after you, PJ."

"Too late," Thistle mocked. "You lied to her. And now she knows about it. You'll never gain her trust again. You're a lousy half-breed without logic. How can your Faery friends make The Ten Acre Wood their new home if you destroy it? Perhaps Alder threw up that force field to keep Faeries out instead of his queen in."

Haywood Wheatland turned and marched away in the opposite direction, back straight, muttering to himself in words Thistle couldn't understand, but a language she recognized.

Faery. He spoke a Faery spell.

❧

Phelma Jo flung open the door to her office suite. "Out. Everyone go home. I'm giving you the rest of the day off, just get out of here right now."

"But I'm in the middle of closing a deal," her best real estate agent protested.

"Finish it on your cell phone in your car." She couldn't bear to lose money, even to satisfy her own immediate agenda. "Just get out!" she screamed at the woman. Twenty years of experience; she should know how to close a deal elsewhere.

The staff of six scrambled to stuff papers into desk drawers, close down computers, and hasten away from Phelma Jo's temper tantrum.

"Lying, thieving, son of a bitch. Delusional, too." She slammed the door to her private office with a satisfying crash. The glass in the upper half rattled.

She didn't care. The bastard was going to be out on his ear. She pulled up the paperwork on the computer for termination of employment before she even sat down. She started typing as soon as the page finished loading.

"Employee number?" She nearly screamed at the computer. It refused to advance to the next line until she filled in the box. Cursing, she opened another window with personnel files. "What do you mean you can't find anyone by that name? I set you up to respond to my needs, stupid software."

More curses escaped her as she rummaged in the file cabinet on the opposite wall. Every neatly labeled, redundant file folder bore a familiar name. All except the one she sought. "I know I had you fill out an application and tax forms." Her fingers flew through the ten folders, hoping it had gotten misfiled. But it hadn't. Nor was it stuck inside one of the others.

"Phelma Jo Nelson," Chase Norton said from behind her.

She spun to face the doorway, feet braced for . . . something aggressive and violent. She didn't know what yet, but the urge to slam her fist into a face, any face, nearly overwhelmed her.

Chase stood in the doorway to her office, too far away to slug, tall and blond and as handsome as ever. His air of calm authority doubled his attractiveness. Not to her. She needed control of her relationships.

He knew that. He looked just as disapproving and hostile as when she kicked him out of her bed and her life because he called her "Dusty" in the throes of wild hot monkey sex.

Passion without rules or limits, as only teenagers can truly indulge.

She was a high school senior then, he home from college for the summer. And he still loved the mousey little brat.

Dick Carrick wasn't much better, still pining after some bimbo who left town when he was a pimple-faced adolescent with a cracking voice.

"What do you want?" she spat at Chase.

"I have here a court order putting a temporary halt to the logging of The Ten Acre Wood, a designated city park."

"Let me see that." She ripped the document out of his hands. He remained calm.

"So what? My work order is signed by the mayor. This minor judge can't override that." She flung the paper on the desk and assumed her chair, as if it were a throne.

"Yes, he can. And he has. If the work crews remove so much as a twig before this issue is resolved, I'll haul them and you off to jail. So will any other officer under my command. Unlike some people, I can't be bribed. And William Tremaine's camera crews will record it all, report names, and dig deep into private files with and without permission." He leaned his clenched fists on her desk and met her gaze with determination. It was the first emotion he'd shown since invading her private space without invitation.

"Fine. I'll grant insignificant Miss Carrick her mo-

ment at the Ball in the park. But I will have those trees.
The profit from selling the lumber to Japanese markets
should fund my mayoral campaign." She scanned the
document.

"What's this?" She placed her finger on a huge number with a dollar sign in front of it.

"I believe Judge Pepperidge has put your deposit on
the purchase of the timber into an escrow account until
the matter is fully investigated. If the city finds against
Mayor Seth Johansen for unauthorized sale of the timber, the money will be refunded to you without
penalty."

"I know that, you idiot. I mean the amount. I never
authorized that much. If I fork over that much, I'll make
no profit. I'll end up in the hole."

Chase blinked several times. "Let me see that." He
turned the paper so he could read it right side up. "That
is a chunk of money. One of the reasons the City Council has second thoughts about this is that the money will
rehire two teachers and fund the free clinic for another
year."

"But I only offered ten percent of that. What you are
holding as a deposit was the full amount I offered—the
salary of one teacher. Not two, let alone funding that
stupid clinic for freeloaders, deadbeats, and welfare
moms." She lumped together all the people who might
turn into her mother.

"That amount of money does sound more reasonable
coming from you." He scowled. "It appears that someone added an extra zero to the amounts you authorized.
Any idea who? Your new assistant, perhaps?" He smiled,
baring his teeth like a predatory animal.

"Who else? I'm in the middle of firing the thieving
bastard except I can't find his personnel file."

"Makes you wonder who he truly is. And what else
he's stolen, besides his file." Chase continued grinning.
Laugh lines crinkled the corners of his eyes. He was getting ready to humiliate her. Again.

"I can't trust any man, it seems. Especially those who have had their hearts stolen by the likes of Dusty Carrick," she grumbled.

"I'll leave you with that thought. In the meantime, I'm going looking for Mr. Haywood Wheatland, if that truly is his name. Seems I've got a case for bringing him in for questioning. He's altered official documents. Maybe embezzled. I'll think of something appropriate."

"Do that. Don't let the door smack you in the butt on your way out."

Fuming, Phelma Jo printed out the termination document and began filling in the blanks by hand. She wanted this official and legal, so the conniving thief of a con man couldn't come back at her for anything.

"I wouldn't sign that if I were you, Phelma Jo," Hay said, quite suddenly appearing at her elbow, as if he'd secretly flown in on silent Pixie wings and grown to human size, unseen. God, she was starting to sound as delusional as Dusty Carrick. Or Haywood Wheatland.

"You can't stop me." She poised her pen over the line at the bottom of the page. The nib bounced up the instant she pressed it to paper. Then it slipped away, leaving a smudge on the pristine mahogany of her desktop.

"Oh, but I can."

"Well, you won't get away with cutting down The Ten Acre Wood."

"I wouldn't bet on that. By now, our friend Sergeant Norton has served cease and desist papers to the work crew. So you are going to have to help me cut down the Patriarch Oak."

"You are out of your freaking mind if you think I will do anything illegal. Underhanded and sneaky maybe. But not illegal." She pushed harder trying to get the pen to follow her orders.

"We'll see about that." Brightly colored sparkles filled the room like a myriad shattering rainbows.

Thirty-one

❧

DUSTY SPENT MOST OF Wednesday night and Thursday morning composing a ream of emails to various committee chairs about a possible change of venue for the Ball. Then she set Meggie and M'Velle to making signs to put in the park that would direct guests to the new address. She'd seen the news crews around town interviewing everyone, from the mayor to the street vendors.

Her stomach still roiled at the assault from half a hot dog on a white bread bun that Hay had bought for her.

Funny, she hadn't seen or heard from him in several days. After that wonderful, sparkling kiss, she thought he'd at least call.

"Dusty, I'm going up to the community college for a meeting," Joe called into the lounge as he headed toward the front door of the museum at noon. "The place is yours for the rest of the day."

"When will you be back?" She ceased typing and pulled a pencil out of her mouth long enough to spit out the words. Her gaze barely shifted from the computer screen to Joe's back.

"Late. Maybe not until closing." He waved casually and disappeared.

For her next chore, Dusty needed privacy. She waited until the girls were elsewhere on the grounds or upstairs with tours. Then she slipped into Joe's office, and closed the door. She'd lock it if she dared.

In a matter of moments she had the complete accounting spreadsheet and her handwritten ledger in front of her. The receipts from the computerized cash register in the gift shop fed all its data from sales and admissions directly to her programs. It printed tickets along with sales receipts.

Item by item, she checked and double-checked, finding redundancy reassuring. Everything matched.

She went through it all again, adding things up on a printing calculator to give her yet another record.

If any money was missing, it hadn't disappeared between the museum and the bank.

She pulled up the banking history via the Internet. All the deposits totaled up correctly. What about debits? Only the treasurer and the president of the Board of Directors had access to the checkbook and each check required both signatures. They kept a separate accounting for expenditures. She recognized the amounts for payroll, insurance, alarm permits, and utilities. They were the same most every month. But the other checks? What were they for?

She'd turned in requisition forms for advertising, decorations, catering, and music for the Ball. Those numbers looked familiar, but she couldn't match them to the penny.

"Well, it looks like you're innocent, Joe. Haywood Wheatland was just stirring up trouble."

"I'm glad you recognize that," Joe said, leaning against the doorjamb.

Dusty jumped in her seat. She'd been so deep in numbers, reality looked a little too bright and, well, real for a moment.

"Sorry to startle you, Dusty. But if you can't find anything wrong with our accounting, then no one can. Because there isn't anything wrong," he said moving into the small room.

"You look tired, Joe." She closed out the computer programs and scooted out of his chair.

"It's a good kind of tired. I convinced the college to

offer teacher continuing education classes centered around the museum, taught by you and me, tuition and fees to be split between the college and the museum. We're looking at a decent source of funds to help us over the hump from losing the grant." He remained where he was, blocking her exit.

"That is good news." Hope brightened inside her that everything could continue on the same even keel. She didn't like the idea of teaching, but she was sure she could push Joe into taking the classes if she did the prep work and designed handouts.

"Now all we have to do is find a way to stop the clear cut of The Ten Acre Wood and all will be well," he sighed. After a moment he reached out and took Dusty's hands. "We will make it all right, Dusty. Trust me."

"I do trust you, Joe. You know that I only checked the books to prove you innocent."

"Yes, I know. I trust you, too. We've been friends for a long time."

She ducked her head, afraid of where this was going.

"Don't hide from me, Dusty." He lifted her chin with a gentle finger. "Our friendship is important. More important than that pretty boy, Haywood. I don't want to see you throw your life away on his lies and con games."

"I know that now, Joe. He was a temporary delusion. He lied to me, and I was just too naïve to recognize it."

"I've never lied to you. And I never will. Because I love you as more than a friend. I need you by my side. The girls love you, too."

"Joe, I . . ."

"Think about it, Dusty. Think about me. About us. We make a good team. Who else do you know you can trust as completely as you do me?"

"I will think about that." Joe was a friend. Chase was a friend, too. Her mother hadn't set up either relationship. Joe was safe. No surprises. Chase was . . . Chase's kiss was magic. Real magic, not the artificial Pixie sparkles that Hay had employed. Chase was volatile.

Chase was real.

She edged past Joe. Her instincts made her want to head for the basement. She mastered her fear and swallowed deeply to remain calm. With hope in her heart, she plastered a smile on her face to greet the last tour group of the afternoon.

Late Thursday afternoon, Chase faced the oncoming CAT-tracked vehicle with front loader forks fully extended. He hoped—prayed—that the driver chickened out before running him down. Steadfastly, he held up the court-ordered cease and desist papers.

A TV camera crew with a satellite truck to back them up and send their footage directly to the station, recorded everything. Chase did his best to ignore them. The court order and his own courage were all that mattered here.

He hoped they were enough.

The driver in the bright yellow hard hat with a discreet F painted on the front, to indicate he was the foreman, glared at him. He kept coming, aiming his CAT for the first line of trees at the edge of the park. He drove over the lawns, heedless of the small circles of shrubs and flowers in his way.

Three uniformed officers held back the five other timbermen bearing chain saws and climbing hooks, by the simple expedient of placing hands on their holstered weapons.

The CAT kept coming.

The camera followed every move, captured every facial expression.

Chase gulped but didn't move.

With a tine of the loading fork on either side of him, the CAT finally stopped a hand's breath from Chase's chest.

"Get out of the way!" the driver yelled over the noise of the diesel engine. A note of desperation crept into his voice.

"I have a court order for you to pack up your gear and vacate the premises for a minimum of two weeks or until the conclusion of the investigation into the illegal sale of this timber," Chase recited in his deepest, most authoritative voice.

With profound determination he kept his hand away from his weapon. He really didn't want this confrontation to turn violent.

"No one said anything about cutting wood being illegal," the foreman returned. He idled the engine down so he could be heard over it, but he didn't turn it off.

Maybe he was hoping the camera couldn't make sense of his words.

"Cutting this wood is illegal until determined by the City Council, the DA, *and* a judge," Chase kept his voice firm. He hadn't realized how powerful the little CAT machine was, or how big "little" was. He hated to think about facing down a full-sized bulldozer.

"I've got a properly signed work order," the driver insisted.

"This court order supersedes that." Chase waved the papers again.

"You're taking bread out of the mouths of our children!" The foreman yelled that directly toward the cameraman.

"Sorry about that. Times are hard for a lot of people. Jobs are scarce. I understand that. This parkland is more valuable than just the price of the timber. It benefits the entire town, not just a couple of politicians and developers."

"Fuck you! I'm calling my boss." The foreman flung off his seat belt harness and jumped clear of the machine.

Had he set the brake? Sweat popped out on Chase's brow, more than the heat could account for.

"Go right ahead. But I need you and your crew to clear off and take all your equipment with you by five o'clock. That's thirty minutes."

"We're supposed to finish the survey tonight and start cutting at eight AM tomorrow. If we take everything off site, we'll be hours late starting, and my work order says I lose dollars for every hour of delay."

"My court order says this park is to be cleared and returned to pre-work order condition by five." Chase looked pointedly at the CAT tracks gouged in the grass and the broken rhododendrons.

A crowd gathered from the neighborhood, milling around, coming closer. The cameras added them to their growing mass of footage.

The afternoon heat intensified. Chase's temper rose closer to the surface. He struggled to keep it in check.

The crowd grew noisier, nerves frayed by tension, uncertainty, and the damned heat.

Sweat coated Chase's back, like an extra clammy skin.

"Ain't fair to tempt a man with work and a good paycheck and then yank it out from under him!" one of the crew called, stepping forward and brandishing his chain saw. Dense perspiration stains showed on his shirt beneath his safety vest.

An officer moved to block his path, weapon half out of the holster. He looked as nervous and frayed as the rest of them.

Please don't draw that, Chase silently pleaded with his patrolman. *Do you know how much paperwork has to be filed if the muzzle clears the holster?* How many people get involved in reviewing that paperwork?

How many thousands would watch it on the evening news?

"I can't afford to not cut this timber," the foreman said, stepping around the CAT to face Chase.

"I'm sorry about that. I do understand. My men and I each took a twelve percent pay cut so we didn't have to lay anyone off or have him go part time and lose his benefits. But the order to cut this timber came through illegal channels. It has to be investigated."

"Who defines illegal?" the crewman with the chain saw shouted. He pulled the rip cord.

A gun fired. The man went down. His chain saw spun across the pavement. Bystanders yelped and jumped back, knocking into others.

More shouts and shoves.

The foreman's fist flew at Chase's jaw. He ducked and slammed an elbow in the man's gut.

People cried out in pain and anger. Fists smacked and thudded. The chain saw continued to spin and roar.

The cameras rolled.

"I have had enough of this," Chase ground out. He grabbed the foreman's arm and twisted it up and back. With his other hand he reached for his cuffs. "You are under arrest for assaulting an officer of the law. You have the right to remain silent."

"I got the right to work, dammit!"

"Anything you say can and will be used against you in a court of law."

The foreman twisted and squirmed.

"Excessive force!" he screamed and dropped to his knees.

Just then, Dusty appeared across the lawn with Joe hovering behind her shoulder.

All the blaring noise faded from Chase's awareness. He clearly heard Joe say, "Can you call a man that violent a friend? Can you trust him not to turn on you next time he loses his temper?" He took Dusty by the elbow and led her back inside the museum.

"Do you have anything to say for our viewers at home?" A reporter shoved a microphone beneath Chase's nose.

Fuck off!

"No comment."

Thirty-two

❧

T HE HOT AND HUMID NIGHT AIR pressed upon Dusty like a thick wet blanket, robbing her of breath and will. Few would sleep tonight in this uncomfortable, swampy air. She fought to take a deep breath before kneeling beside the broken rhododendron.

With all the timbermen in jail after this afternoon's brawl, she had little hope of them restoring the damage their machines had caused. Someone had to fix as much as possible.

At least she'd gotten her park back for the Ball.

Carefully, she trimmed a bent branch, then sat back on her heels to see if she'd cut enough or too much.

The shrub seemed to bounce back and shiver, almost as if it felt a relief with the amputation.

"Wish I could recover so quickly," she murmured.

"Why can't you?" Thistle asked from behind her.

Dusty didn't bother to turn around. She couldn't face her friend with tears streaking her cheeks and turning her eyes a miserable red. "Violence has never been a part of my life. It defines Chase's job. Joe made me think about having to get used to that," she admitted.

Thistle sat cross-legged on the grass on the other side of the rhodie. She trimmed the ragged end of a branch that had broken off. "Since Pixies set up marriage treaties and made the Patriarch Oak neutral ground, we haven't seen much violence either."

"But now Alder has closed off the Patriarch," Dusty

said. "A war could develop if he doesn't come to his senses soon."

"Yeah. He's stupid. A great lover, but stupid, untrustworthy, a liar, and a cheat. Unless . . . Maybe he has a motive he's keeping secret." Thistle bent her head, hiding her face behind her hair.

"Do you still love him?"

Thistle studied the grass in silence for a long moment. "Sort of. I mean that mating flight was fantastic. Not just because of the best sex ever. Because of the mutual trust. We had a glowing aura. Everyone saw it and was amazed. That rarely happens."

"What are you going to do about it?" Dusty asked. She moved over to a patch of mums just coming into bloom. Half of them lay dead, their promise of autumnal rust-and-orange blossoms stripped away.

If the fall flowers died, did that mean summer would never end? She hoped not. She'd had enough of the heat.

"I don't know what to do about Alder. I have to think about Dick, too. I think if he and I ever had a mating flight, it would be even more spectacular. That's not likely to happen. There isn't a lot I can do about Alder in this big body," Thistle said quietly. She looked longingly at the twilight shadows at the edge of The Ten Acre Wood. So close and yet so far away.

"If the barrier prevented you from getting into the wood, that must mean you are still a Pixie, in heart and spirit if not in body," Dusty reassured her.

"Maybe." Another stretch of silence as they worked to restore some of the damage. The lawn was a hopeless cause. But the flowers? Could even Pixie magic bring life back from the vandalism?

"What are you going to do about Chase?" Thistle asked suddenly.

"I don't know. Something. I'm not sure what."

"I expected to find you underground, hiding from reality," Thistle said cautiously. Under her nimble fingers, three sword ferns resumed their upright posture. She squirted them with a mist of water from a little spray bottle she'd stored in her pocket.

"May I try some of that water on the mums? Some of them might revive if I put the roots back into the ground and give them a good drink," Dusty mused.

"I'll get the hose." Thistle rose in a series of jerks and pauses, testing each motion before continuing. When she stood upright, she ambled off to the back of the building. She dragged the long, unfolding coil behind her like a pet snake.

"Hey," Dusty yelled as a spray of cold water filled the air around her.

Thistle laughed as she pulled the nozzle trigger, spraying Dusty as much as the flower bed.

Dusty laughed, too, lunging to grab control of the hose.

Thistle giggled and ran away, carrying the hose with her. As Dusty got close, she turned and sprayed water again.

Dusty stooped and grabbed the hose, yanking it away from Thistle. "Turnabout is fair play!" she proclaimed as she drenched her friend.

Instead of running, Thistle spun, raising her arms high in pure joy. She looked like the little pink ballerina in the music box. Change the tutu from pink to lavender.

Dusty dropped the hose and spun in her own delighted dance. She hadn't danced, really danced free and unfettered for the sheer joy of dancing, since the leukemia diagnosis.

Should she count the dances with Chase at the Old Mill last Friday night? His arms had held her captive and awestruck. But she'd danced, and gloried in his embrace and the movement.

"So what are you going to do about Chase?" Thistle asked again when they staggered with dizziness.

"I thought you wanted me to be with Joe."

"At first I did. Joe needs a mate. But he's acting out of desperation, not love."

"He's still in love with Monica."

"Maybe so. The girls are excited about seeing their mom again—outside the courtroom."

"You've been babysitting them a lot lately."

"Some. Does Chase frighten you?"

"Not Chase. But his job . . ."

"Chase isn't his job."

"But . . . . but . . . you're right." Dusty hung her head and moved on to another drooping rhododendron. "I have to do something, don't I? I can't hide, waiting for someone else to solve this problem."

"Nope."

Dusty took a deep breath. "I'll think of something." She looked around at the grounds. "It's getting too dark to see what we're doing. Let's go find some dinner."

"Pizza?"

"If you want. We'll order in."

"Chase will be down at the Old Mill."

"I'm not ready. I have to think through what I need to say to him so that I don't run away again and ruin everything."

Thistle blew the new whistle Dick had given her to go along with the bright yellow hard hat with the big F on the front. "Snug those floor panels up tight," she called to the three burly men who carried a four-foot-square section of dance floor from a flatbed truck across the grass. Mabel had brought them to the museum grounds among the first volunteers for the setup for the Ball tomorrow night. The three all wore jeans and plaid shirts and looked amazingly similar with the same straight brown hair, tanned skin, and broad, broad shoulders.

She almost drooled over them but caught sight of Dick working his way among the dozen or so men and women unloading the flatbed truck so it could return to the mini storage for more supplies. His lithe body and self-assurance quelled all of Thistle's interest in other men.

"We don't want any dancers tripping on the seams tomorrow night," Thistle said to the burly workers.

"Why not?" the tallest of the three asked with a wide grin that didn't show any teeth. A Pixie grin. For a Pixie to show teeth was an act of serious aggression.

"Because that will be bad for the fund-raiser," Thistle explained patiently, though she also wanted to grin at the idea of tripping up some of the extravagantly costumed guests tomorrow night. She could almost imagine ladies' hoop skirts flying overhead revealing bloomers and gentlemen losing their top hats only to recover them later decorated by Pixies in bright feathers and flowers.

"If it helps Dusty, then we'll do as you say," a second man said on a shrug. He almost dropped his corner of the heavy floor section. His foot had already trampled a rhododendron she and Dusty had healed last night. She didn't want to think about what he might have done to the silver herbs at the edge of the knot garden.

She didn't know the name of the low plant; it wasn't native.

The yellow monster machine still sat at the edge of the tree line. Its treads had carved long tracks in the lawn.

"Mabel said we have to obey you because it helps Dusty," the second man said.

"Nice hat," Dick whispered in her ear as he wandered past with a loop of Pixie lights strung over his shoulder. "I'm going to string these around the covered wagon, and maybe that CAT—decorate it if I can't move it. Then I've got to go back to work. Will you keep an eye on Dusty? She didn't look well this morning."

"I noticed the circles under her eyes were as heavy and leaden as the air. I've seen storm-drenched rose blossoms stand taller," Thistle replied. She worried about her friend. They'd laughed and played last night.

But in the dark hours before dawn, Thistle had heard her crying.

"Maybe it's just the weather. There's a thunderhead growing in the southeast." She paused to sniff the air. "I don't think it will reach the valley anytime soon. The mountains will get rain tonight, though."

"What's wrong with Dusty?" Mabel's three laborers asked in unison. They dropped the floor section, further damaging the gouged grass beside the broken rhodie.

"Mabel told us to help Dusty," the leader said.

Something about his belligerent posture triggered a memory in Thistle. The directionless light cast no shadows or highlights to give her clues.

But . . .

"Chicory? Is that you?"

"Yeah, what of it?"

"Why are you and your brothers here?" Now that she put an identity to Chicory, she recognized Delph and Aster quite clearly. Their human disguises were good but, to Pixie senses, only a thin gloss of magic.

"We told you, Mabel said we had to help Dusty."

"Why is Mabel suddenly so concerned about Dusty?"

Chicory shrugged. "Don't know, but that's the only reason we're taking orders from the likes of you."

"I don't think Mabel is as healthy as she pretends," Aster whispered shyly.

"She doesn't have any children to help her with the garden," Chicory remarked. "That's why she gave our tribe safe haven there."

"Her nephew wants her to sell the house and grounds to a developer who will break it up into smaller lots," Delph added.

"We think Mabel's decided to cultivate Dusty 'cause she knows Dusty won't let anything bad happen to us and the garden."

"Not like what's happening to *your* tribe, Thistle," Chicory snickered. "Falling apart because Alder got selfish about the Patriarch Oak."

"Alder's got a lot to answer for, I admit," Thistle agreed. "Maybe not as much as *you* think."

"Might as well cut it down, since he won't let anyone use it but himself. And rumor has it he's using it a lot, with every female except his chosen queen," Delph added with a knowing glance at Thistle.

"Hmmm . . ." New thoughts circled around Thistle's mind. They made her eyes ache in the glare of light in the thick air. Pixies weren't supposed to think about the future, make plans, or see anything beyond the next trick. "How can rumors have any basis in truth when no Pixie can get in or out to verify them?"

"Ever since the night the policeman came over and asked our help in repairing an old music box, Mabel has been keen on Dusty," Chicory changed the subject. His eyes crossed as if he had a headache from too much thinking.

"Music box! That's it."

Reluctantly, she pulled off the beloved hard hat and lifted the whistle lanyard over her head. "I think that since the Patriarch Oak belongs to all Pixies, not just Alder, we need to make sure no one tribe is responsible for the tree. No one king should have the right to close off the entire Ten Acre Wood to all Pixies."

"Huh?" Chicory looked dumbfounded.

Good. *Make* him think. Pixies needed to think more in order to protect themselves and their territories from greedy and mind-blind humans.

And greedy, uppity, cowardly Faeries.

"What if my tribe moved to a smaller section of The Ten Acre Wood, leaving the Patriarch Oak open to all, and the responsibility of all? It needs to go back to being neutral territory." She looked around at the men.

"I don't know. We've never done things like that before . . ." Aster mused.

Thistle turned to talk to him directly. He seemed more capable of working his mind around new ideas than his brothers.

"Think about it! Think about ending the territory wars among Pixies. Think about kingship being more than privilege. We should all work together for the benefit of all. Build up our strength so that Faeries can't exploit us any more than humans can. And our best bet for preserving the Patriarch Oak is to keep Dusty working at the museum and overseeing the welfare of The Ten Acre Wood."

"Maybe that's why Mabel is suddenly so fond of Dusty!" Delph added. "Mabel's not sick at all, she's just looking out for us."

Chicory snorted at that. But he didn't say anything to dash his brother's hopes.

"Look, you guys are gardeners," Thistle said, handing the whistle and hard hat to Aster. "You guys take charge and make sure these plants get help and the grass is repaired while the humans set up for the Ball. I'm going to go see what kind of help Dusty needs to make sure she continues as guardian of our tree."

She turned and strode sprightly toward Dusty inside the museum, whistling her song. *"Dum dee dee do dum dum."*

Thirty-three

❦

"**G**HOULS," DUSTY MUTTERED, gazing out the front window of the museum at the crowd of watchers gathering along the edge of the grounds. They didn't get in the way of the volunteers assembling the dance floor, setting up round tables and chairs, decorating with lights and garlands. But they watched every move, concentrating on the deconstruction equipment that still littered the street and grass.

The sole cameraman from the TV station wasn't much better.

And there was Chase, looking weary, rumpled, and worried as he ran his hands through his blond hair until it stood on end. Despite the care that weighed down his shoulders and tugged his mouth into a frown, he was still the most handsome man in town.

"How could I have been blinded by Haywood's false beauty?" she asked herself.

"You were blinded because he needed you blind and cooperative. He bespelled you to ensure it," Thistle said softly.

Dusty whirled around, startled. "I didn't hear you come in."

"I didn't intend for you to hear me. Or see me. So you couldn't run away and hide."

Dusty sighed. She halfheartedly flicked her feather duster over a display of cast iron pots and sadirons near the hearth.

"You were happier and more determined last night.

What's wrong, Dusty?" Thistle asked. She stepped over the velvet rope that separated visitors from the artifacts and came up beside her.

Dusty looked out the window again and saw Chase inspecting the intrusive CAT-track machine.

"I don't have time right now, Thistle. We'll talk later." She threw the duster at her friend, then scooted around her and out the door as nimbly as a tabby kitten.

Chase bent over the controls of the machine from outside the cab, his back to her. The crowd thickened around him. Curiosity seekers wondering if there would be a repeat of yesterday's violence.

"Chase," Dusty said gently so as not to startle him. "I owe you an apology."

He straightened without turning toward her, or saying anything.

"I never got a chance to properly thank you for fixing my music box. I'm very happy you did. That was very thoughtful. I'm sorry I neglected that. I'm sorry . . ."

He grunted something and bent over the machine again. "Anyone know where Phelma Jo is?" he called to the crowd from the depths of the gearshift and ignition. "She was supposed to get this stuff out of here last night."

A murmur of questions ran through the crowd like a ripple of a breeze across a meadow.

"Chase . . . I . . ." Dusty wanted his attention but didn't quite know what to say.

"Forget it, Dusty. Apology accepted. I hope you enjoy the music box," he replied coldly and moved away from her with long strides. He hadn't looked at her at all.

"Chase." She darted forward and grasped his sleeve. "Please . . . can we talk?"

"Look, Dusty, I've had a very long and stressful day preceded by an even longer night. One of my men is on administrative leave for firing a weapon. I had to send the county police to the carnival on Thistle's tip about explosives and mushrooms disguised in chocolate because we're so shorthanded. They arrested five teens high on something we can't identify. They tried to blow up a Ferris wheel full of people. Took the rescue squad three hours to get them down. I've got a gang of disgruntled timbermen claiming to be victims. One of them is still in the hospital with a gunshot wound. Thankfully, it was a through and through on his thigh. He'll live with little or no damage. And now Phelma Jo has disappeared, leaving all this junk in the middle of the street making a traffic hazard. I haven't got time for your fragile emotions. Go hide behind your brother, or your new boyfriend, Joe."

Desperate to control herself and not do just that, Dusty swallowed her fears and made eye contact with him, willingly, deliberately. "I really came out here to apologize for turning my back on you yesterday. My only explanation is that I never realized how dangerous your job is until then. It scared me. I was afraid for you. Afraid I might lose you before . . ."

"Forget it. You find it hard to trust people. I get that. You find it hard to share yourself with people. Yeah, I get that too. But you don't realize that trust and friendship is a two-way street. You have to prove that you can be a friend, be trustworthy to those who love you, or that love dies a dirty and disgusting death."

He turned and forced his way through the crowd, thrusting people aside. They surged and formed a new wall between her and Chase.

Dusty hung her head and trudged back to the museum.

"You will pay for this, you miserable, selfish, conniving lump of testosterone!" Phelma Jo screamed as she struggled against the invisible bonds holding her arms glued to her sides and her legs locked at the knees. She sat crookedly against a pile of burlap and junk in a dark shed.

"Ah, I see you are awake," Haywood Wheatland remarked, as if she hadn't just insulted and threatened him.

"Untie me, you bastard."

"Now, now, my mother would not appreciate that title. Though it does fit since she sneaked off with a true Faery the night before she mated with the king of the valley tribe."

"Huh?"

"Haven't you figured out that I am not what I pretend to be?" He looked bewildered and a little hurt. "I thought you were smarter than that."

"You're a con man. You gave me a fake identity, résumé, and recommendations when I hired you. Of course you aren't who you pretended to be," she sneered. "And you will pay for your deceptions. I've already filed fraud and embezzlement charges against you for altering the numbers in my bid for the timber in The Ten Acre Wood."

Hay threw back his head and laughed. "And a warrant will be issued for my arrest. Only I don't exist. I'm not human. After tomorrow evening I will disappear back into Pixie, marry my betrothed Rosie, and become king of Mabel's garden. I have plans for the giant sequoia in her backyard. I think it will make an admirable replacement for the Patriarch Oak. Alder will be left powerless, and Thistle will have no home to return to because my true father's relatives will dispossess them. My sister will be vindicated for their betrayal."

"Huh?"

"Is that all you can say?"

"I can say a lot. I can and will blister the air blue until you untie me. My mom may have been a worthless alcoholic, always dependent upon and submissive to the newest man in her life, but she taught me how to curse with imagination and enthusiasm."

"Tut, tut. We don't want you inadvertently bringing down the forces of darkness. I brought some duct tape to replace my magic bonds. They will begin to wear off soon. And it is quite wearying to maintain them. I'll need all my strength tomorrow night, right after sunset, so it's duct tape for you—and your mouth."

"Huh?" Phelma Jo bent her head as much as possible and looked at herself in the dim light filtering between cracks in the wooden shed. She couldn't see what force kept her immobile, not even a depression in her light linen tunic and slacks.

"Oh, that's right. You were one of the children who never had enough imagination to see Pixies for what they are. You only saw dragonflies. Such a shame. If you'd learned to believe early on, you and I could have conquered this town and all of Pixie *and Faery* years ago."

"You are insane. There is no such thing as Pixies or Faeries or ghosties and ghoulies."

The dirt floor beneath her began to vibrate. A persistent rumble built and rattled the shed.

A look of pure terror crossed Hay's face, turning his clean features into a twisted mask.

"What's the matter? Why does a train scare you so badly?" She knew where she was now. South of town above the falls in the abandoned lumber mill. The train tracks ran right beside it, with a spur backing into the main yard. Lots of odd little buildings falling in on themselves.

"All the iron." He shuddered. "Iron burns us, robs us of our magic, makes us sick, twisted, and insane."

The rumbling faded along with the shaking of the shed walls. Hay relaxed and pulled a fat roll of duct tape out of his inside jacket pocket.

How did he look so cool and calm in the rising heat and humidity? Everyone else went about in as few layers of clothing as possible, sweating profusely. Dark stains around the underarms and along the back had become so normal that few people noticed them anymore. He didn't even have a gloss of perspiration on his face.

"If you are a Pixie, how'd you become so proficient with computers? I didn't think imaginary creatures needed electronics."

"Most Pixies and Faeries don't. That's why so many of us die young these days. The electronics. But Pixies must befriend those who need friends. It's an instinct with us. And I have special powers."

"No one ever befriended me when I needed one," she grunted.

"By all accounts, Thistle tried. All you did was trap her in a jar with a wolf spider. Like I said, you never had the imagination to appreciate an offer of friendship."

Phelma Jo snorted again. She remembered the incident. "It was just a dragonfly. And Dick Carrick spoiled my game. I was pretending the fly was my mother and the spider her abusive boyfriend."

All the pain of those years came flooding back. Phelma Jo felt as helpless now, subject to the control of a man, as she did then.

"I'm stronger than that child. I will get out of this, just as I got out from under my mother's curse. Her boyfriend is still in jail on a thirty-year sentence." Her anger shot new adrenaline through her system. A little bit of mobility came back to her arms and knees.

"Oh, poor PJ." Hay gave her a false pout.

She struggled and rolled again, loosening the bonds a tad more. In another minute she'd be able to jump up and punch him in the family jewels. That should incapacitate him long enough to get away.

"As I was saying, the boys I befriended were all gamers. They learned early on that hacking into another computer system to steal things was just another game. I showed them how to send themselves inside a computer game. They became addicted to the high of explosions. I strengthened their addiction with mushrooms." He laughed and began unrolling the tape.

She fought to move her knees. Anything to get away from this madman.

Her left leg jerked up.

He caught her foot and pushed it higher, throwing her balance backward. "Oh, my, I do enjoy a feisty female. Later, dear. We'll take a nice little flight together later."

Then he used his free hand to expertly wrap the fibrous tape around and around her ankles.

"Anything you want to say before I close your mouth?"

She spat at him; a big gob of saliva splatted against his right eye.

"Too bad that's all you can muster for the moment." He slapped a long length of tape across her mouth and around her head, pulling and tangling her hair in its stickiness.

Thirty-four

❧

THISTLE WATCHED DUSTY CAREFULLY after dinner. Her friend sat listlessly in the bay window, playing her music box over and over. It had returned to its normal tune. No Pixie magic or Pixie music left in it. The ballerina spun around and around, winding down slowly until the music ground ponderously through its last notes.

Dusty sat silently for a bit, letting tears slide down her cheeks. Then she turned the music box key and repeated the process.

The tinny notes irritated Thistle's ears and disrupted her sense of life tuned to the music of wind and rain, and plants talking to bugs, and bugs whispering the news to trees.

Finally, after Dick had gone off to the bar to meet Chase, Thistle yanked the music box out of Dusty's hands before the music completely stopped.

"You've had enough," Thistle insisted.

"Give that back! I can't lose it again. I can't . . ."

"Then come and get it." Thistle held the box high over her head.

Dusty turned her head away, staring out the window.

"You've been listless and boring all day." Thistle curled up in the window seat facing Dusty. She stroked the soft covering the way humans petted cats.

"I . . . can't talk about it." Dusty reached for the music box again.

Thistle held it behind her back, out of Dusty's reach.

"Tell me why you sit here hour after hour crying over this music box. I thought you'd shed all your tears over it when Chase fixed it."

At the sound of Chase's name, Dusty turned her face toward the window again.

Thistle saw a new spate of tears in the reflection.

"You and Chase had a fight. I saw it from the window."

"Worse."

"Worse? What could be worse than a fight?"

"A fight you can make up. He gave up on me just when I thought I'd grown enough to appreciate how much I love him. How I've loved him since we were small children. How I loved him even though he broke my music box. But then he fixed it for me and I thought we had a chance."

"But you ruined it because Hay had bedazzled you and Joe offered you safe haven."

"How . . . how did you know?"

"Because I've watched you for many, many years. Because I was your friend even when you were sick and no one came to visit you but me. Even when you let your cancer define who you were. Because I'm still your friend."

"I don't think even you can fix this."

"Maybe. Maybe not. You'll have to do most of it yourself, though. Now tell me exactly what Chase said yesterday."

"You aren't going to try to talk me out of loving him? I might be better off with Joe because you love his daughters and because Chase was ungentle with you when he arrested you the day you landed in the fountain."

"Well . . . Chase is still not my favorite person. But he's learning to appreciate Pixies. Joe hasn't. His daughters are wonderful friends, and they need me right now. But you need Chase. He's the one you love. And if that's what's right for you, I have to be your friend and help you get him back. Not that I think he's gone far, you understand. But he's going to need a little prodding to get over his blue funk."

"He . . . he said that friendship and trust are a two-way street. I have to prove to those who love me that I can be trusted and that I take seriously the responsibility of friendship."

"You see, he loves you. He said so himself. I don't think I even need any magic to push him back on the right path. You can do that all by yourself. All you have to do is . . ."

"Oh, Thistle, you are the best friend ever!" Dusty nearly fell off the window seat as she threw her arms around Thistle and hugged her tight.

The phone rang. Shrill and insistent.

"I'd better get that. There are a million details to settle before tomorrow night."

Dusty grew very still the moment she answered the phone. "Hello, Ted. My mother told me to expect your call."

Thistle squirmed. Another barrier between Dusty and Chase—her mother's interfering pity dates. What could she do to stop this?

"No, I don't think I can go to the Masque Ball with you. I'm chairing the fund-raiser this year and have too many responsibilities to volunteers and friends to properly pay attention to a date," Dusty said stiffly. Her skin grew cold. Another lie Hay had told her. How had he found out about this delayed call? *Oh, my God*, he listened over the airwaves! Her vision started crowding in from the edges until all she could see was Thistle's face.

"Thank you, thank you, thank you," the tenor voice on the other end of the phone line sputtered. "My mother has been pressuring me for a month to call you because she doesn't like my girlfriend. A pity date with you had to be better than listening to her whine."

"Pity Date!" Dusty bit her lip until she drew blood. That small pain helped her focus, removed the gibbering ape that threatened to take control of her mind and her feet.

Run! it said over and over again. *Run away from the cancer before you become the cancer.* Run away from those who challenge you. Run away from those who only want to hurt you, judge you. Make you less than what you are. Everyone is lying to you. No one can tell the truth.

Hay lied. No one else did.

She ignored the voice, the voice of her cancer trying to protect her from herself. She'd beat the cancer, but not its control over her emotions. Resolutely she settled her shoulders and took a deep breath.

"Ted, you're welcome to buy a ticket and bring your new girlfriend to the Ball."

"I just may. Maybe a date with you wouldn't be about pity, but I really like this girl, in spite of my mother's opinion."

"I look forward to meeting you and your friend there," she said on a laugh. "I hope she's as much your friend as your girlfriend." They said good-bye, and she hung up with relief.

Friendship is a two-way street.

"Thistle, friendship carries responsibility and has to be mutual. Trust has to be mutual. So I'm going to be a friend to you as much as you have been to me. I need to do the same for Phelma Jo."

"Thank you, Dusty." Moisture made Thistle's eyes glisten in the dim light. "Phelma Jo?" she asked then, sounding dubious.

"Yes. Before we had that fight on the playground we were friends. I allowed some other kids, more popular and cliquish, to pressure me into calling her a bad name. I should have realized that she stopped bathing for a reason. I should have taken her aside and offered her the chance to take a shower here, with privacy and safety. Instead I called her 'Stinky Butt' in front of everyone. I owe her a big apology."

"First thing in the morning we'll find her and take care of that."

"I hope tomorrow is soon enough. But I need to deal with Chase tonight."

"Yes, you do."

Dusty looked around for her discarded shoes and purse.

"Chase needs to know . . ."

"That I love him, and I trust him, and that he can trust me." The happiness started in Dusty's toes and brightened as it traveled upward, till she broke out in a huge grin. "Phelma Jo needs to know that, too, but Chase is more important. Will you come with me, Thistle?"

"I bet we'll find Chase and Dick at the Old Mill Bar."

Dusty grabbed her purse and car keys and headed out, a little Pixie tune adding bounce to her step.

Dum dee dee do dum dum, she sang out loud.

Thirty-five

CHASE SCRUBBED HIS FACE with his hands, hoping to banish the weariness of heart and body that plagued him. He stared longingly at his barely-tasted beer.

His attention spread around the bar, seeking malcontents and those normally mild mannered souls with tempers frayed by the heat and humidity.

"God, I wish a thunderstorm would blow in and clear the air," he muttered and took a sip.

The beer tasted sour and didn't help at all.

"Off duty?" Dick asked, settling onto the stool beside him. He signaled the bartender for a beer of his own.

"Barely. I'm out of uniform, but with one man minding a desk and being short-handed to begin with, no one on the force is sleeping tonight. Even the lieutenant and the chief are in cruisers patrolling the hot spots. I've already put in a twelve-hour day. Mabel sent me home." Chase rubbed his face again. He really wanted the rest of his beer—foul tasting as it was—but didn't dare take any more alcohol tonight.

"I don't know why, but normal law-abiding folks think that because they are miserable they have the right to make the rest of the world as miserable as they are," Chase sighed.

"I know." Dick shook his head in dismay. "It's Festival, so abnormal behavior somehow becomes the norm. I had to run a couple of kids off this morning. They had a contest to see who could break the most windows by throwing rocks. I boarded up three broken panes in the basement before I headed out to work. Tomorrow I'll replace them. I know those kids. They're usually well-behaved and respectful."

"I think I've spent more time this past week breaking up brawls and separating loving couples before a simple argument became violent."

"You ever find Phelma Jo? I noticed the CAT still parked beside The Ten Acre Wood." Dick took a long swig of his drink. "Someone draped it in a blanket of Pixie lights." His grin let Chase know he had done the mischievous deed.

"No sign of PJ. And that worries me. For all of her faults and nastiness, Phelma Jo has never done anything illegal . . . that I know of. She claims Haywood Wheatland altered the bid for the timber by a factor of ten, that she's not at fault. I've got the county police patrolling the carnival and keeping an eye out for him, too. God, it hurt my pride to run to them for help."

The local mechanic plugged a quarter into the juke-box and cranked up the volume to ear busting. The whining electric guitars and canned bass made Chase and a few others wince. Previously muted conversations dialed up to an obnoxious roar to top the music.

Chase asked for ice water. It tasted better than the beer and helped clear his head a little.

The high school principal stomped over to the juke-box and deliberately forced the volume back down to one notch above mute.

The mechanic half rose from his seat right beneath the wall speakers. His fists clenched and his brow lowered belligerently. A round of applause greeted the principal's action. That made the mechanic think twice about protesting with his fists.

"Can you ease up the air-conditioning to Arctic?" Chase asked the bartender.

"Sorry, Sarge. We're already running at max, and it's threatening to die." The bartender shook his head as he polished an already immaculate bar. "The mood in this town is scary tonight. We really need a break from the heat. Heard a rumor that the power company is going to brownouts. Too many air conditioners running at full power all the time."

"The place is really jumping tonight," Dick commented. He, too, looked askance at his beer rather than downing it. "Want to talk about it?" ·

"Talk about what?" Chase asked. His spine stiffened defensively.

"About why my sister is sitting in the bay window cradling the music box and crying."

A wild leap of hope flamed within Chase, then died as if drowned by the entire glass of ice water.

"I won't let you hurt her. Not you or anyone else for that matter," Dick continued.

"There is nothing to talk about," Chase replied.

"Yes, there is."

"Nope. Not going to happen." Chase threw a five on the bar and pushed his stool back. "I got work to do. People to find. Tow trucks to call."

"Not yet," Dick restrained him with a firm grip on his forearm.

"Take your hand off me before I arrest you for assaulting a police officer."

"Nope. You aren't in uniform, so that doesn't count. You are going to sit there and wait until my sister says her piece."

"What?" Chase turned toward the entrance cautiously.

Dusty and Thistle filled the doorway. Gentle light haloed them both. The air suddenly seemed drier, easier to breathe.

Dusty took a deep breath and aimed her steps toward Chase. She kept her eyes focused on him. The rest of the room, the noise, the heat, all faded away.

"Dick, ask Thistle to dance," she commanded, never dropping eye contact with Chase.

"Dusty, I . . ."

"Dick, thank you for protecting me all these years. I appreciate it. But the time is long past when I need to stand up for myself. Now take Thistle over there to the dance floor. Give this crowd something to watch, and do other than complain and get angry." She pointed to the empty dance floor.

"Dusty, I . . ." Chase began.

She cut him off with a finger to his lips.

"Chase, I owe you many apologies. But first I have to thank you for telling me the truth when everyone else covered it up in the name of protecting me."

"That isn't true," Dick blustered.

Thistle responded by grabbing his hand and dragging him away. "They need some privacy."

"I'm sorry if I hurt you." Chase dropped his gaze from her eyes to her shoulder and beyond. But his hands crept to her waist, his fingers gripping tightly as if afraid she'd turn and run.

"My days of running away may not have passed entirely, but I promise to do it less often," Dusty said, taking half a step closer to him. The heat of his body and his twitching grin—as if he were afraid to let it dominate his face—banished some of her fears. "All I ask is for the opportunity to prove to you that I accept the responsibility of friendship and will be as faithful and trustworthy as you."

"Oh, you are much more than just my friend," he growled, dropping his head to capture her lips with his own. He kept his caress light, tentative. The tension in his fingers told her how much more he wanted.

She pressed herself against him until she felt as if their skin merged; teased his mouth with her tongue, and clung to him with desperate fingers. Finally, her need to breathe overcame the urgency in their kiss.

"Chase, I have loved you for a long time, from a distance. I was afraid."

"Afraid of the inherent violence inside me?"

"No, never that. I've seen you pull your punches

when breaking up a bar fight. I've watched you help to his feet a football opponent you had just tackled. I cheered you on when you rescued a kitten—who didn't need rescuing—from a tree just to soothe the tears of a small child. I've felt the gentleness in you."

"Then what are you afraid of?"

"Myself. Afraid I could never measure up to Phelma Jo and all the other women you have dallied with."

"Dallied only, while I waited for you to grow up."

"Have I grown up?"

"Yes." He kissed her again, pulling her tighter against his chest, wrapping his arms around her. His mouth pressed hard, intense, and demanding against her own.

She sighed and relaxed into him, cherishing the feeling of completeness.

"I think this is what the kids call Pixie love," he whispered.

"Oh, no, not my Dusty!" Joe wailed from behind her.

Reluctantly, Dusty pulled herself away from the best kiss she'd ever imagined. Better than Haywood's Pixie dazzle kiss. Much better than Joe's safe and undemanding kiss. She had to cling to Chase a bit to regain her balance.

When she turned to face her boss, her spine and chin firmed with determination. "Joe, go home to your daughters. Call Monica and settle visitation or joint custody with her. Then complete your application for the teaching job at the community college."

"But . . . but, Dusty, we're friends. I thought . . ."

"That's all we are, Joe. Just friends. And I thank you for the years of friendship we've shared. I don't love you as you need to be loved. Now go home. We have full schedules all day and evening tomorrow."

"The Masque Ball. Is that all you can think about?" he asked sullenly.

Relief washed through her. She knew for certain now that she'd made the right choice. Joe needed her, but he didn't love her. He'd hurt for a while, more from wounded pride than a broken heart. In the end, their friendship would remain, even if . . . no *when* he moved on to the teaching position at the community college.

"Right now I'm thinking about a whole lot more than the Masque Ball." She turned back to face Chase, rose on tiptoe, and returned his kiss.

A quiet shift in the air pressure told her that Joe had left.

"Um, Dusty, as much as I'd like to walk you home and spend the rest of my life with you, I've . . . uh, got work to do," Chase murmured, barely lifting his mouth from hers.

"Huh?"

"Our favorite mechanic has taken exception to the principal's choice of music. I've got to break up this fight before it spreads." He broke away from her and dove into the fray that had spread to a dozen people.

Thistle giggled.

"Well, aren't you going to spread some Pixie magic and stop this?" Dick asked.

"Don't need to. Chase will handle it, and then Dusty will nurse his hurts."

"And what will we do?" Dick strained against her grasp of his hands.

"Dance. Pixies love to dance almost as much as we love to fly."

Dusty wondered why Thistle sounded so sad when her own heart soared and danced with the fullness of true Pixie love.

Thirty-six

※

THISTLE GATHERED HER ARMY at the museum grounds three hours before the Masque Ball. If Chicory and his brothers and their girlfriends could be called an army.

"Those clouds are sticking to the mountains like dog drool on wings," Thistle pouted. "Or Faery rules on a Pixie." She glared at the towering white clouds with black underbellies that shrouded the big mountain from view.

"Mabel calls it magnetics and talks about shifting air pressure," Chicory joined her scowl. He and his band had grown to human size but kept their wings and flower garb to blend in with the costumed party guests. Of course they couldn't actually fly. All of their magic went into maintaining their size rather than working their wings.

"Can we tickle them over this way?" Thistle asked, missing her wings and her magic more than ever. "If we could just get a little shower this afternoon to cool things down a bit, then they can let loose with everything they've got after moonset."

"I don't think those clouds are gonna bust loose even if every Pixie in the region joined in."

"Hmmm. I wonder."

"Don't even think it, Thistle. Rosie objected mightily to us helping you at all," Aster chimed in.

"She doesn't believe in tribes joining up for anything other than a marriage treaty," Delph added.

"And she's sorely missing her betrothed. Hay hasn't been around in days and days," Chicory said.

"You guys haven't seen him or Phelma Jo at all?" Thistle looked away from the problem of the clouds toward her allies, and hopefully friends.

"Not a sign. And we've been all over town," Daisy said. "Ditch weed flowers can go where royalty can't. And we've been everywhere a Pixie can get into."

"We even peered into The Ten Acre Wood, just in case," Aster said.

"We can't get in there, even from above." Chicory shook his head. "I landed on the top branch of the tallest Douglas fir that sticks above the energy wall, but I couldn't get through the wall, only look for signs of life down below. Lots and lots of activity, but it's all down low, and it's either angry fast, or sullen slow. Nothing bright and happy in Alder's kingdom."

"Hay can't get in there either," Daisy reminded them.

"Okay. I have an idea," Thistle said. "I'm sending Dick into The Ten Acre Wood to take a look around."

"He's human. He should be able to get through the wall," Chicory agreed.

"While he's doing that, I want you six to get back to normal size and go see what you can do with those clouds. Take with you every Pixie from every tribe you can find. We really need some relief in this town, or the Ball is going to break into fistfights just like the bar did last night."

"That will be fun." Delph grinned hugely.

"For you, maybe. Not for Dusty."

"Oh, yeah. Dusty. Mabel reminded us this morning that this is Dusty's day and we shouldn't do anything to upset her."

"Did you hear that Dusty and Chase stayed up after the bar fight until almost dawn, talking and kissing?" Daisy asked. "They are truly in love." Her eyes looked at Chicory with adoration.

"Good. Now go see what you can do about those

clouds. Take with you every Pixie willing to go, no matter which tribe."

"What are you going to do?" Chicory asked.

"Make sure everyone has fun at this Ball. Especially Dusty. Which may mean messing with her cell phone so her mother can't call her *again*."

❀

"Can I have a real gun like yours?" Dick asked as he fondled the toy weapon riding low on his left hip. He pulled his neckerchief up over his mouth and nose like any self-respecting Wild West bandit.

"No," Chase replied firmly.

"Why not?"

"Because I'm wearing a badge and you aren't."

"I can get a badge."

"A real badge?" Chase shook his head in dismay. "No. You aren't twelve anymore. Act like a grownup."

"Oh, you're no fun. The Masque Ball is supposed to be about acting out your fantasies. I want to hold up the stagecoach and ravish the ladies."

Chase snorted. "Can you, just this once, get your mind out of the gutter and pay attention? I need you to walk the perimeter and keep your eyes out for either Hay or Phelma Jo." He scanned the throng of volunteers, some costumed, some still in rough work clothes, as they put the finishing details on the décor and catering.

"And what will you be doing?" Dick pulled his cowboy hat low over his eyes. "Ravishing my sister?" He wasn't sure how he felt about that. Happy for Dusty, yeah. Afraid for her? Yeah, that, too.

Chase hadn't been any better than himself when it came to commitments. He really, *really* hoped that Chase had just been waiting for Dusty, as Dick had been waiting for . . . for Thistle. And it looked like he'd have to wait forever.

"I'll be keeping my eyes on the politicos and my ears open to stray conversations. Everyone is hot and miserable. There's static coming from the electronics, and the food is wilting. This could be a disastrous fund-raiser." Chase carried through his words by keeping his gaze moving and bouncing back and forth from toe to heel, just in case he had to move in a hurry. He had done the same thing on the football field.

"You got a point there. At least the girls can wear those light and airy Pixie costumes." Dick's gaze strayed to where Thistle, wearing bright purple draperies and a tiara, but no wings, was ordering people about.

She was becoming quite the organizer. She'd even managed to get most of her elderly clients here, even if they were in wheelchairs. Mrs. Spencer held court beside the guest book where everyone in town could reminisce about school days with her.

"Yeah." Chase's eyes sought and found Dusty in ethereal white with matching swallowtail wings strapped to her back. She'd dug out the child-sized tiara she'd planned to wear for her first ballet solo and never got to perform because of the cancer. She looked like a fragile doll.

Dick didn't like Chase's possessive grin.

He had to suppress his instinct to cover his sister with a blanket and take her home before a bully could hurt her.

Chase is not a bully on the playground, he reminded himself. He's my best friend and the man Dusty loves.

"Dick?" Thistle's lilting voice intruded on his musing. "Dick, can you do me a favor?" She waltzed up to him and slipped her arm through his.

"Anything to please you," he replied, smiling down on her with an equally possessive smile.

But he had no right to feel that way. Thistle had made it quite clear they had no future together. She wanted to go back to Pixie just as soon as she could. She'd never age, just befriending the next generation of children while he grew old and decrepit and continued his lonely existence without her.

A reverse of Peter Pan.

"Mabel's boys and I think that maybe Phelma Jo is hiding in The Ten Acre Wood."

Both Dick and Chase looked sharply toward the line of trees marking the boundary of the museum grounds and the party area. A web of Pixie lights blanketing the undergrowth and low shrubs among the first row of trees was supposed to deter party guests from wandering deeper and getting lost in the dark.

"Why would you think that?" Chase asked.

"Because none of the Pixies can get in there. Including me. But a human can." She put her hands on her hips and cocked her head, looking at Dick and Chase as if they were totally stupid and thoughtless.

"What about Hay?" Chase asked, still thinking like a cop. "If he is who we think he is, he can't get in there either."

"Harder to find two separate targets than two people as one target," Dick mused. "Best place to stash Phelma Jo until he needs her is a place we won't look for her because we think she's with him."

"Good idea." Chase started walking toward the street and the side path that led directly to the center of the woodland.

"Um, Chase, I think I should go," Dick said. "You've got your hands full here. And with the electronics going all static and crossed, your walkie-talkie might not work in there if something comes up requiring your official presence."

"You're right, of course." Chase stopped abruptly. "Take your cell phone and a flashlight. The big heavy duty one from my cruiser. You can use it as a club if you have to, or to signal an SOS. It's powerful enough we should be able to see it from here. With luck, the cell phone will at least ring mine even if we can't hear each other. I'll consider any call from you as a need for help."

"Be careful, Dick." Thistle reached up and kissed his cheek. "I'd go with you if I could."

Dick's heart beat faster, followed by a sharp stab of regret. "I'll be back to collect more of that as my reward." He walked off, happy to do Thistle's bidding, happy that she turned to him for help.

And looking forward to claiming the first dozen dances with her. He couldn't think of a better excuse to hold her in his arms.

❦

Phelma Jo stared at the arching fronds of a sword fern imagining each branch lengthening and sharpening into a lethal blade. Abruptly her thoughts shifted to seeing tiny jewels glistening in the slanting shafts of sunlight coming in from the west. The facets bounced the light as they moved from plant to plant.

Her muscles ached for her to get up and move. Something she didn't understand bound her to sitting beneath the tall Douglas fir, her attention captured by the wondrous construction of the fern. So graceful, so pragmatic, so resilient . . .

A noise broke her thought. A footstep on the soft ground at the verge of the wetlands. "Damn you for intruding on me and my privacy," she yelled. Her neck snapped back and forth, seeking the source of the intrusion. Her hand clasped a stout branch lying beside her.

She stood up and watched the man in the cowboy hat circle the opening. He peered into shadows every few steps, seeking something.

The world grew quiet. Insects ceased their afternoon gossip session. Jewel-toned Pixies flew to the top of the tree canopy and waited. Or were they Faeries? She couldn't remember which was which, only that there was a difference and it was important to someone.

Who?

Phelma Jo stepped forward. "Go away!" she said, clenching her stick tightly. "You can't be here. We aren't finished."

"Come with me, Phelma Jo. I can help you. I can

make everything right for you again." He held out his hand invitingly. "I can be your friend."

She knew that hand. She'd held it before. She'd slapped it away in anger. She . . . she couldn't remember all the reasons why she hated that hand.

"I belong here now. Hay says I have to stay until he calls me. Then we can finish our job." Something was wrong with that statement. Why would she wait for any man to tell her what to do?

"Hay can't help you. Hay will just cost you money. Hay will take away your control over your life." He took one step closer.

She backed up until she bumped into the fir. The rough bark poked at her spine and scratched her pretty blouse.

"Phelma Jo, you're hurt. I can help you." Again with that entreating hand.

His left hand. She knew he should stretch out his right. What was his right hand doing?

She spotted the iron weapon on his hip and raised her stick.

She slammed the stick down on the side of his head, knocking the ridiculous hat to the side.

His knees gave out, and he sank to the ground.

"Damn, I knew I should have brought a real gun." His eyes rolled up and he fell forward, his face on her feet.

Very good, PJ. Now you can come out of the woods. I have work for you, a tiny voice insinuated into her mind. *I've invented a new game with matches. You can light the first fire.*

Obediently, she kicked aside the man she thought she should know and strode across the grass to the opposite side of the woods.

She wouldn't wait for instructions. She'd light that fire where and when she chose.

Thirty-seven

❦

DUSTY AND CHASE WANDERED the grounds, holding hands. They nodded to the mayor. Dusty waved to Pamela Shiregrove and her handsome husband.

All of the committees seemed to be doing their jobs without supervision. She giggled a bit. "Mom trained them well. But she'd never believe they could do anything without her hovering over them, driving them crazy."

The cell phone tucked into her bra vibrated and jingled. Dusty looked down at her scant cleavage in surprise. A call now could only mean something had gone wrong. Terribly wrong. "Now what?"

She fished the phone out with her free hand, never letting go of Chase. He inspected the procedure with extreme interest, lingering on her breasts even after she freed the phone.

The international exchange on the caller ID told her all. "Hi, Mom. I'm kind of busy right now."

"What time is it there? Has the Ball started? Did you make sure the serviettes match the tablecloths and candles? And I just remembered the big slotted serving spoons are in a box in the attic of the gift shop."

"I know, Mom. We took care of it. And yes, the tablecloths, serviettes, and candles coordinate. We're doing fine. But I've got to get back to my guests."

"Yes, of course. What are you wearing? I do hope you aren't in those musty old pioneer dresses you favor. You need something light and colorful . . ."

"Mom, I'm dressed as a white swallowtail Pixie, complete with tiara. And Chase looks marvelous as the local sheriff."

"That's nice. But did Ted call you? Why aren't you with the date I arranged for you?"

"Ted did call, and we agreed we'd both be happier dating someone else. I'm with Chase tonight. Ted should be coming with his *real* girlfriend."

"Oh." Mom's voice fell flat.

"Mom, I followed all of your instructions for the Ball to the letter." Then she'd tossed most of them and started over from scratch with a less redundant and micromanaged schedule.

"But . . ."

"Not now, Mom." Dusty closed the phone with a decisive click.

It rang again. She ignored it after a quick glance at the caller ID.

"Good for you, Dusty," Chase whispered as he leaned in for a quick kiss.

"I've wanted to do that for a long time. Mom will never let go of me until I cut the umbilical cord myself. Until I define myself and not let her and the dead cancer do it for me."

Chase just grinned and kissed her again.

"Amazing that the food comes out of the kitchens at regular intervals, the musicians play twenty-minute sets and then retire to the punch bowl, and all the guests are behaving themselves," Chase mused. "All without your mother telling people what to do, when to do it, why they should do it, and how."

"I diluted the champagne punch to half usual strength," Dusty whispered. "No one is getting drunk. Mom would never think of that. She insisted we had to follow the 1857 recipe precisely."

"You forgot the mayor." Chase frowned.

"You mean the flask?"

"Yeah."

"Not to worry. Thistle substituted a different one. He's drinking heavily watered vodka."

"Good planning. Good party." Chase raised her fingers to her lips. "I suppose you'll want a formal courtship, lots of dates, making out in the back of my pickup before I can ask you to marry me."

"Oh, I want lots of dates. And lots of making out. But you can ask me before all that happens." She smiled hugely, leaning closer to him, relishing the strength of his arms and the silly grin on his face.

"Later, when this is all over and we both have time to concentrate on the future, I'll get down on bended knee and ask you properly. Then Monday morning we go buy a ring. Won't be very big or flashy, but it will be our promise to each other." He dropped a kiss on her nose.

Her heart swelled until she thought it would burst, spreading her joy to the entire crowd.

"Have either of you seen Dick?" Thistle ran over to them, a deep frown and worry lines making her almond eyes look sharper, her nose longer, and her ears more pointed.

Dusty jumped away from Chase, embarrassed by their public display. "What's wrong with Dick?"

"Dick's a big boy. He can take care of himself," Chase reassured her, drawing Dusty back within the circle of his arm.

"I'm not so sure. He's been gone for hours." Thistle gnawed on her thumb as she stared at the line of trees festooned with tiny lights that added mystery and romance to their dense shadows.

"Has it been that long?" Now Chase looked a bit worried, his muscles clenched where they held Dusty.

"Dick? Where did he go?" Dusty asked. Panic wanted to claim possession of her mind. Not Dick. Dick was always there, ready to protect her, eager to crack jokes, always coming out on top no matter how much trouble he got into—like when he got set back his sophomore year of high school because he partied too much to do his homework. The next year he'd aced all his classes. Or when he quit medical school halfway through because studying interfered with his party time. Maybe that was the excuse, but he really was better suited as a pharmaceutical representative and volunteer EMT.

"I haven't seen my brother since just after he got here at five," she said. A lump formed in her stomach. The same kind of lump that used to send her scurrying to the basement. Now she wanted to range all over the park looking for her errant brother.

"He went into The Ten Acre Wood looking for Phelma Jo," Chase said. He started walking in that direction with Dusty in tow (as if he didn't dare let go of her or she'd vanish into the cursed basement) and Thistle following close behind.

"There's Phelma Jo," Dusty called. "She looks horrible, all rumpled and dirty. Her hair's a mess and she's lost a shoe. That really isn't like Phelma Jo. What's she doing with that match?" Her heart climbed to her throat and cut off her breath.

"And that's Hay right behind her. He's got a chain saw!" Chase dropped her hand and ran as Hay pointedly pulled the ripcord on the cutting tool. His blade bit into the massive trunk of a cedar.

Phelma Jo dropped her match into the dry undergrowth.

A wall of flame shot upward with a roar. Waves of heat spread outward. Shadows twisted into monstrous orange shapes.

Dusty recoiled, throwing an arm across her face.

She smelled gasoline.

Phelma Jo just stood there, entranced by the all-consuming fire.

"Dick!" Dusty yelled. She darted forward, oblivious to the heat, the glare, and the hungry fire. Behind her, voices raised and sirens wailed in the distance.

"Dick!" She had to find her brother.

Chase caught her by the wings. The fabric straps dug

into her shoulders and beneath her breasts as she struggled to go to her brother.

"You can't go!" Chase said, putting himself protectively between her and the fire.

"But he's lost in there, possibly hurt." She struggled some more, knowing her puny strength was useless against his determination.

"Let the professionals do it. The fire department is on its way."

"But it's Dick, my brother, your best friend," she sobbed.

"I know, but I also know that if you go looking for him now, I'll be mourning you both. I can't do that."

Thistle surged forward. "Don't you dare hurt my trees!" she yelled at Hay.

He turned on her, a sneer turning his once handsome face into an ugly mask. Pointed ears and chin turned him into a gargoyle. He brandished the roaring chain saw like a weapon.

Dusty gasped at the pure evil that seemed to roll off him like the waves of heat rising from the flames.

"Did someone call me?" Dick staggered out of the forest, his heavy western boots trampling and subduing the embers where he stepped. He rubbed his head rhythmically and kept his eyes nearly closed. He'd lost his hat.

Chase's heart returned to a normal rate. He didn't think he'd ever felt so relieved in his life.

More embers sprang to fiery life around his friend.

"Dick!" Thistle and Dusty screamed at the same moment.

He looked up and stumbled sideways into Hay, knocking him flat. The chain saw ground to a halt where it dug into the turf.

The fire edged deeper into the woods, ignoring the freshly watered lawn.

Chase pounced on Hay. One foot in the middle of his

back, catching his flailing right hand with his own. "Got
you now, Haywood Wheatland. I'm placing you under
arrest for willful destruction of a city park, threatening
an officer of the law, kidnap, arson, and I'll think of a few
other charges along the way." He slapped handcuffs
around the wrist he held and reached for the other hand.
"You have the right to remain silent . . ."

"You can't hold me! I'll shrink and fly away," Hay
laughed. Then he closed his eyes and screwed up his face
in fierce concentration. The flames cast eerie lights on
the planes and angles of his cheeks and pointy ears.

"Aren't you forgetting your own mythology?" Thistle
sneered at him. She placed a foot on his shoulder, keeping him down. "Those are iron handcuffs. They negate
your magic. You're stuck in that body."

"Huh?"

Chase completed his arrest ritual, making sure the
cuffs fit tightly. No chance the tricky con man would find
a way to wiggle free.

Dusty grabbed Dick by the arm, leading him away
from the spreading flames. She shook him cautiously.
"Are you okay?"

"I will be, when I can get some ice. Phelma Jo packs
quite a wallop. Where is she, by the way? I think she's
been drugged."

Chase turned to where she stood staring straight
ahead, heedless of the flames that licked at her trouser
legs. He threw Hay's hands down and lunged forward in
his best football tackle.

Dusty beat him to it. She crashed into Phelma Jo,
knocking them both sideways, rolling onto the lush
grass, until the flames gave up their fight for life and fuel.

Chase helped Dusty up, a little roughly, as he bent to
inspect Phelma Jo's injuries. "Medic!" he yelled when he
found second-degree burns on her ankles and hands.

Strangely, she remained silent, staring vacantly into
the distance.

Dick joined him.

"Take care of her. You've got the EMT training," Chase ordered.

"The wind has shifted," Thistle announced. It's coming from the east.

"Damn. That will spread the fire downhill, toward town." Chase looked up, taking a tally of where everyone was and how much help they'd be. "We're gonna need more fire trucks." He pulled out his walkie-talkie and barked orders into it.

"The cliff is full of poison oak," Dusty cried. "The smoke is toxic! "

Chase looked at Hay and Phelma Jo in bewilderment. "I've got to get these two locked up. But I need to be on the front lines of this fire."

"The pioneer jailhouse!" Thistle cried, pointing to the ramshackle shed whose wall planks sank two feet below ground level.

"That place won't hold a fly," Chase snorted.

"But it will hold Hay. Between the iron in the cuffs and being half underground, he'll be powerless."

"And Phelma Jo is really out of it," Dusty reminded him, standing up.

Phelma Jo continued to lie on the ground unmoving, humming something. *Do dum dee do*. Not Thistle's song, something else.

"She hasn't moved. Dick, will she be all right?"

"Can't say for sure. But she's acting like he gave her flunitrazepam." He tore Phelma Jo's pant leg from ankle to knee, exposing more raw skin.

"What's that?" Thistle asked.

"Commonly called Rohypnol or ruffies. A date rape drug that has hypnotic qualities," Dick said, not looking up from his work.

"Just looks like a normal magic trance to me," Thistle shrugged.

"Try explaining that to Judge Pepperidge," Chase said, hauling a strangely silent and subdued Haywood toward the primitive shed. "Okay, let's get this guy locked up. Phelma Jo goes in the first ambulance. Dick, find a paramedic among the fire crews for that knot on your head. It's bleeding. Dusty, start organizing people to head downtown and meet the blaze with hoses and shovels as it comes down the cliff. We need the pumper trucks up here."

"Will do!" she saluted him and ran off to the mass of people huddling away from the fire, doing a lot of talking but not much else.

"Don't just stand there. Get out the hoses! Ladies, spray the sides of the buildings and the roof. This is my museum, and I'm not going to let it burn because you can't make a decision. Gentlemen, into town and start wetting down as many of the buildings backing up to the cliff as you can."

She sounded calm and determined, like a mother hen.

Bill Tremaine jumped to obey her commands, Pamela Shiregrove not far behind him.

He couldn't help smiling. The old Dusty, shy and frightened of life was gone for good, because Thistle had taught her to embrace life rather than hide from it.

He heard Thistle call from the distance:

"I'll get the Pixies to rescue who they can from the woods. The barrier came down with the flames." She dashed off barefoot, nearly floating over the grass.

Epilogue

THISTLE BLEW HER WHISTLE, letting the shrill sound open a way for her voice. "Get a move on, buster. If you gotta gawk at the fire, park the damn rig and walk back so you can help!" She waved the driver of the big black SUV around Memorial Fountain and away from the bustle at the edge of the fire.

Another blast on the whistle and she moved another line of traffic forward. Then she danced through the pool of the fountain, letting her bare feet send slops of water onto the street. The hem of her purple party dress dragged behind her. She stood face-to-face with yet another driver, leaning out his window rather than moving out of the way.

Just as she raised her whistle again to get his attention, a fat raindrop splatted against her cheek. Then another, and another.

A wild giggle erupted from her throat. "We did it! We tickled the clouds until they spilled their rain like laughter, right where we need it, when we need it. Pixies rock."

"Huh," the driver looked up at her, bewildered.

"Get your arse and that truck out of the way. Keep it moving, folks. Don't stop to watch. This is a roundabout. That means drive around the fountain. Hey, don't stop in the middle of the road. Get moving before the next fire truck runs over the top of you."

This was her town. These were her friends.

Her bare feet barely touched the ground as she marched over to direct another group of cars into the proper lane. She danced to the Pixie music filling her heart and those of her friends.

Dum dee dee do dum dum.